# THE GUY THAT DOES THE THING -

## Observations, Deliberations, and Confessions

### V O L U M E   1 7

*Fujiwhara Beach*

By
## W. C. Andrew Groome

With Foreword by
Bernard C. Bailey, Ph.D.

iUniverse LLC
Bloomington

# THE GUY THAT DOES THE THING - OBSERVATIONS, DELIBERATIONS, AND CONFESSIONS VOLUME 17 FUJIWHARA BEACH

This is a work of fiction. All of the characters, names, incidents, organizations, and dialogue in this novel are either the products of the author's imagination or are used fictitiously.

iUniverse books may be ordered through booksellers or by contacting:

iUniverse
1663 Liberty Drive
Bloomington, IN 47403
www.iuniverse.com
1-800-Authors (1-800-288-4677)

Because of the dynamic nature of the Internet, any web addresses or links contained in this book may have changed since publication and may no longer be valid. The views expressed in this work are solely those of the author and do not necessarily reflect the views of the publisher, and the publisher hereby disclaims any responsibility for them.

Any people depicted in stock imagery provided by Thinkstock are models, and such images are being used for illustrative purposes only. Certain stock imagery © Thinkstock.

ISBN: 978-1-4917-2006-6 (sc)
ISBN: 978-1-4917-2008-0 (hc)
ISBN: 978-1-4917-2007-3 (e)

Library of Congress Control Number: 2013923793

Printed in the United States of America.

iUniverse rev. date: 01/13/2014

For those who make the world a better place.

To those who don't.

# Contents

# Foreword

Have you ever been a part of a local body of government, let's say in this case a municipal corporation (MC)? Have you ever considered becoming part of one whether as an elected official, an employee, or even a volunteer? Do you know or are a friend to someone who is so engaged? Do you perhaps have an interest in the comings and goings and sometimes antics of such establishments?

If any of the above questions have put even mild pressure on a nerve of the affirmative, by reading this tale you may find yourself reflecting on similarities or analogies in your local real world. Or, just maybe, you may gain some further insight of the inner workings of MCs that some would rather you didn't know.

The author of this, maybe not so far from fact, fiction has laid out in some detail an imagined scenario over a short period in the life of a fictitious local Florida beach community MC. In so doing, characters are followed over this time period that fit into the category of each question asked above – elected officials, municipal employees, volunteers (organizations and individuals), and community locals on the outside looking in.

Beyond being simply a work of fiction, the author provides considerable information on the foundation and operation of MCs and perhaps most importantly, a healthy dose of his own ideas where and how improvements could be made to benefit a community as a whole. After all, he is a self-made successful entrepreneur and businessman who is a firm advocate for free enterprise. Who knows, he may have an idea or two for your local community in your real world.

Bernard C. Bailey, Ph.D.

# Disclaimer

The text that follows might have been inspired by actual events, but all of it is fiction. Though there may be a story or two that seem to correlate to an actual event, this correlation is purely coincidental. The same idea applies to the [FicCha]s in this story. This entire thing is a product of the author's imagination, and any attempt to prove otherwise is the outward manifestation of some neuroses or more serious condition. Please see your doctor immediately if you are experiencing thoughts or feelings that this book was written about you.

To put it another way, if this book upsets you then it is your problem, and therapy at your expense is your most reasonable recourse. Don't even think of coming after the author's [USD], because the author has given it all away and is protected by this disclaimer, a corporate shield, and some really good attorneys that have a passion for destroying the people who file frivolous lawsuits. When it is all said and done, you will end up owing the attorneys a great deal of [USD] and the whole thing will not cost the author a dime. Not to mention that you will have given the author enough material for his next book.

Besides, there are only a couple of [FicCha]s in this story that anyone would ever aspire to be. You don't want to publicly claim that one of the other [FicCha]s was based on you. That would be the same as admitting in public that you have sex with farm animals. Yuk.

# Note To reader

The author uses brackets [] in this story to contain specific items or communicate standard actions or bring focus to a given term. For example, [CC] stands for City Council, [FicCha] is the set of Fictional Characters or a reference to fictional characters in general. [FicChaTen] is an element of [FicCha] that has a set of properties that are unique to that particular [FicCha]. One might use the analogy that [FicChaTen] is a person, but the author would respond that [FicChaTen] is a [FicCha], nothing more, nothing less. There is a list of terms in the back of this book, and you will probably bounce back and forth a little at first, but the author suspects that you will catch on to the coding scheme and begin to know what the items are without having to look them up.

The author's decision to use [] is based on the following rationale:

1. Naming a fictional character deprives the reader from developing an image of that character that is unique to the reader. The author believes trying to name a fictional character and then come up with a hundred different ways to reference that character is an unnecessary distraction from the important stuff.
2. There are certain words, like [LOVE], [FEAR], and [EGO] that really do have universal definitions. However, people might want to become better aquainted with the

definition at the end of the book or a dictionary if they have any hope of being given credibility in a public debate.

3. People elected to public office make decisions about how to spend the money that is removed from the private sector by the people elected to public office. The tactics deployed by some people seeking public office, and those who support them, are intended to keep the public off balance and not focused on the fact that all they are doing is wanting to either take some of your money or to spend that money in a way that helps the politician in some way. The only way to filter through that is to start using a common vocabulary that is based on cascading entities.

4. Brackets, [], simplify global changes and searches for terms.

# The Guy That Does The Thing [TGTDTT]

[TGTDTT] is 'the guy that does the thing.' Nothing more, nothing less.

At least that is what [TGTDTT] is shooting for.

[TGTDTT]'s faith in his Creator is both unconditional and unlimited. [TGTDTT]'s path is revealed to him as his Creator sees fit. In between the occasional pokes from his Creator, [TGTDTT] spends his time doing what he can to be ready for the next poke. At some point, [TGTDTT] is just going to naturally do what his Creator intended, but until that day, the pokes are necessary course corrections.

[TGTDTT] knows that his worth is derived from the merits of his actions as seen from the eyes of his Creator. [TGTDTT] uses his sense of center and peace as a barometer to gage how well he is doing.

[TGTDTT] has lived longer and has accomplished more than he ever thought he would. [TGTDTT] has put his life on the line for the defense of a nation and his name is etched in the annals of history. [TGTDTT] does what he knows he needs to do. The only time he does what other people want him to do is when there is the potential to reveal some kind of truth and no one else is willing to take on the task. [TGTDTT] approaches every action he takes with the pursuit of a higher truth in mind. And yes, I do mean every action. Including many tasks that one might deem to be trivial or even beneath them.

[TGTDTT] knows that buying into the praise that might come from others will lead him to disappointment and criticisms rarely help him understand things that really need to be understood. [TGTDTT] would rather people choose to feel some way that helps them instead of choosing to be offended, but understands that it is their choice that [TGTDTT] has no control over. On the occasions that happiness and joy are experienced by others as the result of [TGTDTT]'s actions, [TGTDTT] is grateful that he has inched closer to manifesting God's intent but [TGTDTT] knows he has more work to do.

Through it all, [TGTDTT] is just 'the guy that does the thing'.

# Old Beach and Surfer Dude [ObandSD]

Beaches are comprised of the calcified remains of living creatures, and stuff that was never alive in the sense of earth based life forms. Whether people originated on the oceanfront or eventually migrated to the ocean from deep inland, not all beaches have been inhabited by people during the beach's existence. There are uninhabited beaches today. But they are few and far between. However isolated a beach might be, the person standing on the beach is far from the first living creature to be on that beach and will definitely not be the last. It kind of makes you wonder why a person might ever think that he could be alone on the beach, or anywhere else for that matter.

Imagine for a moment parking yourself right on the dune of an uninhabited stretch of beach, and there was nobody telling you that being there was wrong. There were other people from time to time that passed by and sometimes visit, but they seem to be fine with you living in your camper trailer on the beach dune.

Imagine further that your mornings are just the sound of the surf and the rise of the sun. Your days are the ocean breeze and the chirping of sea birds. Your evenings are beside a small fire listening to the ocean.

You are known in the community of surfers that frequent your spot and some of the residents and businesses that have begun to spring up nearby. By and large, you get along really well with all people, and they get along with you.

You are perfectly happy sitting atop the dune imagining the energy of each wave you see as though you were riding it. The ocean is your source. The ocean has always told you the truth, and from time to time you get a small taste of its overwhelming power. You would never leave the ocean if you did not have to.

To you, people are a curiosity of sorts. When people come near you or when they speak, any reaction to them stems from comparing the energy coming at you with the type of energy the ocean gives you.

If you can imagine yourself as the person just described, please submit your headshot and video when we start auditioning for someone to play [ObandSD] in the movie.

# Preamble

A long time ago, somebody wrote that God was undecided about whether people should speak the same language because the people might get together and build a tower that would reach heaven. As the story is written, heaven was/is an exclusive place and those in heaven were part of an exclusive club. Heaven was not a place that just anyone could be allowed into.

As the story goes, God was right about the people getting together and starting to build the tower. God destroyed the tower before it actually reached heaven. God also began speaking a different language to each person so that when one person would ask another person what God had said, neither the question nor the response would be understood by the intended parties.

Now you know where [GVBMNT] and those who belong to or support [GVBMNT] get their ideas of how to play God and why they seem to get away with doing so.

# No [BST]

Unlike real cities that have a real history, [MCFLMosFB] is a plot of land that was filed with [GVBMNTFL] in 1957AD so that a few people could prevent the area from becoming a beachside trailer park, or [BST]. After the status of [MCFLMosFB] was granted, the city council, [CC], passed its very first ordinance which prohibited the establishment of [BST]s. Since then, many other ordinances have been passed by [CC], but, for the most part, they are exactly like [MCFLMosFB]'s very first ordinance in that a few individuals want what they want, and they use the governing process to get it.

Rarely, if ever, has an ordinance been passed that really considers an entire community. Not just in terms of what people want, but whether or not people can afford the ever-increasing Ad Valorem Tax Millage Rate that compounds the increase in the amount of Ad Valorem Tax paid because the property values also increase.

With that being said, none of the stuff [CC] has done is stuff [TGTDTT] really cares about. [TGTDTT] would prefer that the Ad Valorem Tax Millage Rate was low, but [TGTDTT] can afford it, and living in a [MC] has a cost and [TGTDTT] has learned that some stuff costs more, and you have to pay the price for what you want.

But . . . [TGTDTT] is uncomfortable with the way in which [MCFLMosFB] business is conducted. [TGTDTT] is uncomfortable with a small group of people deciding who is going to be on [CC]. [TGTDTT] is uncomfortable knowing that [CC] meets in private to decide how [CC] is going to vote before the meetings. If for no other reason, private meetings violate Sunshine Laws. [TGTDTT] is uncomfortable with a [CA] who has been paid a great deal of [USD] to attend meetings but only engages when specifically asked, and then claims he was not involved in the decisions that were made right in front of him. Last but not least, [TGTDTT] is uncomfortable with people who, because they are unable to argue the merits of their particular position, resort to personal attacks. But that is [TGTDTT].

# [LG] and [MC]

In [TGTDTT]'s journey and studies of [MC]s in [GSoF], the approach that seems to keep stuff from getting too confused is to map everything to [B], because everything has to be paid for in some way and at some time. Every park, person, police vehicle, and parade impacts [MC]'s [B]. Any effort to disconnect [MC] service levels and capability from the Budget, [B], is naive if the person is new to such stuff, or dishonest if the person is experienced in such stuff.

Every successful organization has mastery of [B] and all unsuccessful organizations have demonstrated an inability to properly implement [B]. If you don't believe this, the rest of the book has no value to you because you believe in magic fairies that can seemingly create something from nothing and that you can get stuff that nobody has to pay for. If you do see merit in viewing the world through [B], if only for a little while, then continue reading.

The [B]s prepared by [MC] in [GSoF] are required to adhere to the accounting guidelines mandated by [GVBMNTFL]. Every single [USD] that comes in as [MCRev] or distributed, as [MCExp] must be accounted for in a very specific way as defined by Department of Financial Services. These guidelines are extremely specific and comprehensive but they do give [MC] some latitude to do special stuff. It is law that all [USD] that comes into and out of [MC] must pass through one or more defined [MCFUND]s. The list of [MCFUND]s that the FY12-13 [B]s passed by every [MC] in [GSoF] is given below.

[MCFUND] Groups

| | |
|---|---|
| 001 | General Fund |
| 005 | Governmental Activities [GOVBMNT]-Wide Financial Reporting) |
| 050 | Permanent Funds |
| 100 | Special Revenue Funds |
| 200 | Debt Service Funds |
| 300 | Capital Projects Funds |
| 400 | Enterprise Funds |
| 500 | Internal Service Funds |
| 600 | Agency Funds |
| 650 | Pension trust Funds |
| 700 | Investment trust Funds |
| 750 | Private purpose trust Funds |
| 800 | Revolving Funds / Clearing Funds |
| 900 | General Fixed Assets Account Group 1 |
| 950 | General Long-Term Debt Account Group 1 |

The next level of granularity is the Account Code, in which there is a set of Account Codes for the various [MCRev] and a separate set for [MCExp]. For example, Account Code 311000 refers to Ad Valorem Tax (property taxes) and Account Code 518 refers to [PenBen].

The financial people who work for the [MC] must track every single [USD] that comes in and goes out with these account codes and at the end of the fiscal year, everything must balance out. For example, assume the [MC] brought in $5,000,000 in Ad

Valorem Tax Revenue and only spent $4,500,000 on stuff so that $500,000 was left over. The [CM] would be required to notify the [CC] that [USD] was not spent, and to give the [CC] options as to what to do with the excess [USD]. [CC] could pay off some debt (Account Code 517), upgrade some office equipment for the City Clerk (Account Code 511), or do something else. Whatever [CC] and [CM] decide to do, they must account for every [USD] in accordance with this system or get the undivided attention of someone sitting at a desk in [GVBMNTFL]. The person sitting at the desk in [GVBMNTFL] can sign a piece of paper that results in someone being put in the back of a police car at least once in his or her life.

This is how stuff is done in every [MC] in [GSoF]. For every source of [MCRev], there is an equation for calculating current values and therefore a method of predicting future [MCRev]. For every [MCExp], there is data that can be trended to predict future [MCExp]. There is no reason that this information is not made readily available to citizens so that [CitComm]s are informed, and expected future [MCExp] is accounted for... Unless being completely forthcoming is not in the best interests of [CC] or [CM].

[TGTDTT] was sort of wrong about the way the world really worked in the fall of YR11. Not so wrong about the rules, but wrong about how the rules are applied, prioritized, disregarded, or the mastery of the rules by the people who lived by them. [TGTDTT] came to understand that the essential qualities of [MCFLMosFB] were identical to those of the Vatican at the time of the Crusades, Protestant Reformation, Inquisition, and dare I say, silence about the Holocaust in exchange for sparing Vatican City. The difference is in scale and degree, but what you essentially have is a group of zealots that will go to any extreme to achieve glory.

But there is this story that the Vatican likes to tell about a very special person who showed the world that real glory is the complete absence of fear and an overflowing abundance of [LOVE]. Other groups like to tell that story as well. Some of them change it up a little and claim their own author that was divinely inspired, but it is the same story. Where the fun begins is how far the group is willing to go if a person chooses to listen to a different group tell that story.

Then [TGTDTT] met [FicChaTen], who pointed [TGTDTT] in the direction towards understanding stuff a bit better and giving [TGTDTT] the confidence and opportunity to make stuff better for the community in which [TGTDTT] lives and pays taxes.

Right now stuff is not looking very good for future [MCFLMosFB] finances and the people elected in [ELCTN12] to give guidance to [CM] are at best incompetent and at worst, corrupt.

What [TGTDTT] discovered was an awareness that gave some credence to [FicChaTen]'s statements. The general agreement of [FicChaTen] statements with [TGTDTT]'s awareness, [TGTDTT]'s respect for [FicChaTen]'s past record as [ColUSAF], and a sincere affection for [FicChaTen] combined to inspire [TGTDTT] to thinking [TGTDTT] should help [FicChaTen] be successful in what [FicChaTen] wanted to accomplished.

In the case of [MCFLMosFB] in the fall of YR11, there was no detailed reporting or justification of [MCFLMosFB] expenses, [MCFLMosFB] revenues or Ad Valorem Tax Millage Rate used to generate Ad Valorem Tax Revenue. There was also no [USD] or long-term plan for replacing [CapEq]. There was also a history of [CC] approving the purchase of property that [MCFLMosFB] did not need at exorbitant prices. The last big thing that was slapping [TGTDTT] in the face was a great deal of turbulence surrounding [CRA].

[MCFLMosFB] has been controlled since its incorporation by [CLB] which has never had more than sixteen members. There are five (5) on [CC] who represent the public face of [CLB]. Most, if not all of the department heads of [MCFLMosFB] are in [CLB]. The remaining members are distributed throughout the community as required for intelligence gathering. Everybody else; [MCFLMosFB] citizens, [MCFLMosFB] [EMP]s, [OwnProp]s, [OwnBus]s, and visitors are just tools, noise, or entertainment.

Believe it or not, [TGTDTT] is good with all this stuff going on as long [TGTDTT] has no firsthand knowledge that the [USD] [TGTDTT] is giving [MCFLMosFB] is being misspent. By the nature of their employment with the [MC], the Department Head's understand that getting caught in a lie is the end of their career. [MC] [EMP]s can be wrong all of the time, but their statements better be the truth. As least as best they understand it. The same is true for the [CM], and [CA]. The role of the [CC] as it appeared to [TGTDTT] in the fall of YR11 was to be advocates for [MCFLMosFB] [EMP] and not stewards of the taxes and fees collected from the citizens.

Rut Ro. Did [TGTDTT] admit to himself that his confidence in [MCFLMosFB] and [CC] had diminished? Does [TGTDTT] have reason to believe that he could influence the debate and possibly have his confidence in [GBMNT] restored? Is [TGTDTT] buying into his own press and starting to look for shots at glory himself?

[TGTDTT] is just going to put his head down on his desk and wait for the bell to ring so [TGTDTT] can get out of this Political Science class and into Jazz Band where he gets to play the music he loves.

# The Fujiwhara Effect

The Fujiwhara effect, named after Sakuhei Fujiwhara, sometimes referred to as Fujiwara interaction or binary interaction, is when two nearby cyclonic vortices orbit each other and close the distance between the circulations of their corresponding low-pressure areas.

Breaking down the physics of the meteorological phenomena and viewing it from a more general point of view, [TGTDTT] proposes the Fujiwhara effect is present in other facets of his [REALITY]. [TGTDTT] proposes it is also present in the interrelationships between people, to include politics.

Consider a citizen with a goal of making sure that [MC] does not waste [USD]. Then consider another citizen who believe that [MC] Building Inspector is being obstinate when it comes to approving plans to renovate her boat dock. Now let both of these citizens run for seats on [CC] where there are two other candidates who are incumbents.

The first two candidates (A and B) know that for their individual goals to be achieved, they have to upset the status quo. The second two candidates (C and D) are running on a platform centered on the idea that they are doing a good job and things are going well. By the mere nature of things, candidates A and B will likely come together as one force, just as candidates C and D, will come together as one force. Then the election happens. Stuff gets all scrambled up and it starts all over when the next election cycle begins.

What is true about the meteorological phenomena, and an attempt to extend the idea to local politics, is that even the slightest perturbations in the various forces will prevent a merging that produces a single event that is greater than or equal to the sum of the individual events. In most cases, the unification is less powerful than the sum.

What also seems to be true of both the weather and politics is that nothing seems to really end. It is extremely difficult, if not impossible, to say exactly when stuff started, unless we assert that weather started when the earth was created and politics started when Mirror Fogging Carbon Units, [MFCU]s, began to walk upon the earth. However, the forces that created earth existed before the planet became a planet and, if you think Darwin was right, [MFCU]s are derived from something else.

But [TGTDTT] is here now and trying to make sense of at least one or two things. [TGTDTT] believes the Fujiwhara effect is present at every meeting throughout the country and the end result is just a continuation of confused ripples that think they are the ocean.

[TGTDTT] also submits that across the world, the Fujiwhara effect is discernible every time two or more people have ideas that cannot be accomplished without some help from some more people. This is true even when a person decides they want to be left alone. The only way that person can be left alone is if people choose to leave the person alone.

City Council Meetings are the same now as they were in the beginning of this fine nation. It is an opportunity for all citizens to stand up in front of their neighbors and wail -

[GVBMNT] won't leave citizens alone;

Neighbors won't leave citizen alone; and

As an American, a nation founded on the principal of being left alone as a right endowed by God, citizens should be left alone

OR

Petition [GVBMNT] to go bother one or more neighbors because neighbors don't behave as they should

OR

Petition [GVBMNT] to buy something a person thinks [GVBMNT] should have or

OR

Petition [GVBMNT] to stop buying stuff the [GVBMNT] should no longer buy.

There is that word "should" that pops into every statement made by an unhappy person. On a side note, happy people rarely use the word should and use the word "is" instead. But that subject is for another day.

Each of the five people sitting at the front of the room on [CC] promised to uphold a solemn oath and serve the public to the best of their abilities within the constraints of [USFG] law, and [GVBMNTFL] law. These people want to make the world a better place for all of us. Yet none of those five people understand how everybody does not believe that [CC] are helping us and those same five people have decided to believe that we should understand that we need them to keep us safe.

[TGTDTT] imagines taking the minutes of every meeting that has ever taken place in the history of this great nation and processing them in a way toward seeing the commonalities. It is [TGTDTT]'s suspicion that applying a Freudian Dogma Filter would reveal that what is in play during every meeting is a sexual ritual that celebrates and glorifies the life of Oedipus in a very public way.

It is along that line of thought that a plausible case could be made that attending meetings could feed the same need as attending a live sex show. Being a part of the public action would be the same as acting in a live sex show. Assuming such were the case, the candidates elected to [CC] are the [StarPorn]s. The [CA] and [CM] are [ActorPorn] on long-term studio contracts who fill in when called upon by one of the [StarPorn]s. It must be understood that [CA] and [CM] will only be activated at the command of one or more members of [CC]. The people who speak at meetings are auditioning to be [StarPorn] or bit-players. Last but not least, are the people who make sure they get a really good seat in the audience. Well, you know who you are.

If you can hardly wait to sit in the very back of the room at the next meeting, you have a serious problem. The people who make a habit of speaking on "Agenda Items" have a problem too, but at least they don't try to hide theirs.

[TGTDTT] realized that he was not above being a [StarPorn] in YR11 and YR12, but the script had to be really really good for him to audition. When [ELCTN12] changed the line up of regular [StarPorn]s, [TGTDTT] no longer auditioned and stopped going to the theatre at all because he was not going to be the guy who sits in the back of the room. That is what we have [OBandSD] and [FicChaTwentyNine] for.

# [TGTDTT]

[TGTDTT] was there when all this stuff was happening and he could easily convey what he saw and heard as it was all going on. In his quiet moments, he believed he had a real sense of where all the events were leading. What [TGTDTT] did not understand then, and to a degree still does not understand, is why it happened at all; why it happened the way it did, what point in time would he pick to start the story, and what point in time would he end the story.

Confusion, or better stated, lack of precision in matters such as this is not new to [TGTDTT]. Being someone who subscribes to string theory as it relates to the creation of the universe, [TGTDTT] has a sense that everything is connected to everything in the present, was connected to everything in the past, and will also be connected to everything in the future. Even the most mundane or banal events play a role in those events that some would consider monumental. It is because of this connection that one could argue that banality carries the same significance as the monumental.

A person's decision may be recorded as a fact (mundane or not), but the motivations of the person to arrive at a decision can only be speculated. Even the rationale provided by the person who made the decision is to be treated with some skepticism because there is no way to really assess the level of honesty that people have when they engage in introspection.

[FB]'s history as [MCFLMosFB] begins in 1957, but there were already people living there in 1956, and there was a sequence of events that led up to the decision to obtain authority from [GVBMNTFL] to define boundaries, and then tax everybody that reside or conduct business within those boundaries.

[FicChaTen]'s life began in Missouri at about the same time as the creation of [MCFLMosFB] and he did not become a resident of [MCFLMosFB] until he was finishing his final responsibilities as Commanding Officer of 45th Space Wing at the near by Air Force Base in the early 1990's.

[FicChaTwenty] began life in 1944 and was a teenager living in the conservative community of [MCFLLakOca] at the time that [MCFLMosFB] was formed. [FicChaTwenty] did not come to [MCFLMosFB] until after the United States Army notified her that she had no chance of promotion beyond the rank of [MajUSA], and she would be retired.

[MCFLMosFB] maintained a volunteer [FD] until the 1980's when a decision by [CC] put into place a professional [FD]. The author could go on with more "facts" and dates so that everything seems to fit on a timeline, but the meaning of those events would somehow get lost in the shuffle. On the other extreme, the author could leap into a discussion as to why certain decisions were made in terms of "improving" the quality of life in [MCFLMosFB], or satisfying the individual interests of those involved, but that would leave reader and author with an incomplete biased survey and critique of imperfect individuals who have lived their lives in a constant battle between their personal demons and their better angels.

Besides, as much as the author, and possibly the reader, would prefer simple answers to as to how stuff got so screwed up, and why people made bad decisions, the myriad of events, constraints, and emotions involved in the running of a [MC] rarely allow for anything to be simple.

However, there are some basic elements in play that seem to satisfy a number of theories put forth by Sigmund Freud, Isaac Newton, Douglas Hoftstadter, John Maynard Keynes, Benjamin Franklin, the Dali Lama, and many other renowned authorities on the universe in which our planet exists and the human condition that is intrinsic to every [MFCU] that lives on this planet.

Almost everybody has some awareness of the idea of greatness and lives in a manner that gives voice to what that awareness is with respect to how the person is viewed by others. But there are also underlying laws of nature that always override any imaginary construction of [MFCU]s that attempts to counter those laws.

In YR11, the state of [MCFLMosFB] finances was beginning to reveal that some of the decisions made by [CC]s throughout the years did not take into consideration the fundamental elements of sound economic theory of financial planning, yet certain individuals were enriched. The political climate of the past eighteen months, especially the [ELCTN11] of [CC], gave the illusion that wiser minds would prevail, but the [ELCTN12] of [CC] comprised individuals whose histories lack any substantial evidence of true greatness and selflessness but instead contains story after story of selfish, petty, shortsighted, and ill-informed decision making.

[TGTDTT] would prefer to only think about wonderful stuff and terrific people, but [MC]s, even one as small as [MCFLMosFB], are not all terrific and the people are not all wonderful. Even [FicChaTen], the inspiration for this story, failed to complete his final mission by resigning his seat on [CC] because, as he put it,

"Life is too short to bang your head against a wall with nothing to show for the effort but a pounding headache."

[FicChaTen]'s quitting [CC] was both a tremendous disappointment to [TGTDTT] and a wonderful opportunity for [TGTDTT] to better understand what it means to be a loyal and true friend when there was no compelling reason for him to be either.

On the other (not so inspirational) side of personalities are the [FicChaTwenty] through [FicChaTwentyNine]s of the world who never pass up the opportunity to prove they are incompetent, petulant, hypocritical, selfish, and pathetic while trying to portray just the opposite. These same [FicCha]s, and some of their close knit group, are versed in using Alynski tactics to get their way. They are good at it and always have been.

[TGTDTT] gave up wishing stuff was different a long time ago and struggles every day to see the world as honestly as he possibly can. It is his nature to believe there is good in all stuff, including people, but sometimes that goodness is difficult to recognize. [TGTDTT] does recognize that good people can do bad and even stupid stuff. Regardless of their reasons or aspirations, their decisions are still bad and even stupid.

Some people learn from their past decisions, and some people don't. It is the people who refuse to take a long critical look at their actions with the understanding that they might learn something worth learning, which [TGTDTT] allows himself the experience of deciding that they are bad people and that the world would be better off if they would gracefully exit.

# [MCFLMosFB]

---

[MCFLMosFB] is a two and one half square mile bedroom community of about ten thousand people. From the outside, [MCFLMosFB] appears a relatively tranquil place to raise a family or retire. For over fifteen years [TGTDTT] has enjoyed coming home everyday from his office on the mainland and feeling the ocean breeze on his face, talking with his neighbors, and having an occasional meal or adult beverage in one of the few [BusRestLocal]s. Then, one day in September, a neighbor who lives close by came to [TGTDTT]'s door for the first time in both their lives to talk about a candidate who was running for [CC].

Up until this point, [TGTDTT] had taken his voting cues from a friend who is a long time resident and [MCFLMosFB] [EMP]. Now [TGTDTT] is hearing about a candidate who believes he can do a better job than the other candidates.

Up to that point, [TGTDTT] really didn't care who was on [CC] because [TGTDTT] believed the worst stuff [CC] could do had nothing to do with him and that really bad [PubServ]s have a limited lifespan. [TGTDTT] figured voting for the candidates his trusted friend told him to vote for was good enough.

Sitting in his den eighteen months later, following the [ELCTN12] of [CC] results, [TGTDTT] knows that it is not good enough. Today [TGTDTT] knows that bad ideas become a [REALITY] if a person with a better idea doesn't step up and become a human pincushion. [TGTDTT] also knows that a single person with a better idea who is willing to be abused in public is not enough to modify practices and philosophies that have been in place for decades. What [TGTDTT] doesn't know is how to make a good idea a [REALITY] in a way that doesn't involve a great deal of wasted effort where [EGO]s have to be soothed.

For fifteen years, [TGTDTT] did not care about [MCFLMosFB] and focused on being successful as an entrepreneur in a way that avoided getting too involved with other people. [TGTDTT] believed then, as he believes now, that occasionally there are individuals who have merit, but most people lack the qualities [TGTDTT] feels that are necessary to deem their life as significant. In fact, [TGTDTT] doesn't see his life as signicant in the sense that he is somehow important or necessary. But he is here and spends each day doing what he can in the hope that he is as closely aligned with God's intention.

Some people think they are important. Some people even think they are more important than others. But at the end of their lives, two things seem to be pretty true. The first thing is that the person is dead. The second thing is that the fundamental nature of stuff is, for the most part, exactly the same. The entire ruckus people may have caused during their life so that their [EGO] is satisfied was for naught.

Occasionally a person shows up and causes a ruckus. Not for the purpose of satisfying his/her own [EGO], but to manifest a change that lives on well after they have become room temperature. Sometimes the change is imperceptible at first and most of the time it dies off. However, if history has taught us anything, it is that no one in the present really has an honest or accurate appreciation for how his or her actions affect the future. Furthermore, any assessment as to whether something is good or bad has no relationship to whether something is truly good or bad.

The life, up to this point, of [TGTDTT] may or may not have produced anything of any value to those who are alive today or in the future. The same is true of virtually everybody. Try as we might to change that, because we don't know for certain if what we believe is a good thing is really a good thing, we can only hope that our deeds are truly righteous. All of this means that four things are essentially true:

1. What we do is the only thing that really matters.
2. What we think of ourselves and what others think of us does not matter.
3. We all die.
4. We all die unsure if we lived life to our potential.

There are countless resources available to everybody that may guide our actions in a way that turns out to be good. It is [TGTDTT]'s understanding and belief really, that inspiration is everywhere, and that we can simply open our hearts, minds, and eyes in order to recognize it. The problem is that there is as much stuff that is misleading as there is stuff that is helpful, and if we treat all information equally, we honestly have no real idea which is which; especially if the source of information is someone saying something or writing it down. So we might as well be entertained when people who believe wrong stuff decide they have something to say and decide to either say it in public or write it down and have it published.

One last thought on this subject is that there is a "what" component of every event that can be recorded with some precision and relevance to the physical world and is the dominant domain of happy people. There is also a "why" component associated with every event that seems to be the world in which not happy people exist. Happy people will accumulate information and allow the information to point them in the direction that makes the most sense. Not happy people have a very selective and somewhat arbitrary standard for exactly what is information. Happy people embrace information for the wisdom it reveals. Not happy people concoct tales and stories to mislead [GenPub] to a dark place as described in the 1985 British dark comedy *Brazil*.

# [OBandSD]

Coming to Fujiwhara Beach in the early 1950's, after a brief stint in the military, [OBandSD] needed a place to park his camper trailer on the beach. Everything was so cool for the longest time, and then one day [OBandSD] gets a notice that he has to move his trailer because the newly formed [CC] has made it illegal to have a camper trailer on the beach.

On that fine day in 1957, [OBandSD] became a criminal in the eyes of [CC] and [PD] by the 5-0 [CC] vote to approve [MCFLMosFB] very first ordinance. [OBandSD] was looked down upon as a vagrant and low-life by the Mayor, Vice Mayor [CC] Senior Member, [CC] Member, [CC] Jr. Member and the [FBWC].

[ObandSD] could be heard on many occasions saying "That is some funky mojo being sprayed on the peace lovers of the world who want to live off the land and ride the occasional wave. Talk about harshing a buzz. I wasn't bothering anybody, nobody was bothering me. And then powey! Uh Mr. you are in violation of [MCFLMosFB] very first ordinance. You have thirty days to remove yourself and your trailer to a location legally suitable for such purposes, or [PD] will destroy by means of fire this camper trailer under the supervision of the Volunteer [FD]."

The good news for [ObandSD] is that one of his bros let him stash the trailer in his back yard just a quarter mile inland. [OBandSD] could still get the breeze and walk to the surf, but it wasn't the same. It was like all of the wickedness of mankind was beginning to back him into the corner of conforming. It was like how Adam might have felt after he ate the fruit from the forbidden Tree of Knowledge with the exception that [OBandSD] had not eaten from the forbidden Tree of Knowledge. [OBandSD] had been swimming in the Ocean of Infinite Consciousness. Like every ocean on this planet, and this is not a statement about global pollution, there are countless and variant centers of circulation that attract debris.

After [OBandSD] had thought about things a little bit, he kind of put it into perspective that some how either he had drifted into a slick of yucky stuff, or the yucky stuff had drifted into him, which is the same thing if your point of reference is midway between the two elements: [ObandSD] and the yucky stuff. [OBandSD] knows that people go exactly where they paddle as long as the currents and waves behave. [OBandSD] was an experienced enough surfer to know in his heart that he could have paddled back into clean water, but he just wasn't paying attention. Stuff happens when you are not paying attention.

[ObandSD] started attending meetings and listening to what these people were talking about. Meetings are all the same. They begin with some kind of celebratory moment to kick stuff off and get all the lightweights on their way. Eventually the audience settles in with just the diehards and concerned. Some diehards like to read the federal constitution every time they stand up, and they insist on standing up every chance they get. The concerned are the ones that have a [CitComm] they want heard on at least one agenda item. Once the concerned have voiced their [CitComm], the concerned typically bolt. Diehards, on the other hand, are the first in their seats and the last to leave.

Over time, [ObandSD] started to get to know stuff about these people he would see at every meeting. Eventually [ObandSD] learned enough about them to start filling in the blanks with likely or entertaining scenarios.

For instance, there is one diehard, [FicChaTwentyOne], Ph.D., who has something to say about everything. He and his old cow in tow, [FicChaTwenty], used to get paid by [MCFLMosFB] for their opinions, but their contract was not renewed when [FicChaTen] and [FicChaThirty] got elected to [CC] in [ELCTN11].

[FicChaTwentyOne] is this skinny old man whose wardrobe is a small assortment of well-worn plain t-shirts, a couple pair of well-seasoned blue jeans, and one flannel shirt. He seems to live at City Hall. It has been rumored that [FicChaTwentyOne] was given the combination to [MCFLMosFB]'s safe where the important stuff is kept. He has been either a [MCFLMosFB] volunteer or a [MCFLMosFB] contractor, but never a [MCFLMosFB] [EMP] and definitely not a sworn officer of the [GVBMNT] like [MCFLMosFB] City Clerk.

[FicChaTwentyOne] was a retired Lieutenant Colonel in the [USAF] that didn't fly and didn't command anybody. [FicChaTwentyOne] had somehow risen through the ranks to a certain level without demonstrating leadership of any kind. It kind of makes you wonder what compelled [FicChaTwentyOne]'s superior(s) to recommend and approve his promotion(s). [OBandSD] had heard the same thing about [FicChaTwenty]. Anyway, the surprising thing about [FicChaTwentyOne] is that [OBandSD] understands [FicChaTwentyOne] had at least one daughter that was living with him. [OBandSD] was surprised because [OBandSD] cannot see any evidence that [FicChaTwentyOne] was a person that could either attract or perform any remotely affectionate act.

[FicChaTwentyOne] would present his charts and graphs to [CC] and say "can't you see…" and [CC] would go "Wow" but no one ever said, "I do not understand what you are showing me." Instead, because [FicChaTwentyOne] is a celebrity of sorts, [FicChaTwentyOne] gets called in to do the stuff lesser mortals cannot understand. [FicChaTwentyOne] shows his graphs and tells the people what they should do and many oblige.

When [TGTDTT] was out campaigning for [FicChaTwelve], [TGTDTT] would see [FicChaTwentyOne] at least four times in different parts of [MCFLMosFB] throughout the day. Sometimes [FicChaTwentyOne] was talking to a police officer of [MC], other times to [PW] of [MCFLMosFB], and sometimes just peddling along on the bicycle that [FicChaTwentyOne] rode everywhere. There was [FicChaTwentyOne] on a hot sun baked September day wearing his trademark flannel shirt.

[FicChaTwentyOne] was totally plugged in whether anyone wanted him to be or not. [TGTDTT] was sure some people like the fact that [FicChaTwentyOne] stuck his nose everywhere and into everything. But for whatever good [FicChaTwentyOne] might have been doing, there was more than enough data to support that [FicChaTwentyOne]'s word needed to be taken with a grain of salt. And that includes his charts and graphs that [FicChaTwentyOne] liked to quote all the time.

[FicChaTwentyOne] would attend the [COFFEE] meetings and cause ruckus after ruckus after ruckus. [TGTDTT], who was on [COFFEE] invited [FicChaTwentyOne] to join [COFFEE] to make sure [FicChaTwentyOne]'s ideas were given adequate voice and [FicChaTwentyOne] refused. [TGTDTT] asked [FicChaTwentyOne] for his help correcting the perceived horrible injustice being documented in the first draft of the report and [FicChaTwentyOne] refused.

That's when [OBandSD] knew that the diehards who make the most noise are just people who like the sound of their own voice. The diehards that rarely speak seem to be people who have their days free and can attend [CC] meetings.

Another dude that is pretty entertaining is [FicChaForty], [MCFLMosFB] resident town crier in the sense of the old colonial days. [FicChaForty] seemed to like t-shirts, shorts, and flip-flops a great deal as that is what he wore all the time. [OBandSD] also got the impression that doing laundry and taking a bath was a lower priority than being the Voice of the People as the Founding Fathers intended. [FicChaForty] had a flare for the dramatic, his approach to any argument usually began with the statement, "The Founding Fathers never intended ...", and he liked to use the word "codified" as often as he could fit the word into any sentence.

If [OBandSD] were to have a buddy, it would have to be [FicChaTwentyNine]. [OBandSD] and [FicChaTwentyNine] would occasionally sit together in the back of the room and exchange witty banter from time to time. [FicChaTwentyNine] had no interest in making waves. Every now and then, [FicChaTwentyNine] would stand up and say something, but for the most part, [FicChaTwentyNine] seemed to enjoy the show. [FicChaTwentyNine] was one of the people who got to every meeting early so she could get a good seat.

There was this one guy, [FicChaTwentyTwo], who seemed to be a bit pervy. This dude oozed pedophilia. Rumor has it that [FicChaTwentyTwo]'s love of the little boys got him run out of Miami Beach. [FicChaTwentyTwo] is now well past his prime, so he doesn't draw a great deal of attention in that regard anymore, but he does come out of his hole from time to time to spread his lecherous spittle. [FicChaTwentyTwo] kept an "Impeach [FicChaFourteen]" sign in his front yard. The only logical conclusion drawn by those who have no facts is that [FicChaTwentyTwo] was lashing out because [FicChaTwentyTwo] was attracted to [FicChaFourteen]'s sun-bleached wavy hair and chiseled tanned body.

The personalities in the [CLB] were varied, sometimes vile, but generally a great anthropological study in an aging population's adversity to change. Among them were older female citizens who profess to "love thy neighbor" on Sunday at their bumper-sticker-proven churches but who prefer to tell people they don't agree with at [CC] meetings to "shut up," "we don't need your kind here," and other such phrases. There was an old man with some sort inferiority complex who professes to be a former POW from some long ago war fought in a land far, far away-- but wasn't. A retired [PD] Chief who believes citizens should be seen and not heard - especially those who feel as if there might be better ways of spending taxpayer money.

The senior citizens love to wave copies of the Constitution around at [CC] meetings claiming their "First Amendment" rights were being trampled on as they ramble on and on at the podium with no [CC] members stopping them or openly state in [CC] meetings they wish certain [CC] members they don't agree with would get hit by various big machinery with engines...buses, trucks, cars, airplanes, boats, you pick the mashing apparatus. These same people would cry when the [PD] chief takes their boy-scout-pretend-cop-uniforms away for such remarks, only to give them back when the political tides change back to 'normal'. [ObandSD] thought it was lame to wish harm upon anyone, much less people who happened to be in office and could not understand why it was no big deal after they were gone.

As far as grouping people, [OBandSD] would say that the old people seemed to voice their disagreement with actions being taking by young people. Or that the people who were born in [MCFLMosFB] have more of a right to say about what should happen than people who have only lived here for a decade or so. [OBandSD] is correct, but there is more to the story. And this story is not a new one. This is not the first time this story has been told, and it will not be the last time. It is the story of [EGO] feeding itself by using whatever tactics are necessary, including the unfounded exploitation of people's fear and the use of unsavory tactics to scare off any potential threats to the [CLB]'s sovereignty.

Back in the day, some very many days ago, the peasants rose up and stormed the castle when stuff got to be too stupid. With advances in transportation such as sailing ships, a common option to minimize castle storming was to ship off the discontented and undesirables to some colony far away. Today, in every hometown in America, there are people that have nowhere else to go, so the whole shipping them off thing isn't going to work if the natives become restless.

Meetings are a really good place to measure the noise level of a community. The higher the noise level, the greater chance of it developing into a powerful coherent voice that can silence the oppressors. Unless, of course, the oppressors can keep everybody either happy or confused, or both.

# [FicChaTwenty]

The year was 1944 and the place was [MCFLLakOca] that [FicChaTwenty] entered this world. [FicChaTwenty]'s father was one of the town's three barbers and the leader of a local dance band, *The Swinging Hicks*, where he sang and played the accordion. [FicChaTwenty]'s mother, [FicChaFifty], was a middle aged spinster whose primary job was as a clerk at the local library, but she often served as a substitute teacher at [MCFLLakOca]'s two public schools.

The circumstances that led up to [FicChaTwenty]'s conception are part of the town's lore because [FicChaFifty] never married. It was rumored that [FicChaFifty] and the sperm donor were only together the one time, and that one time was when he was drunk and in between musical sessions at the annual [MCFLLakOca] Founder's Day dance. Before that time, and after, no one in the community ever recalls [FicChaFifty] being associated with male companionship.

When he discovered [FicChaFifty] was pregnant, he tried several times to make an honest woman of her, but his efforts were in vain. As the story is told, [FicChaFifty] told him that she got from him all that she wanted and rejected everything else that could be attributed to him or any other man.

Growing up, [FicChaTwenty]'s only refuge was home. The kids at school had heard the stories from their parents and would often tease [FicChaTwenty] about being illegitimate. [FicChaTwenty] excelled academically in English, social studies, and similar courses, but she was always challenged by science and mathematics. [FicChaTwenty]'s foray into the arts and sports were limited to playing the tuba in high school band and [FicChaTwenty] did earn a reputation as a pretty good catcher on the girl's softball team.

[FicChaFifty] recognized that [FicChaTwenty]'s best hopes for a successful life would be found beyond the [MC] limits of [MCFLLakOca], but [FicChaTwenty]'s insecurity limited her prospects for college beyond a reasonable driving distance from home. So in 62AD, [FicChaTwenty] began attending [UoF] where she could discover a new world and still come home when she was homesick.

It was [FicChaTwenty]'s second semester at college that she discovered "Women's Studies" where she learned about Jane Addams, Gladys Bentley, Marlene Dietrich, Barbara Gittings, Audre Lorde, and other women who believed that the male gender was a necessary but undesirable component of the human race that not only oppressed women but were responsible for all of society's ills.

Through the curriculum, [FicChaTwenty] began to understand her mother's life decisions, the source of her own insecurity, and the path she needed to follow. [FicChaTwenty] not only wanted to be one of those women she learned about, she entertained dreams of being in the history books herself while getting even with every boy that ever made fun of her.

The first step was to get a law degree. The second step was to join [USA]. With her law degree in hand and commission as [Lt2JAGUSA], [FicChaTwenty] set out to put all men in their place. [FicChaTwenty] knew it would be long journey fraught with hardships as [FicChaTwenty] elected to immerse herself in a culture that not only glorified everything she held in contempt but demanded that she keep her true inclinations and desires an absolute secret. For [FicChaTwenty] to be successful, she had to be a man among men, but under no circumstances could [FicChaTwenty] reveal that she shared her colleagues' love of women.

[FicChaTwenty]'s zeal to prove she was superior was the subject of virtually every one of her fitness reports. It was suggested on more than one occasion, both verbally and in-writing that [FicChaTwenty] would benefit from learning the practice of law as it is written instead of advancing ideas that were not supported by law. Her case assignments were limited to defending petty criminals who had committed offenses that could not be defended such as failing a drug test or being caught on camera committing the offense, because her commanders felt it was the only way to keep her busy without slowing down the wheels of justice. But even so, [FicChaTwenty] would use every case as an indictment of lesser mortals.

Because [FicChaTwenty] never pushed too far or too hard along the best routes to take, her promotions were few and far between, but the system itself mandated she move up the ranks to a point. The point [FicChaTwenty] could never move to was a position of command. So [USA] waited until she hit the magic twenty-year point to let her know that her services were no longer required or desired. [FicChaTwenty]'s commanding officer had a plaque and a cake made for her so that the base photographer would have some interesting pictures. But at the end of her last day of service, [FicChaTwenty] went home to her McClean, Virginia apartment while all of her former colleagues met at the Officer's Club to celebrate her departure.

[FicChaTwenty]'s roommate at this time was a young college student who was happy to share a bed as long as she didn't have to pay rent. [FicChaTwenty] was happy to use her military paycheck to pay the entirety of the household bills, purchase gifts, and fund the occasional vacation to Miami's South Beach in exchange for the physical affection, but beyond the physical aspects of the relationship, there was no meeting of the minds to satisfy the requirements of a Long Term Contract, which is the idea of agreeing to keep something the same for a long time. After retirement, [FicChaTwenty]'s reduced pay required the nature of the relationship to change, and her roommate interpreted that as meaning a change in address to be with someone who could afford her services. This turned out to be a divorced male professor at the college she was attending.

The break up was hard on [FicChaTwenty]. Deep down she knew that she was being used, but [FicChaTwenty] could not reconcile that a man had upstaged her. It seemed acceptable that an older woman take advantage of another woman's youth and inexperience or that a younger woman take advantage of the neediness of an older woman. But the idea of being chosen second to a man, especially after all [FicChaTwenty] had given her, threw [FicChaTwenty] into a deep depression and anger that still lingers to this very day.

[FicChaTwenty] sulked, cried, drank, and ate for about two weeks before coming to the conclusion that she needed to make a change. All of her plans to be at the top in [USA] had failed. Her attempts at love had failed. Every effort to be praised or even accepted up to this point had failed. Now in her mid forties, all she had to show for her life's endeavors were a pension that would allow her to live modestly, but comfortably, a one bedroom furnished apartment, and a late model travel van. It was time to start over. So [FicChaTwenty] filled her suit cases, a few cardboard boxes, and several garbage bags with her possessions, loaded them into her van, got on I-495 to I-95 and headed south.

[FicChaTwenty] was on a mission with the only objective being to begin anew. She stopped for gas, coffee, and pork rinds about every three or four hours. It took about four tanks of gas to get south of Jacksonville. About an hour after the fifth fill up, [FicChaTwenty] ran out of steam and took exit 195 to [PFB] to get a room for the night using her [USA] retired ID card.

[PFB] is a relatively small facility with a big mission located right on the beach. The command's responsibilities include both [PFB] facilities and [CCAS] to the north. [PFB] facilities is used primarily a refueling and layover for pilots, so its focus is on lodging and recreation. The lodging is waterfront on the riverside of the base and there are houses for use right on the beach. The same is true of its social establishments – mostly drinking spots.

[FicChaTwenty] checked in to her room, cleaned up and headed to [PFB] Marina Tiki Bar. Elbowing up to the bar, she ordered a Cosmo and took inventory of her new surroundings. [FicChaTwenty] saw young men in flight suits and utilities, older men in t-shirts and golf attire, and people dressed in business casual. There were current and former [USAF] personnel, [USMC], [USN], and a couple of Vietnam era [USA] guys. The women there were either wives with their spouses or ex-wives and widows on the hunt.

If there was a conversation to be had with anyone in this place, it would probably not be one that resulted in a lasting relationship that would satisfy [FicChaTwenty]'s desire for emotional or physical release. [FicChaTwenty] took a drink and resigned herself to the notion that the method of meeting her needs on this evening would be in her hands when she returned to her room.

The sun was at treetop level across the river and the sky a combined orange and almost violet hue by the end of her first drink and the beginning of her second. The breeze had settled down to a pleasant and gentle flow, Drink number one was beginning to take effect, the crowd seemed to be less annoying, and [FicChaTwenty] started to take a look around with a new perspective.

Across the bar from where she was sitting, [FicChaTwenty] heard a voice that seemed to be speaking directly to her; even though the person had no idea that [FicChaTwenty] was there. Out of the corner of her eye, [FicChaTwenty] got a glimpse of a smile that was the most inviting she had ever seen. The smile was on a face as beautiful as [FicChaTwenty] had ever imagined. The face was on a body that, even though it was as mature as her own, made her thoughts turn to fantasies involving the two of them beneath a waterfall in a tropical paradise.

The woman across the bar, who was just making her rounds of all the people she knew, began to sense [FicChaTwenty]'s stare and became curious as to who this new face at the bar could be, and why was she looking at her so intently.

"Hello. Do we know each other?" inquired the woman in a southern and genuinely friendly way.

"I don't believe we have met before. I apologize if I appeared to be staring, but I was driving all day from Virginia, and between the road hum, my first drink, and the general mood of my new surroundings, I just found myself completely entranced by the manner in which you moved about the place. My name is [FicChaTwenty]."

"Well honey, it is a pleasure to meet you. My name is [FicChaTwentyThree], but everybody calls me [FicChaTwentyThree]. And if you like the way I buzz around this bar, you really ought to see me on Limbo night."

[FicChaTwenty]'s gaze shifted from looking at [FicChaTwentyThree] to seeing inside of [FicChaTwentyThree]. The thought of [FicChaTwentyThree] assuming the various postures to pass under a stick while calypso music played brought forth an aura that neither woman could deny or escape, but both women realized that [PFB] Marina Tiki Bar was not the place to make it obvious to each other, much less anyone else there.

"So you drove all day and now you are here. Any particular reason? Have you been here before?" [FicChaTwentyThree] asked trying to bring the extent of her own arousal to a more manageable level.

"I retired from [USA] a couple of months ago and I am taking the first steps towards a new life. I had enough of Virginia and thought [GSoF] would be good place to settle down, maybe Miami South Beach. I intended to make it there in one shot, but the drive was just a little long for me, so I decided to stop for the night," responded [FicChaTwenty] in a way that let [FicChaTwentyThree] know that she was accustomed to being discrete while at the same time hoping that there might be some chance to fulfill even the slightest of fantasies that she had been entertaining since the first moment she saw her.

"Have you had supper yet? I was just on my way home and was going to cook something up. I would rather not dine alone and you look like you could use a home cooked meal." [FicChaTwentyThree] offered with a smile.

"I would like that very much. I'll get my car and follow you." [FicChaTwenty] replied.

"That won't be necessary. I'll bring you back to the base in the morning," replied [FicChaTwentyThree].

# [HurcanFran] and [HurcanJean]

It was twelve years after [HurcanAndrw] and a year before [HurcanKtrna] that two hurricanes hit [FB] and the surrounding area within three weeks of each other: [HurcanFran] & [HurcanJean].

The damage from [HurcanFran] was a big deal, especially for the people who live on the coast. All of the weaknesses of the infrastructure were exposed and exploited. With blue tarps everywhere, power just restored, and piles of storm damage at the end of virtually every driveway, there was really nothing left to tear up that could be torn up by another storm of similar or less power. When [HurcanJean] visited, all she could really do was blow all the piles around and dump a bunch of rain. [HurcanJean] still knocked the power out, but the emergency response units from all facets of recovery were still in the immediate area, so stuff did get turned back on quicker than it had with [HurcanFran].

What [OBandSD] remembers the most about [HurcanJean] was the tired but not worried look on everyone's face? [OBandSD] recalls the opposite look on people's faces in the buildup to [HurcanFran].

So with [HurcanJean]'s departure, citizens, [OwnProp], [OwnBus], and [MCFLMosFB] could finally get a chance to clean up this mess. Water was restored within three days. Power was restored to nominal levels within two weeks. Getting back to "normal" took a bit longer. One might think that the incredible kick in the face from two hurricanes would leave a lasting impression on everybody. One would be wrong if one were to think such things.

There are some big differences between a [EMP] private sector and [EMP] public sector. There are some gargantuan differences between the thinking of a person looking to get his roof repaired and a [CM] needing to clear the roads of debris and certify buildings safe for re-entry after the evacuation was lifted and people could return to their homes.

The single biggest difference is that [EMP] private sector must take a couple steps backward financially to recover but [EMP] public sector gets to charge overtime and the [CC] just approves a new [B] with new Ad Valorem Tax Millage Rate and keeps on trucking.

This is all fine as long as [TGTDTT] doesn't hear anything about it.

Eight years after those tempestuous evenings with [HurcanFran] and [HurcanJean], [TGTDTT] began to hear stories as to the precarious financial times during that emergency because [MCFLMosFB] reserves was critically low and [MCFLMosFB], and had to wait for funds trickling their way from [USFG] with stops in [GVBMNTFL] and [GovFLMos]. [TGTDTT] doesn't know if the story is true or not, but the current [MCFLMosFB] reserves will fund nominal [MCFLMosFB] expenses for an estimated six weeks.

In the eight years since [HurcanFran] and [HurcanJean], [CC] went on a buying spree of destroyed property just before the real estate bubble burst a few years later. [MCFLMosFB] shelled out enough [USD] to buy land [MCFLMosFB] did not need to fund [MCFLMosFB] expenses for about a year. Today the property is valued at less than half of what it was originally purchased for.

Whose idea was it that [MCFLMosFB] owning the land was better than a person or business owning the land? Does [CC] have all the convenience stores [CC] wants so [CC] won't let somebody come in and put a convenience store where a [BusRestLocal] used to be. The same is true for strip malls and beachfront hotels and condos. So [CC] approved the spending of funds for the sole purpose of preventing interlopers and unsavory characters from gravitating to our beautiful and pristine beaches. The decisions were met with rousing applause from a consistent few as well as criticism and befuddlement as to the decisions and the manner in which the purchases had been made. Is there anything to the fact that [MCFLMosFB] entered the real estate business when a real estate agent was elected to [CC]?

Now [TGTDTT] cannot vouch with his life the validity, but it has been intimated to him on more than one occasion by long time residents that it was common practice of the [CC] to walk into meeting with the decision made after discussing it amongst themselves. If this is true, meeting is nothing more than live theatre with real backstage tales of woe, greed, hatred, fear, but no love and no respect for the [MCFLMosFB] citizens. You see, in [MCFLMosFB], it is all about supporting the [CLB].

[TGTDTT] is quite aware of the gravity of such an accusation and he will not allow his convictions to be based on conjecture. But in [TGTDTT]'s dealings with everybody in City Hall during the period after the bubble burst, [TGTDTT] could tell when there were five people at the front of the room listening to the people at the podium, and when they weren't.

[TGTDTT] also came to see that when certain people are at the front of the room, [TGTDTT] believes [CitComm] actually helped shape the debate. When other people were at the front of the room, [TGTDTT] could swear that there is nothing anyone could say that would influence the decision that had already been made in private.

It is all about being in the [CLB] and using the [USD] that is taken from [OwnProp] and [OwnBus] to fund [OptProj]. Implementing methodology for funding [OptProj] that places particular emphasis on employment of local private sector resources, one or two of longtime friends will make a little [USD] for all their hard work. Activating [PubReInRePro] level 5 states it can all be done in a way that nobody finds out.

Imagine a group of people and something happens to one person within that group. There will be people who will have no knowledge of the event unless someone tells them about it or they "listen to the tape." Others will remember the event as they wanted to, in the way they wanted to, without accounting for the various filters and attenuators that were applied to the transmitted data and its reception. It is no mystery that policemen and lawyers are very careful about using eyewitness testimony.

Every childhood dream and retaliatory fantasy springs forth from the wicked like vomit from a drunk when the wicked are told [MCRev] is their [USD] to spend however they want and nobody will find out. This is some Faustian stuff.

Before [ELCTN11], there were only about sixteen people at most that had any real say about what our fine [MCFLMosFB] was going to buy this year, next year, or the year after that. Nobody else was in the [CLB]. You could not get in the [CLB] unless someone died and there is a long list of people hoping to get picked before you.

After [ELCTN11], the outpouring of open discussion about the city's finances and interactions between [MCFLMosFB] citizens and [CC] members was immense, and it seemed as though there was an extremely large team of people all working together trying to accomplish something that would allow every [MCFLMosFB] citizen to become more informed and welcomed to become involved, and then there was the [CLB]. The results of [ELCTN12] put the functional operations and all decision making associated with [MCFLMosFB] back in the hands of the [CLB].

Some people don't really like clubs. [TGTDTT] likes teams, but he doesn't like clubs. The reason [TGTDTT] doesn't like clubs is the same reason that George Carlin didn't like clubs. Clubs are exclusionary and distract the individual from his or her true purpose. The members focus on protecting the [CLB] instead of living their life as God intended. [TGTDTT] has better stuff to do, like doing everything he can to live his life as God intended.

[MCFLMosFB] citizens were told before the first hurricane hit [MCFLMosFB] in the year of hurricanes that [GBNMNT] was on top of stuff. But at the time, the [REALITY] was that there weren't any [USD] to pay overtime wages and hire contractors to clear the streets. Well the lessons of that hurricane season were hard learned. We will never forget!

Six years later, the [FD] chief of [MCFLMosFB] asks for some [USD] to buy some new [CapEq] to replace the twenty year old broken [CapEq]. The [FD] chief slides in the idea that [MCFLMosFB] could get a way better [CapEq], but it will only cost three times as much.

Either way, it did not matter because there were no [MCFLMosFB] reserves to buy anything. There was no plan to save any [USD] to buy any of the stuff that [MCFLMosFB] knows will have to be replaced some day. There is no [USD] if Mother Nature elects to send one of her big, fat, noisy, wet children in the form of storms that we name, right into the heart of our fair town.

But all is not lost. [TGTDTT] can still have some fun with this. All [TGTDTT] had to do was to ask [FicChaTwentyFour], the [CM] at the time, how stuff got that way. [FicChaTwentyFour]'s eyes would get big and his leg would start to bounce, then the hummina hummina and the "follow me if you can but since I am just making shit up as I go, you'll be totally lost in 3, 2, 1" dance. [FicChaTwentyFour] was the best dancer that [TGTDTT] had ever seen.

[TGTDTT] really thought he had seen some talented issue dancers before, but [FicChaTwentyFour] made them all look like amateurs. It was no secret to [TGTDTT] why [FicChaTwentyFour] had been able to keep his job for some twenty-five years. [FicChaTwentyFour] was the only person who really knew where and how much [USD] there was and [FicChaTwentyFour] understood the game well enough to be able to keep everyone in the dark about where the [USD] was coming from and what was actually being purchased. [FicChaTwentyFour] also knew who was responsible for keeping [FicChaTwentyFour]'s bread buttered. So when [CLB] told [FicChaTwentyFour] to find the [USD] to buy some property, [FicChaTwentyFour] found it. There was a period of time when [MCFLMosFB] had the [USD] on hand because of the "Real Estate Bubble." Now is a period of time when [MCFLMosFB] does not have the [USD] on hand because the "Real Estate Bubble" burst.

Even so, if someone pumps the well too often, too quickly, or too long, the well goes dry. The [CLB] does not want to hear about some dry well. [CLB] wants to hear "Certainly" to every question they ask and [CLB] aint ever going to ask whether the well is being pumped too often, too quickly, or too long. It is as though there is the absolute expectation that the source feeding into the well is infinite and [MFCU]s needs a good set of rules, so that [CLB] stays in control of the spigot.

Nobody in [CLB] seems to want to keep any [USD] in reserves. [TGTDTT] still doesn't understand how ensuring [MCFLMosFB] reserves is not sustained at a justifiable level to instill confidence in the eyes of the general public is a priority. It just seems that the individual interest of [CC] members was great enough to ignore the voices of dissent and echoes of past lessons and subject matter experts.

A meeting is the only place a group of three to five people can tell a room full of people to bugger off, and there is nothing that anyone can do about it when it happens. It doesn't happen on every episode of meeting, so you have to see all the episodes to really appreciate the dynamic. The [CC] meeting is the only thing playing for free in [FB] and [ObandSD] doesn't have any money or a TV. A person can get a seat most nights, but if the show is expected to be really good, you can only listen to the real time audio broadcast from outside the theatre or catch the web broadcast later.

# Tsongkhapa Passage

*A coiled rope's speckled color and coiling are similar to those of a snake, and when the rope is perceived in a dim area, the thought arises, "This is a snake." As for the rope, at the time when it is seen to be a snake, the collection and parts of the rope are not even in the slightest way a snake. Therefore, that snake is merely set up by conceptuality. In the same way, when the thought of "I" arises in dependence upon mind and body – neither the collection which is a continuum of earlier and later moments, nor the collection of parts at one time, nor the separate parts, nor the continuum of and of the separate parts – is even the slightest way the "I". Also there is not even the slightest something that is a different entity from mind and body that is apprehendable as the "I." Consequently, the "I" is merely set up by conceptuality in dependence upon mind and body; it is not established by way of its own entity.*

Just as [TGTDTT] is convinced that he sees a snake in the dim room that becomes a coiled rope when light is shined upon it, [TGTDTT] can be as equally convinced that he sees a coiled rope that eventually bites him because it was really a snake. At the same time, [TGTDTT] can convince himself that he is right about the snake being a rope because he has come to believe that he is usually right. The fact that [TGTDTT] is now dying from the venom of a coiled rope might be a teachable moment or it might not be. Thus is the human condition.

When [TGTDTT] moved to [MCFLMosFB] in 1998, he saw a tranquil beachside bedroom community. After [ELCTN12],

[TGTDTT] saw a tremendously confused and petty community. When [TGTDTT] looked at the five elected members of [CC], [TGTDTT] saw one person of integrity, vision, and character, saw another person who was mentally unstable and drank too much, a third person who thought entirely too much of himself, a fourth person who was committed to ruining everyone who ever disagreed with her, and a fifth person who could barely spell [B], much less understand [B].

The problem [TGTDTT] is having is that no individual is all good or all bad and that he may not be seeing what is really there. For instance, [FicChaTwentyFour], the former [CM] is one of the most personable, engaging, and friendly people one could ever hope to meet, but [TGTDTT] rarely heard him answer the question that was asked, which always made [TGTDTT] wonder if [FicChaTwentyFour] was hiding something.

Another example is the [FD] chief, [FicChaTwentyFive], that [TGTDTT] considers a personal friend whom he would help in any way that he could, but [TGTDTT] is told by long time residents not to trust [FicChaTwentyFive]. What is clear to [TGTDTT] is that the perception of the moment may not be the same as [REALITY].

The last example is [FicChaTen] who stumbled a little at their first meeting, but he recovered with a well-articulated sense of purpose. Since that meeting, [TGTDTT] has come to trust what [FicChaTen] tells him completely, but only after the signal has been processed using the [ColUSAF] filter.

Of the three examples given, it will take some serious lighting to change [TGTDTT]'s belief that [FicChaTen] is not a snake. With that being said, [TGTDTT] is not willing to bet the farm that he is right. The same idea applies to the other two examples to a lesser degree. [TGTDTT] would be far less surprised to find out if either [FicChaTwentyFour] or [FicChaTwentyFive] is a snake.

But either way, [TGTDTT] has to keep on keepin on. [TGTDTT] wasn't planning on any of these [FicCha]s being in his life, and there is no telling how long they will be. [TGTDTT] just makes sure that he does nothing that would justify any them choosing to be a snake to him. Even for a moment.

Come to think of it, [TGTDTT] pretty much does his best to do that with everyone he comes into contact. But that's [TGTDTT]. [TGTDTT] doesn't want to be a snake, and he doesn't want anyone to see him as a snake. [TGTDTT] figures that if he doesn't see them as a snake, they will not see him as a snake. But if [TGTDTT] must be a snake, even for a moment, to do what he believes is right, then he is okay with that. So if [TGTDTT] is like that, he figures everybody is like that.

If [TGTDTT] can see the hidden inner snake in himself, and can respect the hidden inner snake in a person not himself, there is going to be a bunch of rope in [TGTDTT]'s life. A person can do some really cool stuff with rope, but dealing with a snake is always more trouble than it's worth. So if [TGTDTT] sees that hidden inner snake becoming less hidden, he starts avoiding those people and keeping his distance.

# [FBWC]

[FicChaTwenty]'s evening with [FicChaTwentyThree] was as close to the manifestation of heaven on earth as [FicChaTwenty] could ever imagine. [FicChaTwentyThree] was equal in age but more experienced in the ways of physical pleasure. For the first time in [FicChaTwenty]'s closeted life, someone was eagerly filling her needs. After dinner and throughout the night, [FicChaTwentyThree] guided [FicChaTwenty] from climax to climax where each stop along the way was unique and more meaningful than the one before.

When the sun rose the next morning, an exhausted and invigorated [FicChaTwenty] believed she had found her new home and that, if it was possible, [FicChaTwenty] would never leave. But as the sun continued to rise, the realities of life began to return.

[FicChaTwentyThree] was not only a married woman whose husband was out of town on business, [FicChaTwentyThree] was a pillar of the community. If the general public discovered what had happened the previous evening, the scandal would be overwhelming and would destroy everything [FicChaTwentyThree] had worked so hard to build over the years. In [FicChaTwentyThree]'s mind, last night was going to be the only night and [FicChaTwenty] would be half way to Miami South Beach by lunchtime.

[FicChaTwenty] opened her heart to [FicChaTwentyThree] as she had never done with anyone before. For the first time in [FicChaTwenty]'s life, she was vulnerable and submissive. But it felt so natural and wonderful that [FicChaTwenty] would do anything to keep the feeling and the person who made it happen.

Coffee was brewed, served, and drank. Words were exchanged and tears shed. The two women held each other. Through it all, a realization that would serve both their needs began to emerge. [FicChaTwentyThree] did not have to give up her life and [FicChaTwenty] did not have to lose [FicChaTwentyThree]. But no one could ever know. It was decided that [FicChaTwenty] would find a place to live in [MCFLMosFB] and establish herself in a respectful manner by joining [FBWC] where [FicChaTwentyThree] was a prominent member.

On the surface, [FBWC] is a civically minded service organization that raises [USD] for various charities and causes, promotes women involvement in the political arena, and provides for activities that are run by women for the benefit of women. From the outside, [FBWC] looks the same as the Elks or Rotary Club, where the American Flag is saluted each day and they sing "God Bless America" in perfect unison. However, once you are inside the inner sanctum of the club, you begin to understand that [FBWC] takes on a much more sinister personality.

Hiding behind the auspices of belonging to a national charter, [FBWC] boasts of reaching out and providing assistance throughout the community, the nation, and the world. But these boasts are less about the quality of assistance they provide and more about being able to say they are involved. For instance, [FBWC] sent a check for $100 dollars to the relief fund for the victims of the earthquake in Haiti but refused to get involved in providing any assistance to a local family that had lost their home due to foreclosure and were living in their car. A comparison of the amount of [USD] spent to aid others to the amount of [USD] spent on their monthly luncheons gives a pretty good idea of where [FBWC] interests are. But through it all, the image [FBWC] makes available for public consumption that involves charity for others is just that, image. The [REALITY] is that [FBWC] is comprised of petulant old women that are desperately trying to lay claim to a legacy of moral superiority.

[FBWC] was started by the wives of the founders of [MCFLMosFB], so that the women would have something to do while the men ran [MCFLMosFB]. They planned picnics, parades, fundraisers, and other activities that would bring the residents of [FB] together. But [FBWC] was also the keepers of [MCFLMosFB]'s secrets and it took more than being a woman who lives in [MCFLMosFB] to be a member. A person could not get elected to [CC] or be on any of the [MCFLMosFB] boards without approval by the [FBWC] President. The way to become [FBWC]s President, was to have personal knowledge of the most powerful secrets.

[FicChaTwentyThree] had spent her entire adult life accumulating a vast inventory of secrets that would give her power while making sure no one had any secrets to use against her. [FicChaTwenty] was not [FicChaTwentyThree]'s first one night stand, but it was the first time within [MCFLMosFB] boundaries. There was something about [FicChaTwenty] that put [FicChaTwentyThree] at ease while at the same time, if [FicChaTwenty] was going to stay, [FicChaTwentyThree] needed to keep her where she could keep close tabs on her, and to make sure any threat to her status was dealt with quickly before it got out of hand. [FicChaTwentyThree] knew that bringing [FicChaTwenty] into [FBWC] would ensure that her network of gossipy sycophants would keep her abreast of any potential problems.

[FicChaTwenty] benefited from joining [FBWC] as well. In addition to being able to see [FicChaTwentyThree] on a regular basis without arousing suspicion, club membership would establish her as a power broker and player in the community. [FBWC] is a great networking tool for someone who is looking to make her mark in the community and [FicChaTwenty] could set the stage by establishing the image she wanted to portray without having to deal with her past. So, instead of introducing herself as a frustrated lesbian who was drummed out of [USA] for being a relatively incompetent pain in the ass, her story was modified to that of [MajUSA] retired who devoted her life to [USA] and the pursuit of justice for its unappreciated service men and women. [FicChaTwenty] could tell the tales of her courtroom exploits defending good people who were wrongly accused by incompetent prosecutors. She could tell people that her decision to retire was that after twenty years, she could no longer fight the powerful and corrupt male dominated officer corps that could not stand to be challenged by a more intelligent and capable woman.

[FBWC] was the perfect forum for [FicChaTwenty] to hone her narrative that she was chosen by God Herself to do what man cannot. She saw herself as being sent to help these small town hicks become enlightened and, as funny as it sounds, the women of [FBWC] saw [FicChaTwenty] the same way. As long as [FicChaTwenty] did not challenge [FicChaTwentyThree]'s authority, everything was going work out just fine.

Things were good all the way around. Until one fine day in late summer of YR11:

[FicChaTen]:      I am [FicChaTen] and I am running for [CC].

                  I believe . . . .

                  Active participation by the citizenry in [GVBMNT] is a good thing.

[GVBMNT]'s actions should reflect the best interests and desires of the citizens.

Fiscal responsibility is the key toward true and longstanding progress.

I am for . . . .

wisely using taxpayer [USD] for the ongoing services that this city needs.

pursuing outside funding from [GVBMNTFL] and [USFG]s for [OptProj] that benefit [MCFLMosFB].

Creating an environment that promotes community involvement in fee for service programs that are self-sustaining.

I want to accomplish in my first term . . .

Resolving the matter surrounding the alleged misuse of [CRA] finances.

Applying [CRA] finances and other [MCRev] grant in a manner that improves [MCFLMosFB], not maintain it.

Establish a long-term plan for reduction in expenditures for non-current activities, [PenBen], [MCFLMosFB] debt servicing, etc.

I intend to accomplish these goals by . . .

-A comprehensive internal study (i.e. no paid consultants) and citizen's participation of city [GBNMNT] processes to identify ways to maximize taxpayer value for the same level of service.

-Investigation into ways to reduce the ongoing cost of servicing [MCFLMosFB] debt and [PenBen].

Working closely with [CC] Mayor, [CC] City Manager, and [CC] - Negotiate a satisfactory resolution to the recent allegations surrounding the use of [CRA] finances.

-Prepare and propose a revised set of guidelines concerning the manner in which [B] [MCFLMosFB] is developed and the manner in which [MCRev] grant is spent.

If you agree with what I believe and what I am for, then I ask for your support. If you believe my goals and methods could use some tweaking, then I ask you to join me and work with me.

The ongoing re-election of a small group of people has resulted in a fiscal rat's nest that will take a great deal of effort to straighten out. If we do not straighten this mess out, an increasing amount of your taxes will be spent on legal fees and outside consultants resulting in a general trend towards insolvency.

[MCFLMosFB] was founded by extremely talented, accomplished, and capable people. Today some of its citizens are among the most respected people in their particular field on endeavor. I intend to use my talents and energy to make this city a model for others to admire and I invite you to join me. I want your vote on November 8. I want your presence at meeting. I want you to believe that you can be part of the solution and then act on that belief.

I am [FicChaTen]. I am a candidate for [CC] in [ELCTN11], I am asking you to be a part of the team that will make this city the model for what being a community really means. Thank you.

# The Awakening

[TGTDTT]'s involvement in local government began in late August, when a new neighbor petitioned [MCFLMosFB] to turn her single-family four-bedroom house into an assisted living facility for up to eight people and staff. The house was right across the street from [TGTDTT] on the corner of a relatively busy road and one of the major corridors for the junior and senior high school kids to go to and from school.

Normally [TGTDTT] takes a passive approach to what people want to do with their lives, but he could not bring himself to sitting this one out. There were a number of technical issues that [TGTDTT] thought made the request unreasonable. As such, [TGTDTT] documented his argument as to why the request for variance should be denied and made his case to [MCFLMosFB] planning and zoning board.

During the time that [TGTDTT] had lived in [MCFLMosFB], this was the first one of these meetings [TGTDTT] had ever attended and he had no idea that it would mark the beginning of his ever-increasing involvement in [GBNMNT], specifically [MCFLMosFB]'s politics.

[MCFLMosFB] chair was a 66-year-old woman named [FicChaTwenty]. It was abundantly clear to [TGTDTT] that [FicChaTwenty] was in charge and would make sure the other four members voted as [FicChaTwenty] wanted them to.

The petitioner made her case for the request, and several [MCFLMosFB] citizens, including [TGTDTT], voiced their objections or concerns. Police department head [MCFLMosFB] and [FD] head [MCFLMosFB] discussed their perceived impact to [MCFLMosFB] and building and department zoning head [MCFLMosFB] discussed what would be required to make the facility compliant with law.

When it came time for [MCFLMosFB] planning and zoning board to vote, [FicChaTwenty] gave a summary of the issues from her point of view that led [TGTDTT] to believe that [FicChaTwenty] had not listened to anything that was said during the meeting. As luck would have it, [MCFLMosFB] planning and zoning board voted to recommend that the request be denied by [CC], but [TGTDTT] left the meeting believing that the five people sitting at the front of the room were somehow separate from the fifty or so people sitting in the audience. If [TGTDTT] had self-confidence problems, he would even go as far as to accuse [FicChaTwenty] of thinking that she was greater than he and every [MFCU] not [FicChaTwenty].

[TGTDTT] made the decision to attend the very next meeting of [CC] because there was a chance that [CC] would decide to overrule [MCFLMosFB] planning and zoning board's recommendation. The meeting was well attended, but the petitioner had decided to withdraw her request, so the issue was not discussed.

Having cleared his calendar for that evening, [TGTDTT] decided to stay, watch, and listen. The principal issue on the agenda turned out to be whether to approve the purchase a 110-foot ladder truck to replace a 20 year-old pumper-truck for the [FD] of [MCFLMosFB]. [CM] gave an overview of the issue, [FD] chief provided some history and additional information, individual [CC] members asked questions and gave some opinions, and then several members of the audience began voicing their concerns on both sides of the question.

In listening to all of this, it occurred to [TGTDTT] that the decision as to the prudent course of action was a technical one in terms of capability and cost, but no one had given [TGTDTT] any indication that they understood the long-term ramifications of any decision they made. When [TGTDTT] thought everyone else had a chance to speak, he requested and received permission to address [CC]. [TGTDTT]'s [CitComm]s, which were not prepared in advance, dealt with the idea that any decision made by [CC] would be misunderstood by [GenPub], and that none of the responsible parties had demonstrated a clear understanding of the long term financial impact of the decisions. [CC] seemed receptive to [TGTDTT]'s message and directed the [FD] chief to put together more information.

During the break that followed, the [FD] head of the [MCFLMosFB] approached [TGTDTT] and asked [TGTDTT] for his help in putting together a report that would help [CC] arrive at an informed decision. [TGTDTT] explained that he had no opinion on the matter, but that he would help [CC] in any way that [TGTDTT] could. However, any study that [TGTDTT] did would be comprehensive and honest. The numbers would not be biased towards one option over another. Any effort to degrade the validity of the study would be met with [TGTDTT] walking away from the effort and making a public statement as to why [TGTDTT] finds the study flawed. The [FD] chief agreed with [TGTDTT]'s terms, and they went to work.

The final report was a twenty-year cost analysis of twenty-one different scenarios ranging from doing nothing to buying a $750,000 ladder truck. The night that the report was presented, more than one [CC] member remarked that nothing like this had ever been done before, and that they could not understand why this type of study was not part of normal processes. [TGTDTT] told [CC] that he could only speak to questions concerning this report and was unable to comment as to anything else.

What [TGTDTT] can write now is that while [TGTDTT] was working on the report, [TGTDTT] did discover there is no long-term plan for [MCFLMosFB]. There are long term zoning plans to be sure, but the financial management of [MCFLMosFB] was on a year-by-year basis with no view to the financial needs of [MCFLMosFB] in years to come, or any review of past spending to assess the efficacy of operations. Being a [OwnBus] and a project engineer, [TGTDTT] found such a short-term view troubling. Not that there was anything [TGTDTT] could say was wrong, but that those with the responsibility for ensuring the smooth [MCFLMosFB] operations never gave serious consideration to what was going to be needed five or ten years down the road. [TGTDTT]'s inquiries into [MCFLMosFB] finances gave [TGTDTT] reason to believe that there was no [USD] in the bank to buy stuff [MCFLMosFB] knew it was going to need. What [TGTDTT] also found was that [CM] was resistant to anyone finding out how [USD] was really being spent.

For what it is worth, just because [TGTDTT] sees something that is contrary to his worldview, doesn't mean that [TGTDTT] is going to lose sleep over it. [TGTDTT] lives his life the way he lives it, and other people live the way they live. As long as his way does not mess them up, or their way doesn't mess him up, [TGTDTT] usually doesn't give the matter a second thought.

If [MCFLMosFB] goes bankrupt as a result of mismanagement, [TGTDTT]'s life goes on virtually unchanged. If the [MCFLMosFB] [EMP] pension fund runs out as the result of mismanagement, [TGTDTT]'s life still goes on virtually unchanged. [TGTDTT]'s concern for others extends only as far as the other person's desire to improve his/her situation. It is rare that [TGTDTT] ever refuses a request for his help, but [TGTDTT] cannot want to solve other's problem more than they do. That might seem a little callous, but [TGTDTT] has limited time on this earth, and he would prefer not to waste a moment of it trying to help people who do not want his help.

In the process of helping the [FD] chief, [MCFLMosFB] citizens began to approach [TGTDTT] to discuss other issues. One of [TGTDTT]'s neighbors, [FicChaTwelve], came to [TGTDTT]'s door for the first time in the thirteen years that [TGTDTT] has lived there to talk about a candidate for [CC] that [FicChaTwelve] was supporting. Candidate was a [ColUSAF] retired, whose platform was "Efficient Government." The candidate is [FicChaTen], and his official military biography explained he was a [USAF] Vice Wing Commander and Operations Group Commander, graduate of the [USAF] Fighter Weapons School, flew missions in Desert Storm 1, and led many as a Strike Package Commander at his deployed locations, and after retirement, his civilian job is as a functional equivalent of a [CM] for [CCAS]. Electing [FicChaTen] to [CC] would bring some serious talent to the team, so without knowing anything else, [TGTDTT] was going to vote for [FicChaTen]. Besides, some of the other candidates had already been there awhile, and it was time to bring in new people.

[FicChaTwelve] offered to introduce [FicChaTen] to [TGTDTT], and not wanting to be rude the next day they went to [FicChaTen]'s house. [TGTDTT] asked [FicChaTen] why he wanted to be a human pincushion.

At first [FicChaTen]'s answers didn't speak to anything [TGTDTT] could readily understand. [FicChaTen]'s repetition of the word "efficiency" didn't convey anything meaningful to [TGTDTT], but eventually [TGTDTT] got [FicChaTen] to talk specifics. [FicChaTen] outlined some of his concerns, which mirrored [TGTDTT]'s awareness to that point. [FicChaTen] wanted to do something about it, and [TGTDTT] respected those who see a problem and step in to fix it.

[TGTDTT] supported [FicChaTen] from the sidelines, wrote a couple letters to the editor that got published, and signed a nominal check. [FicChaTen] won the election with room to spare. [FicChaTen]'s first act was to create [COFFEE] to perform an honest and comprehensive study of [MCFLMosFB]. He wanted to document what they are doing, how they are doing it, and compare it to other communities and organizations. [TGTDTT] was on [COFFEE]. In fact, [TGTDTT] was the principal author of the [COFFEE] charter and the final report.

The charter essentially outlined the scope of responsibilities but didn't specify exactly what studies were going to be performed. The charter did make it clear that [COFFEE] was strictly an information gathering function, and it was up to the department heads of [MCFLMosFB], [CM], and [CC] to decide if and what changes should be made and how to go about making those changes. The final report documented the studies performed, listed specific items that warranted public discussion, and identified several areas that would benefit from further study.

The final report was well received by [MCFLMosFB] citizens, [CC], [CM], and department heads of [MCFLMosFB]. It also served as the catalyst for [B] for [MCFLMosFB] [FY12-13] negotiations. The results of those negotiations were a 0.5% reduction in Ad Valorem Tax Millage Rate, 7% reduction in [MCFLMosFB] expenses, $150,000 dollars put into [MCFLMosFB] reserves and the purchase of much needed computer equipment. All without cutting or reducing services of any kind and without laying off or firing [MCFLMosFB] [EMP]s.

Everyone involved in the effort and everyone affected by the effort felt good about working together and helping each other. Countless [CitComm]s of support drowned out the few detractors who seemed to have an agenda that had nothing to do with bringing the community together. [TGTDTT] was genuinely surprised as to the impact of their efforts and believed that [COFFEE] was something that would really make a positive difference in how [MCFLMosFB] was run and perceived by [MCFLMosFB] citizens and surrounding communities.

There were editorials in the [FlaTo] praising [COFFEE] and [COFFEE] was even mentioned on the [MicBil] radio show as a good thing. Everyone in [TGTDTT]'s new circle believed a corner towards a brighter future had been turned.

Then [ELCTN12] happened, and everyone in [FicChaTens]'s group was left confused. [FicChaTwenty]'s group was elated, and everybody else felt like they felt, but the 'everybody else' group wasn't really making anything happen so they don't count. The [MCFLMosFB] voters decided to return [FicChaTwenty], [FicChaTwentySix], and [FicChaTwentySeven] to [CC] instead of newcomers [FicChaTwelve], [FicChaFourteen], and [FicChaFifteen].

The reason for the confusion is that [FicChaTwenty], [FicChaTwentySix], and [FicChaTwentySeven] were all directly involved in creating the environment and conditions that [FicChaTwelve], [FicChaFourteen], and [FicChaFifteen] were working to modify and potentially improve. How could people not understand this?

So three days after the election, [TGTDTT] sits trying to see the greater truth. One question [TGTDTT] has to ask is whether the stuff he perceived as problematic were really problems at all. Another question is that if the problems [TGTDTT] perceive are really problems, why did the majority of the voters think otherwise? The last question [TGTDTT] will deal with is what changes does [TGTDTT] need to make in his life so that his actions achieve the intended and truly beneficial results?

Before the polls closed on November 6th, YR12 [TGTDTT] was cautiously optimistic that [MCFLMosFB] voters agreed with much of what [TGTDTT] thought was important. After the votes were tallied and reported, [TGTDTT] was in a state of disbelief. When [TGTDTT] had emptied his second glass of Knob Creek that evening, [TGTDTT] was a little angry. When [TGTDTT] woke up the morning of the 7th, he was uncertain as to whether he should abandon any future involvement in the community. Yesterday [TGTDTT] began to see a glimmer of what he is supposed to do. Today, [TGTDTT] begins his journey to help himself become a better person and hopefully help the little town of [FB], [GSoF], and possibly other communities as well.

# Welcome to [FBResMailGrp]

Hi [TGTDTT],

Thanks for the beer and the chat! You won't regret supporting [FicChaTen]... [FicChaTwelve] promises you that. [FicChaTwelve] will be by Saturday morning around 11:30AM. Oh, [FicChaTwelve] also wanted to know if [TGTDTT] would mind putting one of [FicChaTen]'s signs on your property along the main road? [FicChaTwelve] has an extra sign.

This is some additional information on [FBResMailGrp], [FicChaTwelve] maintains. [TGTDTT] will be Bcc'd on all future correspondences, and no one will be able to see [TGTDTT]'s email address. Below are "rules of engagement" for [FBResMailGrp]. If [TGTDTT] has questions or concerns, please let [FicChaTwelve] know.

As the responsible entity for [FBResMailGrp], [FicChaTwelve] considers these rules of use and ethics to be important:

1) [FBResMailGrp] is an information conduit and individual email addresses will be protected (not public record) because [FBResMailGrp] is a private-citizen's initiative and not a [GVBMNT] one.
2) Information sent out will be just that-- information. It will be non-partisan and will not espouse a particular belief or outcome.
3) If someone asks to be removed (or added) to the list, it will be done so at [FicChaTwelve]'s first opportunity,

and [FicChaTwelve] will acknowledge all requests. [FicChaTwelve] does not retain email addresses that have been removed from [FBResMailGrp].

4) [FicChaTwelve] will verify facts, figures, and information sources by providing citations, links and other publicly available references. If [FicChaTwelve] makes a mistake, [FicChaTwelve] will correct it.

5) If [FBResMailGrp] member seeks additional information, [FicChaTwelve] will route the question (leaving the source anonymous) to appropriate sources for answers.

6) If [FBResMailGrpMbr] seeks contact with another [FBResMailGrp] member, [FicChaTwelve] will obtain specific permission to share ONLY the approved contact information and nothing else.

7) [MCFLMosFB], to include [CC], may request relay of information through [FBResMailGrp] pertaining to [MCFLMosFB] operations, general public sentiment of [MCFLMosFB], general public opinions regarding [MCFLMosFB], and general public queries of [MCFLMosFB].

8) [FicChaTwelve] will not engage active [CC] members directly nor share dialogue among [FB] resident mail group members of [CC].

9) Information will be current, uncensored, and complete... if you ever feel [FicChaTwelve] has left something out, he will correct it.

You can share [FicChaTwelve]'s email address with other [MCFLMosFB] citizens who would like to stay abreast of our city's business. [FBResMailGrp] is open to all residents, [OwnBus], and [OwnProp] of [MCFLMosFB].

Very Best Regards,
[FicChaTwelve], [FBResMailGrp]

# Meeting [FicChaTen]

It seems that native Floridians are few and far between. Second or third generation Floridians are even fewer and farther between when compared to the almost twenty million people that currently live in [GSoF]. When people meet [TGTDTT] and find that he was born in Naples, it is more common that they make a reference to Italy than the relatively small Gulf Coast community of [MCFLColNa].

With the exception of a six-year hitch in [USN] and business travel, [TGTDTT] has lived in [GSoF] his entire life and he loves it. [TGTDTT] loves the humidity, the swamps, the beaches, the rivers, the food, and so much more about the state he calls home.

What [TGTDTT] doesn't embrace is the influx of people from other places who complain about the perceived inadequacies when compared to where they are from. [TGTDTT]'s reaction is always a certain gratitude that he is happy where he is and the desire that the malcontents go back to wherever they came from. This is true when people mention they can't get an Authentic Philadelphia Cheesesteak Sandwich, [APCSS], here, which seems perfectly obvious to [TGTDTT] for no other reason than this is not Philadelphia.

[TGTDTT] went to a university faculty dinner with his wife one time and sat with the Dean and a few other couples. One of the couples began droning on about moving down here and the troubles they have had adjusting. It turns out they were from Philadelphia, and they made mention of the lack of [APCSS]s. [TGTDTT]'s wife gently squeezed his arm because she knew of his intolerance of whiners, had witnessed his lecture on the subject many times, and because they were sitting with her boss, hoped he would not engage the conversation and embarrass anyone.

As [TGTDTT] was mentally preparing his approach to shutting them down in a tactful and powerful manner, the couple mentioned there was this one place that did serve an [APCSS]. They told him the name of the shop, exactly where it was, and suggested [TGTDTT] go there if he ever got the chance. Accepting the need to acknowledge their suggestion as his cue to take part in the conversation, [TGTDTT] asked how it was possible that a local diner could serve an [APCSS]. Did they fly the sandwiches already prepared down from Philadelphia? The husband looked confused by the question, and the wife replied, "No silly. They make them fresh right there."

[TGTDTT] replied that if the sandwich was created using locally made bread with meat and cheese that was purchased locally, then the resulting product was not an [APCSS]. It may have properties that are similar, if not identical to an [APCSS], but it is not an [APCSS] if, for no other reason, it was not made in Philadelphia.

Some days later, [TGTDTT] happened to be driving and saw the shop the couple was talking about. He was hungry and decided to stop in. Going to the counter, the young man asked what [TGTDTT] would like to order.

"I was told by some people from Philadelphia that I could get an [APCSS] here."

"Absolutely." Replied the young man.

"Great. I would like one [APCSS] to go."

"What do want on it?"

"I would like an [APCSS]. Whatever that means. So please prepare my sandwich exactly as an [APCSS] is prepared."

There was some more back and forth that was going nowhere, so the young man went and got the manager. The manager came out from the kitchen and asks [TGTDTT] if there is anything he can help [TGTDTT] with. [TGTDTT] explained that his goal was to have the experience of an [APCSS], and that he was led to believe that he could have that experience by making the proper purchase in this establishment. [TGTDTT] further explained that if he were to assert any bias into the process, it would prevent him from achieving his goal. The manager seemed to understand more than the young man whom first tried to take [TGTDTT]'s order, and said he knew what to do.

[TGTDTT] eventually got and paid for the sandwich. When he took his first bite, he realized two things. The first is that there is no such single thing as an [APCSS]. The second thing he realized was that this sandwich was not better than most of the steak sandwiches he had eaten before.

The point of all this is to make clear that people decide to believe stuff that is not true in the sense that "two plus two equals four" is true. People also tend to assign importance to things that may be out of whack with what is really important. This was on [TGTDTT]'s mind when [FicChaTwelve] picked him up to go meet [FicChaTen].

[FicChaTwelve] and [TGTDTT] pulled up to [FicChaTen]'s house just as [FicChaTen] was putting air into some bicycle tires. [FicChaTen]'s six-foot plus height becomes quite apparent when he stands up because he stands up straight. Knowing he was retired military, [TGTDTT]'s immediate impression was something along the lines of DC and not Little Creek. [FicChaTen] extended his hand, they shook, and [FicChaTen] led [TGTDTT] through the house to the boat dock where they could talk. Respecting that his time was limited, [TGTDTT] got to his point quickly, which was "Why do want this gig?"

[FicChaTen] believed that [MCFLMosFB] could be more efficient and that he would work to introduce efficiencies into [MCFLMosFB]. [TGTDTT] told [FicChaTen] that [TGTDTT] had no idea what [FicChaTen] was talking about and that repeating the word "efficiency" wasn't helping [TGTDTT] understand.

[FicChaTen]'s tact went from the general idea to specific initiatives that would reduce [MCFLMosFB] cost. [TGTDTT] responded that he did not need to be on [CC] to make those suggestions. Was he using the [CC] as a stepping-stone to [GovFLMos], [GVBMNTFL], or [USFG]?

[FicChaTen] realized that [TGTDTT] perceived his narrative as unconvincing. [TGTDTT] told him that [TGTDTT] would vote for him because [FicChaTen]'s resume was sufficiently impressive and getting a new voice on [CC] is a good thing, but as of yet, [FicChaTen] had not inspired [TGTDTT] at all. [TGTDTT] suggested [FicChaTen] consider some soul searching to better understand why [FicChaTen] was running and how [FicChaTen] being on [CC] would benefit [MCFLMosFB] citizens because up to this point, it was the [APCSS] thing all over again.

[TGTDTT] suspected [FicChaTen] wasn't accustomed to [TGTDTT]'s comfort in telling [FicChaTen] the fallacy of [FicChaTen]'s argument up to this point in such a calm, clear, and blunt manner. [TGTDTT] remembers how the look on

[FicChaTen]'s face and the tone in his voice changed. He stopped talking at [TGTDTT] and started speaking to [TGTDTT].

[FicChaTen]: A small group of people that serve the interests of a small group of people run [MCFLMosFB]. [CC] rubber stamps the [B]s put forth by [CM] and As Valorem Tax Millage Rate and [MCFLMosFB] expenses keep going up with nothing to show for it except increasing debt and unfunded liabilities. The tax paying citizens of this community are seen as subservient to City Hall and citizens are treated with contempt and disrespect. There is no reason for it to be this way, and I am working to bring sensible representative [GVBMNT] to our [MC].

[FicChaTen] then began detailing his understanding of the facts that led him to this conclusion. It seemed to [TGTDTT] that [FicChaTen]'s running for [CC] was not a vanity exercise. [TGTDTT] found himself being drawn in to accepting that what [FicChaTen] thought was important was really important, and that [TGTDTT] had a personal responsibility to becoming part of the reform movement. Knowing [FicChaTen] had places to be, [TGTDTT] thanked him for his time. [FicChaTen] then took [TGTDTT] by the arm to shake his hand and said, "I would certainly appreciate your vote, but there is something more important that I would like you to do."

[TGTDTT] gave [FicChaTen] the "What's that?" look. [FicChaTen] responded to [TGTDTT]'s look by saying, "Don't take my word for it, do your homework and figure this out for yourself."

# [FicChaTen] [CC] [ELCTN11]

[BeginTrans FBResMailGrp]

Subject: Highlights meeting [CC]
Date: Sunday, September 25, 11 9:13 AM
Wednesday night was a lively session.

After a presentation/proclamation to the Daughters of
the American Revolution recognizing the week (17-23 Sep
11) as Constitution Week, the first order of business
was adopting [B] [FY11-12]. One councilman requested
that [CC] continue to look into keeping the [MCFLMosFB]
newsletter somehow. When the dust settled, our Ad
Valorem Tax Millage Rate (and many tax bills) went
up AGAIN. [B] [FY11-12] passed at its second reading.

[CC] adjourned and then reformed as [CRA] board. [CRA]
board talked about when they were going to meet with
the [GVBMNTSTATE] Redevelopment Association regarding
their visit report. There was lively [CitComm] and
discussion on the upcoming [GVBMNTSTATE] Redevelopment
Association Conference in [MCFLOraOr]. It was finally
decided that, since [CRA] board has $2500 budgeted for
travel expenses for the year, [CRA] board can use UP
to THAT AMOUNT to send [MCFLMosFB] representatives
to the conference this year.

On a different agenda item, while the current grant
writers clearly give the city a great return on
investment, there was much discussion on the Grant

Writer's Contract contents. Essentially, [CC] approved an open-ended contract (that can be terminated by any party with 30 days notice) that only stipulates the base cost for the 12 fiscal year (plus an undetermined amount and type of reimbursable expenses and travel). After the 1st year of the contract, the cost for the Service will be whatever the city wants to budget. Now that's a contract! Excerpt of [CitComm]:

[FicChaTen]     It is fundamentally irresponsible to rely on [GVBMNTFL] or [USFG] funds to meet the ongoing needs of [MCFLMosFB]. [USD] made available by [GVBMNTFL] or [USFG], in the form of grants, is a great tool for one-time [MCFLMosFB] expense that meet the conditions of the grant, but not to pay [MCFLMosFB] salaries of police officers and professional fire fighters. We need those [MCFLMosFB] [EMP]s, and we need to pay them using [USD]. We must rely on [USD] that cannot be taken away at the whim of [GVBMNTFL] or [USFG].

There is a recent issue that, if improperly handled, will adversely affect all [MCFLMosFB] taxpayers and may result in a reduction in the quality of service provided by [PD] and [FD].

Electing me, [FicChaTen], to [CC] this November 8, [FicChaTen] will work with [CM], [CA] [MCFLMosFB], and the other members of [CC] to ward off potential legal action that may come from the misuse of [MCFLMosFB] Revitalization Fund, and to ensure that the taxpayers of [MCFLMosFB] are paying for the services we need. It is wrong to run [MCFLMosFB] in a manner that has us worrying about [GVBMNTFL] or [USFG] taking [USD] away from us or coming back to us after the fact and requesting a refund of [USD] we already spent. Those who are running for [CC] [who have previously been on [CC]) or asking to be re-elected have been doing just that. Bringing sanity and responsibility to [MCFLMosFB] is just one of the many reasons [FicChaTen] is running for [CC] and asking for your support."

The non-discharge of firearms and BB gun ordinance repeal passed. [GVBMNTFL] law applies to this and cannot be further restricted without significant fines to [CC]. Excerpt of [CitComm]:

[FicChaForty]:          We are protected by the Second Amendment of the Constitution of the United States of America. The Founding Fathers knew that the tyrants in waiting would resort to devious and seemingly harmless actions to control the citizenry.

In a 2-to-2 tie, the renaming of our barrier island was defeated (we made the front-page of [FlaTo]!). [CC] joined [CCFLMosCC] in seeking more historical proof of the claim that Ponce de Leon landed in Melbourne Beach and not St. Augustine. Excerpt of [CitComm]:

[OBandSD]:          Where is the merit in renaming something to remind us that Europeans have syphilis and other diseases that killed the native population?

There's going to be a special meeting of the [CRA] on Tuesday, 27 Sep 11, at 6PM at City Hall. [FicChaTwelve] will send out a separate announcement on that on Monday. [FicChaTwelve] has requested [CM] post the DETAILS of [CC]'s response to the [JLACFL] Letter.

Best Regards,
[FicChaTwelve]

(End Transmission)


(BeginTransmission)

From: [TGTDTT]
Sent: Sunday, September 25, 11 12:16 PM
To: [FicChaTen]; [FicChaTwelve]
Subject: Getting Involved

Gentlemen,

Thank you both for your time this morning.

I think it is great that you are going door-to-door to meet the fine [MCFLMosFB] citizens. I also think that the effort is necessary but might not be sufficient to get [FicChaTen] elected.

Not knowing [FicChaTen]'s current time commitments or anything else for that matter, I can see value in speaking to groups and delivering a message that is pertinent to that group.

Suppose the campaign had knowledge of the various clubs, civic groups, Religious Organizations, businesses (and business groups) etc... and you prepared a speech or short remarks that were specific to each of those groups as to why their support for your candidacy would further their interests.

So within the realm of [CC] participation and the matters that are coming before the [CC], how is your participation going to benefit . . .

> Each of the schools in [MCFLMosFB]
>
> Each of the churches, temples, synagogues, and Montessori schools, etc.
>
> VFW, Elks, Rotaries, etc.
>
> [OwnBus]s current [MCFLMosFB] [EMP]s

Having made that suggestion, I don't know if the idea holds any water because [CC] might not have anything to offer or that a particular organization that I mentioned off the top of my head doesn't even have a chapter in [MCFLMosFB].

I do believe that if [FicChaTen] were to go in a room filled with veterans and give a five or ten minute talk that . . .

> honors their service
>
> gives credence to a well justified empathy
>
> illustrates the value they bring to [MCFLMosFB]
>
> identifies at least one matter handled by the [CC] that directly affects them
>
> clearly articulates your position and how [FicChaTen] would vote on the matter

that when [FicChaTen] left the room, [FicChaTen] would have earned the respect of the majority of the attendees.

That formula, or something like that formula, could be repeated for every group [FicChaTen] would speak to.

I would also suggest considering an event for the detractors so that [FicChaTen] would have the opportunity to address their misconceptions or potential fears.

Now having made that suggestion, in addition to the list of questions made earlier, I don't have a clue how to make it happen in a reasonable amount of time. However, there are people in your camp that knows a person who knows a person.

Should this idea have merit to you, please forward it to those in your camp who might be able to take the next step.

What I can offer is that if I knew

> who you were speaking to,
>
> why you were speaking to them,
>
> and what you wanted them to know

I would be willing to create at least the first draft of your remarks. Putting me in the same room with those who can put [FicChaTen] in the various rooms I described might have some value. But in making that suggestion, I need to be put in a room with people who have a reasonably firm grasp of the particular group and their issues.

Be well,
[TGTDTT]

(End Transmission)

(Reply)

Very well put and delivered. We talked about your
suggestion at length and see its real value. Perhaps
you and I should talk about this, too? As we discussed,
there's no pleasing everybody, but if you do the
RIGHT thing, it's hard for folks to fault you for it.

I'd like to hear what [FicChaTen] replies with. Let
me know.

Cheers,
[FicChaTwelve]

(End Reply)


## September 26, 11

| | |
|---|---|
| [TGTDTT] | Don't be surprised to hear that I pummeled [FicChaTwelve] with a baseball bat for coming to my house last week and getting me involved in this whole thing. |
| | Spending some time looking over the other candidates, the [MCFLMosFB].org web site, and re-reading your stuff to get my head around some of the [CitComm] and understanding a way to make them translate into specific items you can speak to. |
| [FicChaTen] | I see. Interesting. |
| [TGTDTT] | Anything I share with you needs to be vetted because I still don't know what I am talking about. |

In pouring over [B] [MCFLMosFB] [FY11-12], I see that [MCFLMosFB] is servicing [MCFLMosFB]'s debt with annual payments on the order of 1.2M or about 10% of the total [B].

Storm Water Utility 312K

[CRA] 465K

Capital Asset Fund 289K

My first question is what [MCFLMosFB]'s plan to retire [MCFLMosFB] debt? Is there any opportunity to make the [MCFLMosFB] debt go away sooner to free up a million [USD] a year to do other stuff?

General [GVBMNT] Services [B] is 400K for retirement (almost 30%)

My second question is what is [MCFLMosFB]'s plan for reducing the ongoing and potentially increasing burden of paying retirement benefits in perpetuity?

Why does [B] [MCFLMosFB] [FY11-12] have 25K for professional grant writers?

What can we do to reduce [MCFLMosFB]'s insurance premiums?

Can 70K be justified for Internet and telephone services when I pay about 2K annual for broadband to run my business?

Building and zone department [MCFLMosFB] pays an annual $1,200 for permit software annual license fee.

[MCFLMosFB] recreation contract instructors for classes were paid 323K. How much of this was subsidized or covered by fees for the various classes?

10K for printing and binding services.

Take a look at page 82. If it is telling me what I think it is telling me, I am going to throw up. A professional grant writer is getting 34 K where engineering is getting 15K. That just seems like a lot of [USD] going for professional grant writing. You might want to look at some of the leases as well.

I won't even touch [CRA] because it is unclear as to what is going on with that.

By and large [MCFLMosFB] does not have a great deal of [USD] to waste but there are some line items that are philosophically inappropriate (debt servicing and pensions) from my point of view and I suspect [MCFLMosFB] will be sued by either [GVBMNTFL] or [USFG] for misappropriating the [USD] they get in the form of grants.

In all honesty, I still don't know how you are going to be effective in manifesting a change that improves the fiscal management of [MCFLMosFB] and improves [MCFLMosFB] itself. I will share that the other candidates might benefit from at least asking the people to look into the details.

[FC01]    [GOB]'s are not interested in any of this.

[TGTDTT]   If this stuff doesn't help you sort out your thoughts, please let me know. Because the biggest question I have is "Other than attend the meetings and cast the occasional vote, what can you get done in your first term on [CC]?" You don't need to tell me, but if you don't have some idea of what levers you can pull, then you are just a guy who goes to the meetings and casts the occasional vote. I am still going to vote for you this time and I am thinking that [FicChaThirty] might make the meetings interesting. But unless someone can make a good case for re-electing any of the people who have previously been on the [CC], I want new thinking because the old thinking is not going to get [MCFLMosFB] management modernized.

[FicChaTen]   I value your insight. My bike travels this weekend, visiting 800 homes, has convinced me the population wants change. They are unhappy with [GOB], ever-increasing Ad Valorem Tax Millage Rate funding non-efficient government activities, perceived intrusiveness of code enforcement, building dept making it difficult for small businesses to move into [MCFLMosFB], etc. It was tiring, but a real eye-opener.

The secret to success will be if these dissatisfied citizens actually get out and vote. Historically, only 10% of [MCFLMosFB] citizens vote . . . their votes drive what [GOB]s like to refer to as 'overwhelming citizens' mandates.'

I have asked to speak with probably the largest opposition group in [MCFLMosFB]—[FBWC]--for exactly the reasons you wisely lay out. I was turned down. It seems those entrenched in their status quo beliefs are unwilling or unable to debate issues. This idea is constantly confirmed when 'status quoers' get up in meeting [MCFLMosFB]s and berate those with other views rather than discussing issues in an unemotional and fact-backed manner, and some turn downright mean-spirited about it. Throughout it all, we of the 'efficiency movement' persevere and grow in our numbers.

This week I am working on your great idea for a FAQ section to my campaign website. I look forward to receiving questions you have or have heard. I am coalescing same from my weekend bike riding.

Thanks again for your support. I am glad to have your intuitive council on our side.

[TGTDTT]     I am done for the day. Have meetings tomorrow for my stuff.

(BeginTransmission)

Subject: Following the [USD]
From: [TGTDTT]
Date: Tue, September 27, 11 1:33 pm
To: [FicChaTen]

For your benefit, my questions are to spur your thinking so that you are prepared. Taking the time to reply to me with these answers makes me think that I am taking you away from getting the message out to those that need to hear it. You have my vote, or will have it come November 8 so don't waste any more time on getting back to me.

It is important to foster an environment that would get the good [MCFLMosFB] voters to the polls on November 8.

Does everybody in [MCFLMosFB] know who you are and is aware of at least one compelling reason to vote for you?

What is your campaign's plan to get people to the polls? I might suggest, and be willing to participate in a door-to-door campaign the night before the election reminding people that tomorrow is Election Day and that

"[FicChaTen] is a competent candidate who would bring a message of fiscal responsibility, continuous improvement, sound judgment, and honorable service to [MCFLMosFB] citizens as I hand them a pamphlet that has you on one side and the voting locations and hours of operation on the other side with a phone number they could call if they need a ride to the polls.

Everybody who is intent to vote for someone else is going to vote for someone else. You are going to be elected by those who are already going to vote for you and those who realize you are serious about being elected. What is your plan for the next 40 days? (Don't answer that, just make sure you have a plan and people to execute your plan).

On a side note, you might want to consider attending all the upcoming [CC] and [CRA] events but not speaking unless you see a clear path to saying something that would make the audience see you in a favorable light and not so self-serving. Somehow it has to be conveyed that you deserve to be on [CC], should be on [CC], and are politely (humbly and eagerly) waiting until the results of the November 8 election puts you in one of the chairs.

[TGTDTT]

(End Transmission)

# [CRA]

---

*Former Prime Minister of England, the late Margaret Thatcher, is credited with the quote, "Socialism is great until you run out of other people's money."*

[OwnProp] or [OwnBus] receives tax bills from four governmental entities if their stuff is within the boundaries of a [MC]: [MC], [GVBMNTCNTY], [GVBMNTSTATE], and [USFG].

The bills come in many ways, but that is the jist of it. When it comes to the distribution of the [USD] given to [GVBMNT], remember that all levels have to get their cut. So when [MC] collects taxes on property or a business, some of that [USD] is paid to [GVBMNTCNTY] by [MC], some of the [USD] sent to [GVBMNTCNTY] is then redistributed where some of that filters up to the [GVBMNTSTATE] and [USFG]. Everybody has to get his cut. If you are a smart [CC], you can play a little game called [CRA] so [CLB] can spend more [USD].

The idea is that [MC]'s portion of the taxes that go to [GVBMNTCNTY] normally get pooled with all other [MC]s and [GVBMNTCNTY] then does a couple projects and throws a few dollars back to the [MC]s. So what if [GVBMNTSTATE] let an [MC] designate one or more areas as needing Redevelopment which creates a formula allowing the [MC] to keep more [USD] at the local level. The problem is that the rules say that if the [MC] does that, the designated area becomes a separate entity and any revenue within the [CRA], stays in the [CRA].

There are five voting members that decide how [CRA] revenue is going to be spent. There are five voting members who decide how [MC] revenue is going to be spent. In [MCFLMosFB], it is the same five people.

[CC] mayor bangs the gavel and announces, "We are now [CRA]." and magically transforms into [CRA] chair. After some time, the gavel is banged again and [CRA] chair announces, "We are now [CC]." and [CC] mayor becomes the current state of the [MFCU] with the gavel.

The support cast is the same people as well.

[CC] has a history of publishing and approving an optimistic [B] in September after publishing amendments to the current [B] in July. Sometimes the adjustment approaches 30% or more and this has been going on for years.

Now if one were to look at real expenses for the last several years, one would see that there is a general trend with spikes. Filter out the anomalies of random purchases, the curve becomes even smoother. Filtering the data even further to a very specific cost, for instance, the average total annual cost of a single police patrol element that is operating twenty-four-seven, and the curve becomes almost perfect. The same is true for revenue sources as well. For instance, the average Ad Valorem Tax collection rate per residential property has been pretty consistent in the low to mid seventy's with a fifty percent chance of changing.

So how hard is it to project contracted expenses to trend [MCFLMosFB] [EMP] costs? When [TGTDTT] first proposed the idea, the people in the room thought he had gone bananas. Then [TGTDTT] presented a chart that showed [MCFLMosFB] revenue minus [MCFLMosFB] expenses using trended data out fifty years. Then stuff got real interesting. But we need to return to the topic at hand. The bottom line is that this same group of people tells us what we want to hear in September when everybody is paying attention, but the [B] amendment in July usually happens when fewer people are paying attention and there is not much anybody can do about it anyway.

[CC] mayor banged the gavel one July night in YR10 and said, "We are [CC] and [MCFLMosFB] aint got no [USD]."

[CM]:     [CRA] has some [USD]. Maybe we should ask them for some [USD]. It won't hurt anything.

Mayor:   Is that so?

[CM]:     It's so.

Mayor:   What do you think [CA] [MCFLMosFB]?

[CA]:     I'm sorry, what were you discussing?

[MCFLMosFB] Mayor] banged the gavel and announced, "We are [CRA] and [CC] is asking us for some [USD] to spend on [MCFLMosFB]. I say we give it to them."

In the audience, [FicChaTwelve] raised his hand to be recognized and approached the podium. He cautioned [CRA] to be extra vigilant in making sure the [CRA] revenue is spent in accordance with [GVBMNTFL] law 163.

Murmurs were heard throughout the room, and the vote was four to one for giving [MCFLMosFB] the [USD] [CC] wanted. The "No" vote was cast by [FicChaFourteen]. It wasn't the first time [FicChaFourteen] was the only "No" vote in his first two years on [CC] and he was looking forward to any shift in the political will that would slide stuff in a good way. What a glorious day it would be for [FicChaFourteen] to be on the winning side of a three-to-two or a four-to-one vote. But those days were just fantasy as [CRA] board members voted to give [MCFLMosFB] some [USD] for the seventh year in a row.

A few days later some people got together, with [FicChaTwelve] being one of them, and decided to do something about [CRA] channeling funds to the [MC] that should have been used for other purposes. Through public information requests and the documents in the reference section of the local library, the group was able to assemble a credible story that describes how the [CRA] has been in direct violation of [GVBMNTFL] law 163 on multiple points. Those points spell out how the [USD] was not spent per plan and that the [USD] paid to [MCFLMosFB] was an illegal transfer because it was used to keep the lights on and not to build something new as defined in the approved [CRA] plan.

The concerned citizens sent their case to [GVBMNTFL] Attorney General and [JLACFL] with the request for some guidance as to a proper approach to straightening all this out. The Attorney General replied that as long as [CRA] and [CC] does what [JLACFL] tells [CRA] and [CC] to do, Attorney General [GVBMNTFL] is good. [JLACFL] came back with a "Woe Nelly. You all better make sure you got your facts straight. [CC] mayor, is any of this true? And you better not be lying to me."

```
(BeginTransmission)

[FB] [ResMailGrp]

There is a special meeting and [CRA] meeting at City
Hall starting at 6PM on Tuesday.

[CC] is supposed to cover [CC]'s response letter to
[JLACFL]. [FicChaTwelve] requested that [MCFLMosFB]
```

post the letter on its website so citizens could have a chance to review it prior to the meeting. However, [FicChaTwelve] will save you the trouble of looking - it's not posted yet.

Please try to attend this meeting. This is going to be the ONE chance [CC] gets to justify the diversion of [CRA] finances into the General Fund over the past 7 or more years for purposes that appear to be against Florida Statutes. The more eyes on the document, the better; but I don't hold much hope to see it before the meeting.

[FicChaTwelve] suggests you check out [MCFLMosFB]'s website tomorrow morning and other times throughout the day to see if the letter was posted. I will not be able to get word to you in time if it posts during the day.

Best Regards,
[FicChaTwelve]

(End Transmission)


[MCFLMosFB] Mayor, [FicChaSeventeen], banged the gavel and announced, "We are [CC], and I would like to know what I can tell [JLACFL]."


[CM]:     We are under no legal obligation to respond.
Mayor:   What do you think [CA]?
[CA]:     I'm sorry, what were you talking about?
Mayor:   What can I tell [JLACFL] in response to this letter?
[CA]:     Well, I am going to have to study the history of all this before I can give you any counsel on the matter.

Mayor: Well would you please do exactly that and get back to me as soon as practical?

[CA]: Certainly.

That evening, back in the quiet confines of the suburban home of [CA], [FicChaTwentyFour], was relaxing on his sofa with a drink in hand, his tie loosened, his belt unbuckled, and his trousers around his ankles.

[FicChaTwentyFour] Ohhh. What to do, what to do? Yeahhhh, that's right. The key is to establish the document trail so that anyone in [GVBMNTFL] can reference that document because it will have a sentence that helps them politically.

[FicChaTwentyThree] Mmmmmm, that, mmmm, sounds, mmmmmm, about, mmmmmm, right.

[FicChaTwentyFour] Don't stop, no. Oh my goodness. Aughhh. Thanks. Now I know exactly what to do.

Some time went by and [CA] announces a solution at another special meeting. After the formalities, [CA] reads the draft of the response letter:

Dear [JLACFL]:

In response to your letter of August 17, [CC] and [CRA] have done nothing wrong and to prove their full compliance with the law, we promise to never do any of that stuff you mentioned ever again.

Sincerely,
[CC] Mayor, [FicChaSeventeen]

The Mayor, [FicChaSeventeen], about had a heart attack right then and there. [FicChaSeventeen] might have thought, "How did get I dragged into this. "I will not be the only signature on that letter. We are all going to sign whatever we send."

The other members of [CC] shifted in their seats. [FicChaFourteen] is said to have remarked, "I haven't been on [CC] long enough to get embroiled in a scandal, and I damn sure don't want to be signing no letter." [FicChaEighteen] just grunted. [FicChaTwentyEight] just sighed and thought, "Well, it would seem that those noisy little fuckers have made a new friend at [GVBMNTFL]. I am so going to screw them if I get the chance." [FicChaThirtyThree] just wondered what he had to do to finish out his one term now that the city is no longer buying Real Estate.

The decision was made to make some edits to the proposed draft to better reflect the interests of [CC] as a single voice:

> Dear [JLACFL]:
>
> In response to your letter of August 17, [CC] and [CRA] of [MCFLMosFB] have done nothing wrong and to prove full compliance with the law, we promise to never do any of that stuff you mentioned ever again.
>
> Furthermore, we have been doing this stuff for some time and you guys haven't said anything. We just thought everything was cool. So if we have done anything wrong, which we haven't and aren't going to do again, it would be your fault for the lax in oversight on the part of your organization. After all, the word Auditing is in the frickin' name for Pete's sake. You had better get your house in order before even thinking about looking in our yard.

Lastly, and most important, some of us just got here and I am the sole "No" vote on all that stuff you mentioned that we did.

Sincerely,
[CC] Mayor, [FicChaSeventeen]
[CC] Vice Mayor, [FicChaTwentyEight]
[CC] Senior Member, [FicChaEighteen]
[CC] Member, [FicChaThirtyThree]
[CC] Junior Member, [FicChaFourteen]

The [FlaTo] started dedicating column inches in the Front, Space Coast, and Editorial Sections for all stuff [MCFLMosFB]. The local AM morning talk-show host and the show's listeners had something to say about the developments in [MCFLMosFB].

Hold on to your hats, this could get interesting.

# Meet [FicChaSixteen]

| | |
|---|---|
| Your Host: | Good Evening to all of you out there. Tonight we introduce to you, the audience, someone who plays a very important role in our story. His name is [FicChaSixteen] and he is an unemployed accountant type of person who relocated to [FB] from the Gulf Coast of [GSoF] after his marriage and business interests went straight in the proverbial crapper. Good Evening [FicChaSixteen]. |
| [FicChaSixteen]: | I used to be somebody. I used to have stuff. But then some shit went down and now it is all in the past. I know I like my smoke and drink. From time to time I like to really like my drink and then I call people to tell them that we have to bring all this forward because there is some shit going on. We have got to get up in their faces and let them know we are not going to back down. |
| Your Host: | Well that is all very good, but would you mind telling our viewers what shit is going on and what are we bringing forward. |
| [FicChaSixteen]: | You know man. |
| Your Host: | No. I really don't. |

[FicChaSixteen]: Don't tell me you don't understand. You're better than that.

Your Host: OK then. Well [FicChaSixteen], what would you like to talk about since you did call me.

[FicChaSixteen]: That bitch, [FicChaTwenty] and her sidekick [FicChaTwentyOne] are up to something and we had best get started bringing it forward. Fucking [FicChaTwentyFour] has all those assholes eating out of the palm of his hand. We have got bring this shit forward.

Your Host: As a regular attendant and speaker at both the [CC] and [CRA] meetings, what changes are you really trying to get implemented?

[FicChaSixteen]: These people have not taken into consideration the information that I did not bring with me but will make it available as soon as practical, that clearly shows a misinterpretation of the intent of my [CitComm]s at the last meeting. And on that note, I will sit down and return to my game of "Angry Birds."

Your Host: Well that is all the time we have this evening. Thank you for tuning in.

And remember, we let you know WHAT TO THINK ABOUT and WHAT TO THINK ABOUT what you think, so YOU DON'T HAVE TO. Good night. Aaaaaand, we're out.

[BeginTransmission]

Subject: Something to consider
From: [TGTDTT]
Date: Wed, September 28, 11 9:16 am
To: [FicChaTen]

There are 39 days left until the election. If you win - great. If you don't win - Why? From what I have seen in the two meetings I have attended, it will be because you failed to get your message out. Any time spent countering anybody else's criticism is time wasted. Any time spent trying to get ahead at the expense of someone else is time wasted. People have a right to feel good about the candidates they support without feeling as though they have to criticize the other candidates or even defend the candidate they support.

As far as the debate is concerned, I believe the following:

When asked a question, you should answer the question using clear facts that are justified and assumptions that are clearly stated as assumptions. If you use a number, you had better be right.

Sarcasm is very rarely affective. Personal attacks are also genuinely frowned upon. It seems you have some cause to bring attention to the votes and behaviors of some of the other candidates, but it might be a better approach to frame the idea in the form of a question. For instance "[FicChaTwentySix], would you be kind enough to explain to this audience how your votes for increased Ad Valorem Tax Millage Rate and resulting Ad Valorem Tax Revenue has served to benefit [MCFLMosFB] service levels and capability?" or something to that effect.

All statements you make should be meaningful and informative. Cliché and hollow rhetoric will alienate people.

Your campaign needs to be about electing people who can make a difference that will make stuff better. You are not running against anybody. You are running for something and you are going to need a great deal of help if you get the job. Imagine for a moment if you established such a presence that the other candidates voted for you, or at the bare minimum privately admitted that you are the person who should get the job.

It is absolutely critical that when you walk into a room, it is because you have a command of the facts, knowledge of how to be an effective [CC] member, and a plan to fix at least some of the broken stuff.

With your permission, I would like to discretely meet with some people, starting with [FicChaTwelve] and possibly [FicChaFourteen], to help line up some more facts that might be of use to you. What you have now is almost good enough to get you to second base, but we need to get you geared up for a home run.

Unless of course you are proud of what you have and don't want the help, which I would respect.

[TGTDTT]

[EndTransmission]

# [FBWC] Candidate Forum YR11

18 Oct at 7:00pm at [TSCMuniCom] the [FBWC] hosts a "political forum" wherein each candidate gets a few minutes of intro, then fields questions from a moderator (which I understand the moderator picks from those submitted by the audience). Each candidate fields each question in some sort of rotating order.

Your Host: Welcome to [FBWC] Candidate Forum YR11. This year, there are four candidates vying to fill two [CC] seats. One candidate is seeking re-election, another candidate is a former Mayor, and the other two candidate's are first timers. Let's meet the candidates.

[FicChaTen]: Step right up ladies and gentlemen because there's trouble. Trouble with a capital "T" which also stands for taxes, and when you take that almighty "T" away, all you have left is rubble like bubble so its spelled r-u-b-b-l-e. You know exactly what I am talking about. You have felt it in the air. If you don't believe me, look at this fine graph. See those two lines? If we don't do something really smart really soon those two lines are going to cross each other and that would be really really bad.

But seriously folks. "First of all, I love our City's small town atmosphere and the plethora of available activities the area offers. The entire reason I am running for [CC] is to maintain our town as OUR town.

At the rate we are going (43% tax rate increase in just the last 5 years . . . taking us within 1.4 mills of [GVBMNTFL]-mandated maximum Ad Valorem Tax Millage Rate of 10 mills), we risk losing our City. Please do an internet search of Florida cities that have had to declare a financial emergency due to reaching 10 mills and not being able to meet their obligations... it is ugly and takes control of City resources and activities away from the cities (and could even result in complete city bankruptcy). By the way, the only city in worse shape in our county is [MCFLMosPB] . . . and [CCFLMosPB] (influenced by their [EMP] unions) recently voted their Ad Valorem Tax Millage Rate this coming year to a full 9 mills . . . only one mill away from disaster.

If it weren't for the efforts of an ever-increasing group of concerned citizens, our Ad Valorem Tax Millage Rate would have been almost 9 mills (8.88) . . . even closer to our state mandated maximum. To me, that's scary.

The answer, in my opinion, is "efficiency." Efficiency doesn't mean less service. Contrary to what the [GOB]s are saying, I do not want to shut down [RecFLMosFB]). It means maintaining services at the lowest possible cost to the taxpayer.

I run a contract for a private company maintaining a military base (many times larger than [MCFLMosFB]) that requires we meet strict performance criteria while saving [USD] via efficiencies in order to make a profit . . . .so I know its doable.

I could go on and on about this concept, but I have written substantially about it on my website. I have an "Issues" section that will soon--if it doesn't have it yet (a tech-savvy buddy is putting it together for me)--have sub-issues wherein I delve into these concepts (and others).

My basic concept is to maintain our small town atmosphere at the lowest possible cost to the taxpayer . . . and plan to do that through ensuring every department is being run as efficiently as possible and getting [GVBMNT] out of the way of our small businesses. Once we can demonstrate that we take efficient and limited [GVBMNT] seriously, our tax base will increase via increased business activity and new families moving in.

I am appalled when I talk with small [OwnBus]s in the local area who tell me they will not locate their businesses in [MCFLMosFB] because of perceived intrusive [GVBMNT] and the highest municipal tax rate in the county (second highest now that [MCFLMosFB] hit 9 mills). Even more alarming, I recently talked with a small [OwnBus] who may be moving out . . . He rented his facility versus buying it because he'd heard the stories about trying to run a successful business in [MCFLMosFB] and he's glad he did.

[FicChaThirty]: I did not prepare any remarks and just got back into town from a business trip, so let me just say that [MCFLMosFB] is being run like a private club that doesn't let all of the dues paying members actually use the pool, or the golf course, or that great weight room. But most of all, you can't sit in the dining room or at the [CLB] bar enjoying the fine fare prepared fresh daily. I think that is just wrong. I know what it is like in every [MC] in the country, but we are better than everybody else because we live in [FB]. My children know some of your children so I care more than these other people.

[FicChaTwentyEight]: I am the single most qualified person on this stage. My demanding and complicated day job helps me keep my skills sharp so my decisions are good decisions. I have no idea what all this talk about [CRA] and [MCFLMosFB] reserves approaching zero. If there was any truth to this stuff, I would know about it because I am the single most qualified person on this stage.

[FicChaTwentySix]: I don't agree with anything [FicChaTen] and [FicChaThirty] have said. [MCFLMosFB] does have some problems, but they are not the problems these two are making such a fuss about. The real problems [MCFLMosFB] have would already have been solved if you people would have listened to me when I had an idea that would end up being meaningless. Besides, you people know me and I support Fall Prevention programs.

Your Host: Well okay then. What say we move on to the audience questions where every member of the audience had the chance to complete a question card? The questions asked will be selected totally at "random". So the first question from a member of our audience that all the candidates must answer is, "What is your favorite thing about [FB]?

[FicChaTen]: Communities such as ours are becoming increasingly rare. Since the [MC]'s founding some forty-five or fifty years ago. I can't remember exactly how long ago it was because it is not relevant at this point so forget I even mentioned it. As I was saying, it has been the citizens who have made this a wonderful [MC]. But today, we are at risk of losing that community spirit to a few immature and petulant [MFCU]s who have been allowed to sit at the adult table. [MCFLMosFB] spends more [USD] than it really needs to, and my commitment to each of you is that I will work to increase the efficiency of our [GVBMNT]. Doing the same amount of stuff but using fewer resources and allowing [MCFLMosFB] to build up its reserves. I will do all of this with your help. Thank you.

[FicChaThirty]: What a great questions. Let me see. Well, my kids play sports in this town and I think that is wonderful. My husband is a commercial pilot who is having trouble getting work and my business as a [MC] planner is having some challenges so I know what tough times are. It is wrong that struggling people have to pay the high cost of [MCFLMosFB] [EMP]s. I mean really. One [MCFLMosFB] [EMP] drives a Lexus, another [MCFLMosFB] [EMP] drives an Infinity and her husband drives an Audi. I mean come on. Really? Vote for me and I will work hard to spread the pain as much as I can.

[FicChaTwentyEight]: As the single most qualified person on this stage, I can say with the confidence that only comes through years in a demanding and complicated job, that I am more informed about everything than any of these other candidates. Except well maybe [FicChaTwentySix]. In fact, we are kind of together. Not together together but together. Vote for me and [FicChaTwentySix].

[FicChaTwentySix]: I had nothing to do with any of that stuff you people said I did, and besides, it was perfectly legal, and I have already promised never to do it again. Oh, and if I am asked a specific question about something to do with something in the city, I will not answer it specifically because I don't care about specifics because its not my job.

Your Host: Well folks, that is all the time we have. A special thank you to candidates for their riveting answers. Our sponsor this evening was [FBWC]. I do hope you enjoyed tonight's show.

And remember, we let you know WHAT TO THINK ABOUT and WHAT TO THINK ABOUT what you think, so YOU DON'T HAVE TO. Good night. Aaaaaand, we're out.

# [ELCTN11]

*First they ignore you,*
*Then they laugh at you,*
*Then they fight you,*
*Then you win.*
*                    - Gandhi*

(Begin [FicChaTen] Campaign Press Release)

October 20, 11 at 6:18 PM

As interesting as drama and gossip are, to view those who are sticking their neck out to run for public office with anything but respect for doing something most of us can't be bothered to do seems out of character for those people I do know. Furthermore, the recent reports of improper behavior regarding signs, petty criticism of candidate brochures, and possible coercion of business owners and citizens by those who used to be 'somebody' in our city, are a gross distraction from solving real problems that face our city.

At present, [MCFLMosFB] is facing a possible repayment of 2.2 million [USD] of [CRA] money that [JLACFL] has deemed inappropriately spent. [MCFLMosFB] spends 1.2 million [USD] annually on [MCFLMosFB] debt, over 300K [USD] for pensions and is attempting to pay the salaries of [PD] and [FD] using [MCFLMosFB] revenues from Grants that may be taken away at the whim of [GVBMNTFL] or [USFG]

[RecFLMosFB] spends 3 [USD] for every 2 [USD] it takes in.

There are virtually no reserves to respond to a natural disaster such as a hurricane without running to [USFG] which doesn't have the [USD] either. All on a current 12 million [USD] [B]. And this is just the stuff I know about right now.

For the stuff I have stated as facts, they are facts as I understand them through my own research. I welcome the education necessary to set me straight. The candidates that have my attention right now are those people who are also trying to get to the truth and asking for our support to put them in a position to do something about the stuff that doesn't make sense to me and many others.

There are candidates who understand the problems we are facing. Some of them can be shown to be directly responsible for some of those problems. There are candidates who might have a particular reason for running that has nothing to do with putting [MCFLMosFB] finances back on sound footing.

Whomever you choose to support and for whatever reasons you choose to support them is your business and the only person who will know who you vote for on November 8 is you.

Regardless of who you support and why you support them, I urge everybody to take a breath and remember that on November 9 we are still neighbors and, in some cases, friends. Many of the residents of [MCFLMosFB] are attorneys, engineers, executives, doctors, teachers, and so many other professions that demand respectful and meaningful discourse to do their jobs. I can't imagine that such behavior must end when we leave our place of work at the end of the day.

If I could persuade any of you and anyone else of anything, it would be to dig into the issues that

[MCFLMosFB] is currently facing, understand how we got in this situation, and then engage the candidates to determine who among them has a clue about solving those problems.

I am willing to tell all of you that I support [FicChaTen] in his quest for a seat on [CC]. [FicChaTen] has thrown his hat into the ring to be selected for a job that needs to be done and I absolutely don't want to do it. His entire adult life has been in the service of our country and now he is standing up to be of service to [MCFLMosFB]. [FicChaTen] has to earn his seat on [CC] and once he is there he has to prove he was worthy of my trust. From what I have seen, read, heard, and know about some of the people who are supporting him, I am comfortable with my decision.

Should you support [FicChaTen]? Why don't you do as I have suggested and get a handle on why supporting [FicChaTen] might be a really good idea. Are the other [CC] candidates any better? Again, get a handle on all the issues [MCFLMosFB] is facing and see how they intend to handle those matters that are important to you.

My support for [FicChaTen] says nothing bad about any of the other [CC] candidates. All it says is that I view [FicChaTen] as competent, capable, and dedicated and I believe he deserves the chance to reverse some pretty scary trends in our city's financial health. Some of the other [CC] candidates have had their chance and have either helped create the problems or were ineffective in helping the other [CC] members make more responsible decisions.

So for all of you, support the [CC] candidates you want to support. On November 8, vote for the [CC] candidates you want to vote for. All I ask is that between now and then, please conduct yourselves in a manner that ensures we can all live with ourselves and each other on November 9.

Be well,
[TGTDTT]

(End [FicChaTen] [CC] Campaign Press Release)


(BeginTransmission [FBResMailGrp])

While this isn't specifically associated with [GVBMNT], there appears to be a growing problem in our community regarding the upcoming [CC] election.

[CC] candidate's campaign signs are being removed from properties within [MCFLMosFB]. Also, residents are being pressured and businesses threatened to sway votes or remove signs or suffer consequences.

If you are being pressured, if you are a victim of this activity or if you see or witness this activity, you can call me or email me ([FicChaTwelve] will guarantee your anonymity) and [FicChaTwelve] will address it with the proper authorities.

[FicChaTwelve]

(End Transmission [FBResMailGrp])


Your Host:    Today we are here with a local legend. The word about town is that he is one of the last honest men in the world. It is no small feat to get the man, known only as [TGTDTT] to publicly endorse a candidate. So [TGTDTT], who are you supporting in the [CC] race this year?"

| | |
|---|---|
| [TGTDTT] | I am supporting [FicChaTen] because he understands that the fundamental nature of how [MCFLMosFB] is being run needs to be changed. [FicChaTen] has a plan ready to be put in action that will put [MCFLMosFB] back on track towards sound finances. I am reluctant to support anybody who is seeking re-election or has previously held a council seat because they are responsible for the current situation and they made it a point of keeping the necessary information from me and others. Bringing in new thinking by competent and accomplished people who look to the citizens to be a part of the solution through an honest and critical assessment of the issues seems the smartest thing we can do right now. |
| Your Host: | Well okay then. But you know that making your support known in a public way exposes you to ridicule and criticism. |
| [TGTDTT] | I don't know that. |
| Your Host: | Sure you do. I mean come on. Everybody laughs at the douche bags on television. Especially the nut jobs trying to make a name for themselves during the hoopla of campaign season. |
| [TGTDTT] | Are you saying that my talking to you will make me into something I am currently not? |
| Your Host: | I suppose that is what I am saying. |

| | |
|---|---|
| [TGTDTT] | I don't understand. Is it that I am being interviewed on camera that this magical transformation will take place? |
| Your Host: | Forget about transforming for a minute. Did you know there are rumors that you are [FicChaTen]'s conscience and voice. |
| [TGTDTT] | So you believe that [FicChaTen] has a conscience and [FicChaTen] has a voice? |
| Your Host: | My point is that [FicChaTen] would be lost if it were not for you. |
| [TGTDTT] | So you believe that [FicChaTen] is not lost? |
| Your Host: | Look Yoda. My point is… |
| [TGTDTT] | Please. We agree that [FicChaTen] has a conscience and a voice. We agree that [FicChaTen] is not lost. We also agree that the source of [FicChaTen]'s conscience, voice, and sense of direction comes from someplace to be appreciated. You assert that the source is me. I cannot refute the assertion as we are all connected. But is it also possible that the source of my conscience, voice, and sense of direction is [FicChaTen]? Please forgive me if I shutter at the thought that you are somehow involved. |
| Your Host: | Are you always like this? |
| [TGTDTT] | I can't be or this interview is not really happening. |

Your Host:  Well folks, that is all the time we have. A special thank you to [TGTDTT] for his riveting answers.

And remember, we let you know WHAT TO THINK ABOUT and WHAT TO THINK ABOUT what you think, so YOU DON'T HAVE TO. Good night. Aaaaaand, we're out.

(Begin [FicChaTen] Campaign Press Release)

October 28, 11

[FicChaTen] and team - I wish I could say "Good Morning" but I can't today. They took [FicChaTen] and [FicChaThirty]'s signs from my neighbor's house and maybe one other house in the neighborhood. I am so ashamed of their behavior, whoever they are. It is so unfair, so corrupt.

I am going to draft a letter to [FlaTo] today but it won't be about the issues everybody is running for, it is going to be about why we have no honesty or integrity or professionalism with many on our current [CC] members. Now it is no longer about the [B] on the table, the 750K fire truck, the [CRA] misused funds, or even the 140 acres of land destined for ugly condos. It is about saving our city from evil people who only want to better their own businesses or those of their contributors.

In the future I hope we pass a bill that inhibits previous mayors, or any [MCFLMosFB] [OwnBus]s from serving on the council at all. I also hope that after a 4-year term a council member has to vacate his/her seat. It is the only way we will get clear, honest thinking on [CC] and perhaps then stuff will filter back to [MCFLMosFB] citizens and not be decided just on what 5 people want. It is time we attended [CC] meetings and got more involved. Shame on us a bit for actually being ignorant, and complacent, and trusting [CC] with our hard-earned tax [USD]. We know in life that can be a gamble.

You may send this to our supporters and maybe others will write [FlaTo]. Folks, be sure not to slam people by name because we are above that as a group and need to remain professional and fair. It is the mature thing to do.

Thank you,
[MCFLMosFB] citizen

(End [FicChaTen] Campaign Press Release)


(Begin [FicChaTen] Campaign Update)

October 29, 11

Folks

As you know, a local business supporting opposition candidates to the [MCFLMosFB] [EMP]-backed [FicChaTwentySix]/[FicChaTwentyEight] team was threatened yesterday by phone calls claiming potential city retaliation. Police were called and reports were made, though it took quite a bit of effort by [FicChaThirty] to get a decent report filed (noting specific threats and targeted candidate) [FicChaThirty] has been leading the inquiry into discrepancies in local [FOP] endorsement of the aforementioned team.

I know this sort of nefarious activity on the part of [GOB] is disconcerting and some of you may be feeling overwhelmed and threatened. Don't be discouraged . . . be invigorated.

This should be a clarion call to redouble our efforts to clean up our city in more ways than just efficiencies.

We obviously are facing and experiencing the [GOB] network in earnest. That tells me one thing . . . we are over the target area . . . and they are telegraphing it's a high value target!

We will not succumb to such 'mob' tactics. We will hold firm and support each other. 'They' want us to roll over and quit . . . we have not (which scares them) and will not (which will scare them even more and probably cause even more such threats).

Our cause is just and our motives pure. With those fundamental characteristics we cannot be defeated.

BTW—[MicBil] covered this issue on today's 6:00AM segment of his radio show.

BTW2-- I see today's [FlaTo] letter to the editor complaining about [FicChaTen] not using a disclaimer on his campaign photo as just another [GOB] tactic . . . though he is correct, I missed the requirement in the regulation. First-time campaign screw-up (and probably only-time because I've figured out politics is very nasty and I ain't running again!). I realized the error on Monday and we are now applying a sticker with the disclaimer to our literature. Hopefully, that'll untwist their panties, but somehow I doubt it.

Hang tough
[CC] 11 Candidate, [FicChaTen]

(End [FicChaTen] [CC] Campaign Update)

(Reply)

I have heard some of the same is happening in
[MCFLMosWM]. A [MCFLMosWM] citizen placing a sign in
his yard was for a new [CCFLMosWM] candidate (who
is one of his good friends) was told that he could
not put campaign sign in his yard, code violation.
He is afraid to say who approached him. We cannot
let them intimidate us or the bullies win.

Citizen

(End Reply)

[MCFLMosFB] is going to spend about 3,300 [USD] today and
every day this year to service [MCFLMosFB] debt incurred by [CC]
and about 1,000 [USD] today and every day this year for pensions.

At present, there is a mindset among [CC] that incurring
[MCFLMosFB] debt and raising Ad Valorem Tax Millage Rate
to address shortfalls in planning is more acceptable than working
more closely with [CM] to fine tune the various procedures, [B]
s, policies, and agreements the tax payers of [MCFLMosFB]
have to pay for.

Would it not be great if the individual members of [CC] were
to perform a detailed study and subsequent optimization of
[MCFLMosFB] expenses?

At least two of the five people running for [CC] think stuff is
fine as it is.

How will the [MCFLMosFB] citizens react to a [CC] candidate
who told them that revising the relationship between [CC] and

[CM] to allow for direct participation in the development of departmental [B]s; determination of need for various purchases; realignment of resources to reduce unnecessary duplication of efforts and excess inventory; renegotiation of various agreements in order to reduce [MCFLMosFB] expenses; establishing an environment that would promote the full utilization of un-occupied store fronts; transition to pay-as-you-go operations for unnecessary but desirable services; transition the funding of necessary services to revenues obtained from stable tax revenues instead of relying on [GVBMNTFL] and [USFG] grants, and; encouraging the private sector to participate in the funding and completion of [OptProj] that make [MCFLMosFB] a better place to live but can be done more efficiently and cost effectively with a minimum participation of [MCFLMosFB] [GVBMNT].

A new member of the [CC] has about 12 meetings in the first year in office to get some really good stuff accomplished that serves the greater good, addresses the counter arguments of any detractors, promote the reasonable voices of the incumbents on the [CC] who may or may not seek re-election, encourage new voices to pursue seats on the [CC].

```
(Begin [FicChaTen] Campaign Update)

November 7, 11

Teammates-

Tomorrow is THE day! All of our preps, walking,
riding, driving, visiting, etc. comes down to tomorrow.
[FicChaEleven] and I will be staking out our areas
tomorrow at 0530 or so. We need as many people as
possible at both locations.
```

Please come as early as you can . . . polls open at 7AM. The major times we'll need wavers is from 7-9AM, 11AM-1PM, and 4-6PM.

I am proud of our effort in this race. Together, we have run a campaign of integrity and honor . . . debating issues versus making personal attacks on opponents. I hope the [MCFLMosFB] citizens see fit to make a change in our city's governance.

Regardless of tomorrow's outcome, we have made many new friends and have established even deeper relationships with friends we already had. We have met many wonderful members of our community who share the same wish for small, Efficient Government to maintain our city's unique seaside community atmosphere.

I have been honored and humbled to have been associated with all of you and I look forward to spending the rest of our lives together here in our great town.

See you at the polls!
[CC] 11 candidate [FicChaTen]

(End [FicChaTen] Campaign Update)


(BeginTransmission)

Subject: Hurtful statements
From: [TGTDTT]
Date: Tue, November 08, 11 9:41 am
To: [FicChaTen]
Cc: [FicChaEleven], [FicChaTwelve]

During the relatively short period that I was in uniform, it never occurred to me that anybody owed me anything for my military service. I never lost sight of the idea that I was defending my country by choice, but the idea that the civilian population owed me anything never occurred to me. Today when I see someone wear the uniform, mostly kids, I tend to think that I owe them something. From time to time I will pick up their bar tab or let them go in front of me at the grocery store. But these small efforts do not come close to balancing the ledger with regards to the life I have today because of the service that these young people provide.

Everybody who has ever worn the uniform and served their country honorably is worthy of our respect and gratitude. Those who continue to serve through running for elected office deserve such renderings even more so.

This person who remarked to you this morning that you have disgraced the uniform could not be speaking from a place of understanding. I do not think it would be a stretch to comment that his mental state at the time was questionable.

It is beyond my comprehension that you would ever have to defend yourself in such a manner and my prayer is that someday this person will reflect on his words today and come to understand that unless he apologizes voluntarily, he has obliterated any good he might be remembered for and that his words today have rendered his entire life meaningless.

I am appalled beyond measure and there is no retaliatory act that would ever even the score. Making the demand for a public apology will accomplish nothing. This person has said something so hurtful and demeaning that his soul is doomed to an eternity of torment unless he undergoes a change of heart. I pray I never meet this person and connect him with this event because I will not be silent as to his ignorance.

I wish I had words that would put all of this into perspective or could see a path that would make this right other than this person realizing the complete stupidity of his statements. But I don't. All I have to offer is that the reason I became an engineer and a software developer instead of something that dealt more closely with people is that I have first hand knowledge of how incredibly and unnecessarily hurtful people can be. Just when I think it is safe to give the human race some credit, somebody behaves like a completely unadulterated total asshole.

Six hours and 20 minutes until the polls close!

Be well,
[TGTDTT]

(End Transmission)


(Reply)

Thank you very deeply my dear friend. I needed to read these words.

[FicChaTen]

(End Reply)


(BeginTransmission [FBResMailGrp])

[CC] election results:
[FicChaTen]: 1,299,
[FicChaThirty]: 1,228,
[FicChaTwentySix]: 1,070,
[FicChaTwentyEight]: 949,
[FicChaThirtyOne]: 340

```
Now the work begins! Congratulations [FicChaTen]
[FicChaThirty].

Best Regards,

[FicChaTwelve]

(End Transmission)
```

The crowd cheered and the glasses were raised.

[FicChaTen]:         Teammates--

WE did it! [MCFLMosFB] citizens are no longer subjects. Councilman [FicChaFourteen], Councilwoman-select [FicChaThirty], and I will ensure the cesspool that has been [MCFLMosFB] politics for years is cleaned up rapidly. The win for the [MCFLMosFB] citizens tonight was overwhelming.

[GOB] is no longer in control . . . [MCFLMosFB] citizens are. Please join us to help govern our city in the most efficient way possible . . . the more people present at [CC] meetings, the better. Additionally, I would like to see all [MCFLMosFB] Boards stood down and stood back up with new, fresh people aboard.

We are a liberated people tonight. I remain humbled by your support. God bless us all!

[TGTDTT]: I'd like to propose a toast to [FicChaTwentySix] and [FicChaTwentyEight]. This election would not have turned out the way it did without their full cooperation and assistance.

Crowd]: Here Here!

[FicChaTen]: Our campaign raised the level of debate in this city and brought to the forefront those issues that affect each and every person in [MCFLMosFB].

My voice was really your voice and we have been heard by those who needed to hear it the most. Our positive message was received by many but not all.

Our work has just begun because there are real problems that need to be fixed. It is time for all of us to turn our attention beyond [ELCTN11] to doing all we can to make our [GVBMNT] of the people, for the people, and by the people. Whatever obstacles that now remain, I did not embark on this journey to reach a single short term goal, but to accomplish several long term goals:

A solid fiscal foundation for [MCFLMosFB]

A business friendly community

An involved citizenry and a transparent [GVBNMNT]

This was a victory for [MCFLMosFB] in many ways. Let us hold our heads high and greet tomorrow with renewed zeal and enthusiasm.

[TGTDTT]:

Thank you so very much for sticking your long neck and prominent chin out so that cowardly and ignorant people could throw punches that weakened them and strengthened you. If Teddy Roosevelt were alive today, he would be running around your house right now yelling "Bully" in celebration of a good man who stood tall in the center of the arena.

It is my sincerest hope that this is just the beginning of a friendship that I will cherish and honor for all the days to come.

[FicChaTen]:

I look forward to many great years as very close friends and confidantes. THANK you so much for your friendship and comradery during this trying time. A wonderful woman gave me some sage input during the campaign when former friends were showing their true colors . . . she said her sainted Scottish mother once told her that "you never knew the worth of a friend until you have eaten salt with him." I have eaten salt with you and found you to be a true, true friend.

(BeginTransmission)

From: [TGTDTT]
Subject: Congratulations. Breaks over
To: [FicChaTen], [FicChaFourteen], [FicChaThirty]
Cc: [FicChaTwelve]
Date: Wednesday, November 09, 11, 10:23 PM

"Now what do we do?" is a question that comes to mind. I had been giving the matter some thought prior to yesterday but did not want to get too far ahead of events. Now that [ELCTN11] is over, it is time to govern.

Much of the turnout was based on [MCFLMosFB] voters taking ownership of their city. All of you have communicated advocacy for citizen's involvement. [FicChaTen] has even suggested we join [MCFLMosFB] Boards and [MCFLMosFB] communities. Being someone who loathes meetings in general, I don't see myself trying to get on any boards or committees but I have a personal obligation to [FicChaTen] to do what I can.

The change that you all seek will not be the result of a decision made by any [MCFLMosFB] Board and recommended to [CC] for consideration. It will have to be the result of grass root efforts that are introduced to the boards and [CC] for consideration.

Each of you has a set of issues that you would like to make progress on. All of you could benefit from assistance in research and development of the issue based on your communicated understanding.

Specific proposals will be presented to the various boards and [CC] by the citizens and voted on by the boards and [CC], instead of you being the person that presents the issue.

There is overlap in the various things you three want to accomplish so coordination of effort would be useful. There are also priorities that must be assigned to everything because we can't do everything at once. There is also a calendar that we have to live by.

When we cut through all the rhetoric, everything boils down to specific proposals that you will either say "Yey" or "Ney" so you guys need a stack of stuff you can all say "Yey" to and it needs to be presented in the proper order, by the right person, to the right group and at the right time.

Now to my point,

I am offering to make my services available to the three of you for the purposes of consolidating those issues important to you, developing a plan based on specific steps that can be implemented, turning those steps into specific proposals presented by [MCFLMosFB] citizens [MCFLMosFB] Boards and [CC] for consideration; coordinating the grass roots efforts to present those proposals; developing a calendar of events associated with the issues, proposals.

None of the above will happen in a vacuum or without your knowledge and approval. Each of you will be a active participant and no one will be left out of the loop.

Please talk amongst yourselves to see if any of this makes sense. Feel free to call or write with any questions or concerns. Should you deem this a good idea, your first step is to communicate to me what is important to you and any specific items that come to mind. It may be something as simple as "Go read my website" or it might be valuable to take a few moments on your own to prepare something specific to governing the next 12 months or your first term. I prefer you each prepare your thoughts without coordinating so as to get the greatest coverage.

The sooner we get started, the more time we have to generate advocacy for the specific initiatives and make sure we are doing the right stuff in the right way. You had last night to bask in the glory of victory but this morning you became a do-nothing politician until you can say you have done something.

[FicChaThirty], we only met briefly at [FicChaTwelve]'s after [FBWC] Candidate Forum YR11 so I don't expect you to trust me out of the gate, but am sure that if you were to speak to [FicChaTen], [FicChaTwelve], and/or [FicChaFourteen], they will vouch for me.

Be well,
[TGTDTT]

(End Transmission)


(Reply)

Hey [TGTDTT],


I appreciate all of your hard work, support, and encouragement in this endeavor, as I'm sure the others do. I need to talk to you in person about a few issues before we get started. Are you available to talk in person in the next day or two? Let me know as my schedule is pretty flexible.

[FicChaFourteen]

(End Reply)

# We Need [COFFEE]!

*Follow the [USD]!*

The Citizen's Observational Fact Finding Efficiency Exercise, or [COFFEE], as it became to be known was the brainchild of [FicChaTen] and [TGTDTT]. During one of the [CC] meetings in FY11, [CC] agreed to budget thirty thousand dollars for an efficiency study of [MCFLMosFB]. As part of [FicChaTen]'s campaign platform, efficiency in [GVBMNT] was the dominant theme that wound its way into every specific initiative he advocated and was a guiding force in the manner in which he approached how he would solve problems that were of concern to [MCFLMosFB] citizens. Shortly after [FicChaTen]'s election, [FicChaTen] and [TGTDTT] were having beers at a [BusRestLocal], to chat about "What's next?" When the efficiency study was mentioned, [TGTDTT] made it clear that the 30K allocation was a joke that doomed the project to failure. When [FicChaTen] asked why, [TGTDTT] laid it out.

- ❏ First, to do a study of this nature properly by an outside consultant would cost [MCFLMosFB] a buck fifty to a quarter mil ($150,000 to $250,000, or put another way, at least the averaged annual loaded salary of [CM], [FD] Chief, [PD] Chief, [PW] Head, Building and Zoning Department Head, Recreation Department Head, and City Clerk. [MCFLMosFB] doesn't have that kind of [USD].
- ❏ Second, because the study was done by an outside organization with no vested interest or intimate

understanding of the community, the results would be suspect at best and rejected outright at worst.

It was [TGTDTT]'s belief that individuals who had a vested interest in the community and an expertise in organizational management, fiduciary responsibilities, and strategic planning should perform such a study. [TGTDTT] also believed that such individuals lived right here in [MCFLMosFB].

That [FicChaTen] was persuaded was a "good news, bad news" thing for [TGTDTT]. The good news was that [TGTDTT]'s argument was well received by someone [TGTDTT] had respect for and wanted to be successful in his efforts to make [FB] a better place to live. The bad news for [TGTDTT] was that it was unlikely that [TGTDTT] would be able to remain on the sidelines and would end up being one of the people involved in this study. As it turns out, [TGTDTT] was right about getting involved but totally clueless about the amount of extra energy that would be required to complete the job.

[TGTDTT]'s internal clock is always ticking and [TGTDTT] always thinks he is behind the curve far more often than he thinks he is ahead of stuff. The impact of such thinking has resulted in [TGTDTT]'s curricula vitae being over 50 pages long and his financial statement being something to envy. However, [TGTDTT] also thinks stuff should not take as much time as it does. So if a couple of days go by and [TGTDTT] doesn't see any progress, he assumes nothing is being done. As it turns out, most of the time [TGTDTT] is right, so he ends up just taking care of stuff because that way stuff gets done. This was the case for getting some kind of coherent statement that could be presented to [CC] for consideration. Not knowing anything about how to get something approved by [CC], [TGTDTT] decided to draft a charter so that others could comment, edit, amend, and eventually approve.

It took all of forty-five minutes to create the first draft of a charter and get it to [FicChaTen] for initial reactions. [FicChaTen] suggested a few other [MCFLMosFB] citizens that should probably be involved in the project and said it was a good start. After a half dozen or so group edits, the draft charter seemed in good enough shape to present to [CC]. On Wednesday December 21, YR11 a subset of the authors made a presentation to [CC] that was now comprised of the following individuals

[CM], [FicChaTwentyFour]
[CA], [FC02D]
[CC] [FB] Mayor, [FicChaSeventeen]
[CC] [FB] Vice Mayor, [FicChaFourteen]
[CC] [FB] Senior Member, [FicChaEighteen]
[CC] [FB] Member, [FicChaTen]
[CC] [FB] Jr. Member, [FicChaThirty]

For reasons surpassing understanding, [CC] did not know what to do. There was a big debate as to whether or not [CC] should even agree to accept a proposal into public record. Once that was settled, the debate shifted as to what to do with the proposal at all. When [CC] realized they had no idea as to how to proceed, the Mayor opened up the agenda item for [CitComm].

After a few people got up and spoke, [TGTDTT], the principal author of the charter made clear that the proposed draft charter was intended to be a starting point to help [CC] decide what it really wanted to do. [TGTDTT] told [CC] that he believed the document was sufficiently detailed to be used "as is" if the study was to be done in the private sector, however, the requirements and limitations associated with performing the study for a governmental organization compelled additional review and consideration by the [CC], [CM], and [CA].

[TGTDTT] made it clear that it was fully expected that the document would be revised, if not completely rewritten. All in all, it took about an hour for [CC] to decide to have [CC] members make whatever changes they wanted and to have [CA] prepare a clean copy that could be voted on by [CC] at the next meeting in January.

The January [CC] meeting presented a final copy of the charter that was almost identical to the draft charter with the exception that [COFFEE] membership went from 3 members to 7 members. The final charter also included meeting requirements intended to ensure that Sunshine Laws were not violated. [CC] approved the charter and then debated the process for selecting [COFFEE] members. A half-hour later, [CC] decided that interested citizens would submit their resumes for consideration and the selection would be made at the next [CC] meeting.

[TGTDTT] wasn't trying to be on [COFFEE]. [TGTDTT] saw the merits of the study, but was more than happy to let others do the work and that they get the credit. During a break, [TGTDTT] talked to [FicChaTwentyFour], the [CM] and said that if a dozen resumes were submitted that [TGTDTT] was not going to throw his hat into the ring. [FicChaTwentyFour] agreed to call [TGTDTT] the day before the deadline to let [TGTDTT] know how many people signed up for consideration. [TGTDTT] got a call from the City Clerk on January 25, YR12 to let [TGTDTT] know that only six people had submitted resumes. So [TGTDTT] filled out the form, attached his resume, and poured himself a glass of Knob Creek to drown his new found despair.

In retrospect, it seems somewhat curious that [TGTDTT] received a call the day before the deadline and there ended up being some fifteen or so applicants. Or has somebody been slipping [KoolAid] into [TGTDTT]'s drinking water?

# [COFFEE] Charter

## Proposal to [CC]
## Citizen's Observational Fact Finding
## efficiency Exercise [COFFEE]

## Abstract

Contained herein are the purpose, description and advisory scope of the volunteer [COFFEE] to be considered by [CC]. Though considered feasible by the authors in its current form, this document is intended to serve as a catalyst for the formulation of [COFFEE], by [CC] to benefit and enhance [MCFLMosFB] Operations, Management and [CC] members' decision-making process, and thus consequentially resultant citizens' positive long-range quality of life in [MCFLMosFB].

## Background and Introduction

Follow future Prudent & Solutions Driven Revenue Management

Given the economic conditions of the last several years and with minimal likelihood of a significant improvement in the near term, [MC]s must pursue greater focus on performing as efficiently and effectively as possible. As such, it is essential that [CC] form [COFFEE] to examine [MCFLMosFB] finances, including near and mid-term fluid financial projections analysis not excluding operations and procedural practices, to ensure the future efficiency and long range effectiveness of [MCFLMosFB] while maintaining an acceptable [MCFLMosFB] quality of service.

While [COFFEE] will be a formidable effort, the level of interest shown by the voters of [MCFLMosFB] in the recent election clearly shows there is widespread support for such a study initiative.

On November 30, 11 during remarks made by the two newly elected [CC] members, [FicChaTen] made progress on one of his campaign commitments to seek approval for an efficiency Assessment and Increased Citizens Involvement by proposing [COFFEE].

It is in the best interests of [MCFLMosFB] to establish [COFFEE] for the following reasons:

1. Restoration of confidence in [MCFLMosFB] [EMP] and [CM].
2. If the Initiative results in recommendations to increase the efficiency of [MCFLMosFB] management, Operations, expenses, and Ad Valorem Tax Millage Rate, the residents of [MCFLMosFB] will benefit from the savings.
3. If the Initiative finds that [MCFLMosFB] is operating in the most efficient manner, then it can and will restore public confidence in [MCFLMosFB] management and Operations.
4. The Initiative will also take into account the desire to sustain [MCFLMosFB] quality of service to the benefit [MCFLMosFB] citizens within reasonable parameters given current financial and constraints to [B].
5. [COFFEE] will pursue a path for building [MCFLMosFB] reserves having clear solutions to extinguishment of debt

service burdens that only diminish current and future [MCFLMosFB] revenues resource value.

[COFFEE] will be volunteers working without compensation. It is anticipated that this Initiative will have a minimal cost impact to [MCFLMosFB].

The fundamental purpose of [COFFEE] is threefold:

1. Perform a comprehensive assessment of all [MC]'s governmental funded activities via processes, including but not limited to: [MCFLMosFB] regulatory (non)/mandated objectives with related policies, staffing, operations, management, external/internal contracts, financial and cost accounting, [B], and financial/management reporting, and create a model that accurately reflects the current state of affairs with respect to [MCFLMosFB].
2. Utilizing the results of such assessments, recommend updated modeling initiatives for governmental processes that are intended to meet all applicable regulatory and fiscal requirements while improving the overall efficacy of [MCFLMosFB].
3. Recommend improvements to governmental objectives formulation, policies and practices for the purposes of validating assumptions and ensuring net positive results.

## Panel Purpose

[CC] shall approve [COFFEE]'s purpose by a simple majority in its entirety.

[COFFEE] shall conduct assessment audits, inspections, and any other activities reasonable in order to assess, improve, and validate the efficacy of [MCFLMosFB] processes. [COFFEE] members will be entrusted with the handling of confidential information as required to best understand and make sound recommendations to [CC] for consideration.

All actions performed by [COFFEE], to include individual members, shall be approved in advance by [CC] during the regularly scheduled [CC] meetings. A simple majority vote by [CC] constitutes approval.

[COFFEE]'s purpose may be renewed annually on the last actual meeting of each calendar year. A simple majority vote by [CC] constitutes renewal of [COFFEE]. If [CC] does not renew [COFFEE], [COFFEE] is disbanded.

All members of [COFFEE] shall act in the best interests of [MCFLMosFB] and within the statutory boundaries of [MCFLMosFB], [GovFLMos], [GVBMNTFL], and [USFG]. The [COFFEE] members shall be fully indemnified and held harmless from any liability associated with [COFFEE] work and findings.

**OBJECTIVE & SCOPE**: The [COFFEE] overall objective is to assess practices, processes, procedures, composition, and staffing levels—current and historical—to identify change opportunities and create long-term efficiencies and/or reduce [MCFLMosFB] expenses and optimize [MCFLMosFB] departmental performance. All recommendations and related efficiencies solutions will be forwarded to [CC] on a study-by-study basis to ensure [COFFEE] is creating a seamless approach to solutions.

**COMPOSITION**: [COFFEE] shall be composed of no more than seven members. Each [CC] member shall appoint one [COFFEE] member. The remaining members may be appointed, by majority vote from [CC], from applicants volunteering to serve on [COFFEE]. Each appointed [COFFEE] member may request subject matter experts for specific purposes pertinent to [COFFEE] efforts. [COFFEE] member subject matter experts must be approved by majority vote of [CC]. There will be no limit to the number of subject matter experts who support [COFFEE] efforts.

**APPOINTEE QUALIFICATIONS & RESTRICTIONS**: [COFFEE] appointees must be residents of [MCFLMosFB] and/ or majority [OwnBus] currently operating in [MCFLMosFB]. Appointees shall possess skills in professions relating to [MCFLMosFB] services, management, accounting/finance, law, engineering, administration, information technology, and Quality Assurance. [COFFEE] nominees must execute a Confidentiality Agreement/Non-Disclosure Agreement in order to participate on [COFFEE] and have access to [MCFLMosFB] [EMP] records.

**APPOINTMENT PROCESS**: [COFFEE] candidates shall submit a professional résumé that clearly delineates professional competency in one or more qualifying occupations. [CC] member shall evaluate [COFFEE] appointees by considering both professional and character references. Appointee information shall be made available to each [CC] member. A majority vote of [CC] shall be required for each [COFFEE] candidate. [CC] shall also appoint a Chair for [COFFEE] who will report progress and findings to [CC] during the course of [COFFEE]'s work. The Chair shall be selected by majority vote of [CC].

# Access to Files, Data, Records

[MCFLMosFB] shall make available at no cost to [COFFEE] members a networked computer, printer, workspace, and uncontrolled access to all media, files, active and inactive electronic records, and personnel. [COFFEE] will perform its function during normal [MCFLMosFB] business hours of operation when access to workspace is necessary. No records shall be exempt from provision to [COFFEE].

## Access to [MCFLMosFB] [EMP]

[COFFEE] is authorized to interview [MCFLMosFB] [EMP] at all levels to gain insight into governmental objectives, operations policies and procedures, schedules, and other information germane to efficiency discovery. [COFFEE] may electronically record interviews with personnel, as need dictates. At no time is [COFFEE] required to divulge sources of information. Confidentiality shall be ensured to all persons interviewed by [COFFEE] and any person may report information to [COFFEE] with the expectation of confidentiality.

## Reporting

At least one representative of [COFFEE] will attend regularly scheduled [CC] meeting's for the purpose of delivering a progress report and/or efficiency Initiatives for [CC]'s immediate consideration and implementation. The contents of such reports will be provided in advance of the meeting in electronic soft-copy to [MCFLMosFB] city clerk via email for distribution to the individual members of the [CC] and publication to [MCFLMosFB]'s web site.

## Expenses

Prior approval by [CC] must be obtained for reimbursement of any expenses incurred by [COFFEE] or any of its individual members. Any reimbursements will be processed in accordance with currently established practices and documented in progress reports to [CC].

# Panel Membership

[COFFEE] is the creation of, and answerable to [CC].

[COFFEE] shall have no fewer than three and no more than seven working members. Members shall be appointed by the [CC] to serve no more than twelve (12) calendar months, or until disbanded by majority vote of the [CC], whichever occurs first. [COFFEE] Members may be asked to continue to serve for longer than twelve (12) months by majority vote of the [CC].

In appointing members to [COFFEE], [CC] shall make its best effort to meet the following objectives:

1. At least three (3) members representing businesses operating in [MCFLMosFB]. These individual do not need to be residents of [MCFLMosFB], if they are not residents they must be the majority owner(s) of a business operating in [MCFLMosFB] at all times while they are serving on [COFFEE].
2. At least three (3) members who are residents of [MCFLMosFB] and have at least 3 years experience managing and operating a business in the county containing [MCFLMosFB]
3. At least three (3) members who are residents of [MCFLMosFB].

Panel may establish Task Units, each of which shall be chaired by a voting member of [COFFEE]. There is no limit to the number of Task Units that may be established however membership on the Task Units shall not exceed seven individuals.

# Meltdown

"This can't be right. Nothing lines up. I can't do anything with this."

Sounds pretty bad, but it gets worse. Public apology worse. But not to [TGTDTT]. He did what he did and took full responsibility for the entire incident. [TGTDTT] told [CC] that he would not resign because it would deny [CC] the opportunity to remove him for cause. When [OBandSD] heard [TGTDTT] speak to the room that night, [OBandSD] couldn't help think that [OBandSD] is seeing the kind of thing that ends up being a story that becomes considered sacred texts.

The back-story and specifics are that [COFFEE] was approved and before it could even get started, the snakes began an all out assault on [COFFEE]'s Chairman, [FicChaTwelve]. The leader of the local chapter of the [FOP] threatened to go public with [FicChaTwelve]'s single arrest (medication DUI) that happened the previous year. (And this guy calls himself a "law enforcement officer"? More like a "union thug.") There was huge public outcry where the majority of the voices were supporting [FicChaTwelve]. Some of these voices were pretty eloquent. One of the most eloquent was [TGTDTT]. In three minutes he calmly persuaded [CC] to reverse its decision to accept [FicChaTwelve]'s resignation as a member of [COFFEE].

(BeginTransmission)

Fellow [COFFEE] Members,

I tendered my resignation from [COFFEE] to the [CC] today. Pressure from outside sources precipitated this; but please let me assure you: The people on this team are a focused, loyal, devoted, and astute corps—not just "core"—committed to blazing a trail for future City planning. The task is a shared one—which is why we sought (and valued) audience participation during our first meeting. It was an opportunity—not a mandate—for our community to offer their personal stake and brainpower in the process.

Tomorrow night I will update [CC] on highlights of our first meeting—a meeting that was (unquestionably) a resounding success and promises to be a defining moment in the process for sustaining [MCFLMosFB]. I ask you for just one thing: stay the course

Use your intellect, camaraderie, skills, and intuition to capture data of real value. Ask good questions and chase the answers…and when the process is over be able to say, "We made a difference…we made community history by making our community achieve more." Report what you see…report what you feel…and use your data to support it.

I extend my sincere apology to each [COFFEE] member—I can imagine no greater honor than to have been one of you through to the end—but even the start was a central event in [MCFLMosFB]'s future.

Sincerely,
[FicChaTwelve]

(End Transmission)

(Reply)

I was stunned when I received [FicChaTwelve]'s email . . . I have known [FicChaTwelve] for many years when [FicChaTwelve] worked with my ex in his [USAF] job and then with him in many other official functions and awards that [FicChaTwelve] made and brought to my workplace.

I was a bit taken back today when I received [MCFLMosFB] city clerk email about [COFFEE] emailing each other about questions we had...such as appointments, questions and skills bank. I thought that this was agreed at the meeting last week that if we were to correspond we needed to include [MCFLMosFB] city clerk and [CM] so we would comply with Sunshine Laws. It appears now that we must also include the entire city. Then I come home and have a message from Recreation Department Head, [MCFLMosFB] on my voice mail about meeting and that she had received an email and phone message from [CM] about FC012's . . . .okay.. I get it.

And also some people that I converse with at various local businesses and that I would talk to along the street when I walked my dog are now ignoring me . . . . . . I am not even known in this city. It is almost like no one wants us digging into their business. I will be there tomorrow night and hopefully we can at least say "HI" to one another without being scrutinized by our fellow [MCFLMosFB] citizens

You did not get this email from me so delete it!

[COFFEE] member

(End Reply)

(Reply)

I read the [FicChaTwelve]'s note after returning from a nice meal at Neptune's with my wife and after having a tremendously productive meeting with the [MCFLMosFB] Finance Department earlier in the day. My heart sunk and I felt as though all of the wind in my sails had died.

I spoke to [FicChaTwelve], not knowing the details of his reasons and expressed the sentiments that warriors understand, and that is never quit, never give up. I let him know that if quitting was an option I would have done so long ago because being on [COFFEE] and trying to improve government processes is a huge pain the ass.

Then [FicChaTwelve] told me his reasons and my emotions got the best of me.

Why are the accusations of divisiveness coming from people who overtly try to hurt others?

Why are the most impassioned lectures on Sunshine Laws coming from people who have enjoyed privileged conversations for the longest time?

I have been [FicChaTwelve]'s neighbor since 98. We have had dinners together, we have attended social functions together, and he has been in my home to discuss matters that were important to [MCFLMosFB].

Not once have I ever heard [FicChaTwelve] speak an irresponsible phrase. Not once have I witnessed anything that did not reflect well on [FicChaTwelve]'s character. The longer I know [FicChaTwelve], the more respect I have for him and the more I trust him. And since I am not someone who readily trusts or believes in people, the fact that I trust [FicChaTwelve] to do the right thing and respect others is not just rhetoric. It is saying something very important.

[FicChaTwelve] was the one person on the team who could bring the members together to speak with one voice. [FicChaTwelve] was the one person I trusted to keep my passions in check and the project on the right path. [FicChaTwelve] was the one person that I wanted most to be with me when this project was finished and we could enjoy a job well done as colleagues, teammates, and friends.

Why on earth would someone do something so unnecessary and downright evil to hurt this man? Why anyone would tolerate or experience any joy at the thought of doing something so evil or knowing that such evil was done.

It is more likely than not that the damage and public display of small-minded, selfish, irresponsible, and hateful behavior that [FicChaTwelve]'s resignation was trying to avoid has already been done and that, once again, the [FlaTo] is going to publish something that has no business being published. To that end, these hateful people will once again bring harm to a decent person to advance their self-interests and I am denied the opportunity to work alongside my friend doing something that will bring the city together.

My role in helping [FD] head, [MCFLMosFB] put together a comprehensive study that allowed [CC] to render an informed decision was [FicChaTwelve]'s doing. [FicChaTwelve] never read a word of the report until after it was published. [FicChaTwelve] never suggested that I accept [FD] head, [MCFLMosFB]'s request for assistance nor did he influence my research in any way. But it was [FicChaTwelve]'s example that made my answering the call to service mandatory.

Bringing [COFFEE] together so that [CC] could vote on it was [FicChaTwelve]'s doing. I know I wrote the first draft and most of my words made it into the final draft, but it was [FicChaTwelve] that made it all happen.

Leadership is not always doing something or telling others what they should do. Leadership is also creating an environment that inspires others to do more and to be better than they ever thought they could be. [FicChaTwelve] is, without a doubt, such a leader.

Please join me and encourage others to let [FicChaTwelve] know that we need his steadfast leadership. I invite every [MCFLMosFB] citizens to stand up at this Wednesday's [CC] meeting to publicly state that [FicChaTwelve] did not deserve what has been done to him and that we absolutely believe he is the one person with the vision and character to bring the other six members of [COFFEE] together so that we may bring [MCMFLMosFB] together as one community.

I have not decided what I am going to do about all this. My prayer is that between the time I go to sleep tonight and the time I go to sleep tomorrow night after the [CC] meeting, I will find within myself a renewed capacity to continue with this exercise. If I were to see an outpouring of support for my friend and a repudiation of hurtful behavior, I might be convinced that my efforts are worthwhile. If I don't see such an outpouring of support tomorrow night, then my inclination is to say "to hell with all of you". But as I said, I haven't decided.

[TGTDTT]

(End Reply)

(Reply)

Without doubt, your words are the kindest and sincerest vote of confidence I have ever received. My only wish is that they meant the same to those who resist everything. Stay the course…I am still behind you (and [COFFEE]).

Thank you for this unforgettable acknowledgment.

Your Friend,
[FicChaTwelve]

(End Reply)


In the next [CC] meeting, [TGTDTT] asked calmly, "Which one of us is next?" Then [TGTDTT] made the point that all of this effort to prevent a person from doing something the person has no intention of doing and is not authorized to do anyway is hysterical fear. The people involved in [COFFEE] have been totally forthcoming in what their goals are and have gone to the trouble to make sure the scope of inquiry is limited to information that is clearly not sensitive and pertains specifically to [B] and policy/process.

Everything worked out well and [FicChaTwelve] remained the Chairman. The time wasted just made the task more difficult. [COFFEE] had sixty days to say something important and the rules imposed by [CC] at the advice of [CA] caused even more delays. The last time [CC] approved something like this was called the Right Sizing Committee (RSC). The RSC had as many as twenty-one members at one time and performed their study over an eighteen-month period.

[TGTDTT] wanted to get his hands on the raw financial data so that he could answer relevant questions using the answers the data provided and not what people are telling him. When he finally got the data, it corresponded to the beginning of a weekend where his wife was at a conference out of town.

If a project is really cool, [TGTDTT] loves all-nighters working on really big data sets. But in his excited and sleep deprived state; he completely failed to recognize that his data set had become corrupted and the results were meaningless.

[TGTDTT] had no perspective to assess the merits of sharing his findings with anyone under the premise that it is telling us something. In short, Elvis had left the building. [TGTDTT] went into overdrive discussing his findings with a close circle in the hope that someone would influence his thinking in a manner that made sense. Those who saw the data came to the conclusion that something is wrong, but it is probably something [TGTDTT] did to it and that no action should be taken other than [TGTDTT] getting some sleep.

In [TGTDTT]'s sleep deprived state, he began to embrace the perception of incompetence and corruption and adjusted his receiver of all incoming messages accordingly. The result was that the message [TGTDTT] received was, "You should not show this to anyone."

But [TGTDTT] was running on pure adrenalin and probably should have been tranquilized because he told each person who advised him that he agreed with them, and then released a rant of rants to a large and public audience.

It wasn't until the following day that [TGTDTT] had discovered that it was indeed [TGTDTT]'s error.

So like a man, [TGTDTT] went to each person individually and apologized for his conduct. [TGTDTT] laid himself wide open to the possibility of being privately and publicly humiliated and crucified. [TGTDTT] stood before [CC] and apologized to the entire community.

[TGTDTT]:     I, and I alone, am responsible for the authorship and release of the Ledger Analysis report that was distributed via email to the members of the [COFFEE], [CC], [CM], and City Clerk. Not a single aspect of the report's release, including the way it was released is excusable.

There is no defense for what I did other than to let you all know that it was culmination of events that included extended periods without sleep or food and working in a complete vacuum. What had begun as a round the clock effort that was producing great progress in the development of a long term financial planning model for the city ended in a miserable attempt to reconcile corrupt data. In those last few hours before the report was released I lacked the cognitive skills to put any of my findings in context but my determination to complete the exercise prevented me from taking a step a back and get some sleep so that I could revisit the problem with a fresh set of eyes. However, everything associated with the matter is of my making and I am the only person responsible for my actions and decisions.

Upon realizing the extent of the technical errors in the data analysis and coming to grips with the extent of my breach in professionalism, ethics, and trust, I immediately issued a written apology to those I knew were most affected by my lapse in judgment. I have since met with them in person and expressed how shameful I feel at having hurt them. I now come to apologize publicly to [CC], [COFFEE], and to each and every one of my fellow citizens for my actions.

Much, or maybe all, of this could have been avoided had I been afforded the opportunity to openly collaborate with my colleagues and those that I have made the commitment to serve. I believe that had I spent my time working with others instead of in isolation left to my own inclinations of sleep deprivation and tunnel vision, my findings would have been questioned and reviewed in real time.

I will not volunteer my resignation from [COFFEE] because it would deny those who have just cause and the opportunity to demand it. If asked for such, consider it given. To the extent [CC] is inclined to terminate my participation for cause, you are both justified in such action and have the authority to do so.

Whether I resign, am terminated, or am allowed to remain on [COFFEE], I have no intention of going forward under the structure and limitations associated with being a member.

What I will do, to the extent that the [CM] and [MCFLMosFB] [EMP] permit, is to work with them directly and quietly to fix problems that need fixing. My involvement will be limited to actually making a difference instead of attending public meetings. If it were to become that nobody ever knew I was involved in something that helped this city, then my service was appropriate to my comfort zone and values.

My actions of Sunday March 5, YR12 mark the lowest point in my personal and professional life. There is no criticism of my actions that is not warranted and any credibility I may have had has been damaged. From the time I got appointed to [COFFEE] with its structure and limitations, I had been going about doing what I know is right in the wrong way. As of right now, I am going to do what I know in my heart is right but I am going to do it in the way that allows me to work with people to solve problems in the most efficient and compassionate way I know how.

There were some people who nipped at the blood in the water, but they were very few in number and if you were not really listening for them, you couldn't hear them. When [TGTDTT] was done apologizing, virtually everybody in the room decided that [TGTDTT] should be allowed to keep working and that he should be able to do stuff his way if they want to understand anything worth understanding.

From the point of the disinterested bystander who goes to [CC] meetings instead of watching television, [OBandSD] thought that this drama playing out before him is definitely being produced by one of those small independent film companies. There is no way the corporate weenies at Warner Bro's or MGM would be behind this project.

People were crying. [TGTDTT] was on the verge of being inconsolable. All because Microsoft Excel does what Microsoft Excel does when the operator does not allow adequate clock cycles between mouse-clicks. There is a point where the software can't store the commands for the next thing while it is doing the thing it is doing right now. The end result is that the software will abandon what it doing right now and start working on the next instruction using a partially processed data set. In short, everything falls apart. In this case, the repercussions affected an entire town.

# Fair Winds and following Seas

"Who has to die around here before I can get some more of my people on this council?" was a thought [TGTDTT] could never imagine any of the people [TGTDTT] was coming into contact with, much less himself, ever having. But if someone does die, we might as well make the best out it.

[CC] Senior Member [FicChaEighteen] was a World War II veteran. Fought in the battles planned by Admiral Chester Nimitz and Bull Halsey as a private first class [USMC] in the Pacific Theatre. [FicChaEighteen] was also a retired airline executive who had a beachfront condominium in a building with a bunch of other retirees of substantial means.

[FicChaEighteen] was a good man who spoke for those of his peer group. [FicChaEighteen] would always support stuff that can be framed as helping make life better or safer for senior citizens. He always behaved with dignity and elevated the tenor and quality of the debate. [TGTDTT] did not always subscribe to his point of view, but [TGTDTT] could see where [FicChaEighteen] was coming from.

At age eighty-six, [FicChaEighteen] got his orders for a permanent change in duty station to report on May 8, YR12.

Right before [COFFEE] was to release the Final Report and just before the fiscal year 12-13 [B] process is scheduled to start,

[FicChaEighteen] checks out. In retrospect, a plausible case could be made that [FicChaEighteen]'s departure was a foreshadowing of events to come.

But [FicChaEighteen]'s gone and someone needs to replace him. There is important work to be done so the sooner we replace [FicChaEighteen] the better. Sincerest regards to his family. Now let's see who we want to put in ole [FicChaEighteen]'s seat.

And with a bang of the gavel, the Mayor called to order the special meeting of [CC] because it was the first time in [MCFLMosFB]'s history that a sitting member of council died and no one was really certain as to how to handle things. Would [CA] please tell us what to do?

"But of course," answered [CA] [MCFLMosFB]. "The short answer is that you have thirty days to find a replacement."

| | |
|---|---|
| Mayor: | Well I propose we take a week to think stuff over. |
| [FicChaTen]: | Mr. Mayor, as a combat veteran yourself, certainly you see the benefit of handling this matter immediately so that we can get on with our mission. |
| Mayor: | I do understand your point of view [FicChaTen], but coming back in a week does not hurt anything. Besides, [FicChaEighteen]'s service is the day after tomorrow. Can we show [FicChaEighteen]'s widow some respect? |
| [FicChaFourteen]: | I agree with the Mayor. The list of people on our lists is not going to change and |

most of us have a pretty good idea the names on every body else's list so making a decision next week shouldn't be a problem.

[FicChaTen]: Mayor, I make motion that we appoint [FicChaTwelve] to [CC] Jr. Member seat due to the recent demise of [FicChaEighteen].

[FicChaThirty]: I second the motion.

It is at this time that [OBandSD] saw the best impression of the TV [FicCha] Lieutenant Colonel Blake by Mayor [FicChaSeventeen] on the television series M*A*S*H when Pierce and Macintyre are sparring it out with Burns and Houlihan. "Ah jeez guys. Can't you just wait a few days to do what you are going to do anyway?"

What makes this analogy so important to our story is that the closest impersonation of Major Burns was being done by the now [CC] Senior Member [FicChaTen] and the role of Houlihan was being performed by the new [CC] Member [FicChaThirty]. The other thing is that in this episode, Burns and Houlihan got their way and just like on TV, the antics of [FicChaTen] and [FicChaThirty] came back to haunt everyone.

With the motion seconded, a vote was taken. The Mayor voted "No" and the other three voted "Yes". [FicChaFourteen]'s dream had come true. For the first time in his political career he was on the winning side of a controversial vote, but he did not want to be. He said he wanted to wait a week but when a decision had to be made, he showed his mettle, swallowed his pride, and cast his vote in the best interests of [MCFLMosFB] even though he would have preferred to wait a week. That stinging feeling

[FicChaFourteen] is having is the wound left after a small piece of his soul is torn away and fed to two hungry demons.

Are you buying all this? From the cheap seats it looks like a shift of one set of cronies to another set of cronies. From up close, it doesn't look a whole lot better. Over the last few months, [FicChaTwelve] and [TGTDTT] worked closely together and were the driving force for a number of positive steps towards transparency and efficiency. Since there was no way humanly possible for [CC] to make a decision that would be accepted by a majority, or at least the loudest screamers, one might as well get it over with as soon as possible. As far as picking someone [TGTDTT] could have confidence in, they made the best choice they could have with [FicChaTwelve]. To some, [FicChaTwelve] was their Jackie Robinson. To others, it was the idea that this can't be good. It can't be good for the people who have no respect, trust, confidence, or affection for [FicChaTwelve] and it can't be good for all the people that do have that stuff, because it really does look like cronyism.

Just prior to the start of [FicChaEighteen]'s memorial service, [FicChaTwelve] received his first hand-delivered councilman's briefing book and was holding it while standing in line to express condolences to [FicChaEighteen]'s widow. By and large [FicChaEighteen]'s widow was a good woman from another time who forgot that hearing the same old stories from the same five people, does not mean that a lot of people have come up and told you something. [TGTDTT] is in front of [FicChaTwelve] because [TGTDTT] wanted to introduce himself as being the person whose quote was in the paper. [FicChaTwelve] was just being polite.

What [TGTDTT] saw in [FicChaTwelve] was a guy who did not appreciate the symbolism of extending your condolences to the widow of the councilman's seat you were just appointed to while holding the briefing book that used to be delivered to her husband. Or was [TGTDTT] reading too much into the situation?

Regardless, [TGTDTT] was able to get [FicChaTwelve] to let [FicChaThirteen] carry the book in her purse.

So as of July 1, YR12 the makeup of [CC] was two reformers, one debt-settler, one excited kid and one "Colonel Blake." [TGTDTT] and [OBandSD] sensed a storm brewing on the horizon and [TGTDTT] was going to be player in a little dramatic comedy [TGTDTT] likes to call, "A Glorious and Divine Celebration of the Magic of Hubris."

# [COFFEERpt] (Excerpts)

Report of Activities and Findings
of
[COFFEE]

Made To
[CC]

Created for
The Interested citizens and Dedicated [PubServ]s
In [MCFLMosFB]

## Executive Summary

Contained herein are the observations and a portion of the data collected to date. The data was provided by [MCFLMosFB] [EMP] or obtained from reliable public sources. From all of the research and efforts put forth in this initiative, the most important conclusion that can be offered at this time is that the mere publication of this report in no way constitutes completion of an in-depth assessment and that an ongoing and continued effort is required in order to achieve and sustain efficiencies while eliminating excess and extravagance.

[COFFEE]'s findings indicate that a firm and continuous commitment by the dedicated and professional [PubServ]s to eliminate all unnecessary expenses would reduce the total cost of business. However, [MCFLMosFB] can never materialize much savings without a corresponding increase in citizen's involvement and potential decrease in level of service.

[COFFEE] determined that:

- Policies that tend to create financial liabilities that accumulate over time reduce the efficiency and availability of revenue.
- Increased citizen volunteerism can decrease public sector costs, inject new process models, and increase public awareness of [GVBMNT] [B] challenges and methods.
- Increased operational expense/effort can be mitigated by greater citizen involvement, reduced consumption, and reassessment/understanding of needs.
- Reductions in [MCFLMosFB] revenues are the result of economic influences both within and outside the control of [MCFLMosFB]'s decision-makers.
- Paid consultants and vendors from outside the community provide services that the citizens of [MCFLMosFB] may be capable of performing with an acceptable degree of competence and expectation of success.

The pages that follow detail specific issues in an effort to identify paths for reducing [MCFLMosFB] expenses without risking the long-term financial viability of [MCFLMosFB] or reducing the quality of life in [FB]. But unless the magnitude and nature of community involvement improves, [MCFLMosFB] expenses will always be higher than what some of the citizens think it should be.

[COFFEE] suggests that consideration and public discussion to obtain a widely accepted solution be associated with the following items:

1. Incorporation of detailed long term financial planning in [B] process that is transparent and available to the public

2. Deeper examination of vehicle usage, subsidy, and necessity
3. Evaluation of [MCFLMosFB] [EMP] Cell Phone Subsidy policy
4. Evaluation of the pay increase for special skills.
5. Examination of the Department Program cost structure
6. [EMP] Sick Leave sell-back policy
7. Optimizing the number of active Credit Cards issued to [MCFLMosFB] [EMP] and members of [CC], including retail accounts and credit cards.
8. The needs of the Administration and Finance Department (IT and software).
9. Identifying repetitive tasks that can be sufficiently defined in order to solicit competitive bids that are compared to the estimated project costs of performing the service using [MCFLMosFB] [EMP].
10. Native data electronic format (Word, Excel, PowerPoint, etc.) and standardized software data sharing.
11. Implementation of electronic measures for the archival and retrieval of selected records processed by the Building and Zoning department.
12. Examination of IT infrastructure, state-mandated capabilities for the [PD], and related software, firmware, and hardware.

The [COFFEE] charter was sufficiently broad, and the principal task was of such enormity that areas of interest were identified but time and resources prevented adequate study. In addition to the items recommended for public discussion and possible action, [COFFEE] identified several matters where additional study is required. The items below are a subset of the total:

1. Transitioning all business with the community to on-line processes and electronic payment including implementation of e-payment methods for services and fees

2. Examine how [MCFLMosFB] owned facilities are utilized and their potential to enhance [MCFLMosFB] revenues.

3. Clarify [MCFLMosFB]'s real estate holdings and identify opportunities to enhance [MCFLMosFB] revenues.

4. A comprehensive wage and benefit analysis of [MCFLMosFB] [EMP]

5. Fleet Management, Procurement, and Utilization

6. Evaluation of all public lands with respect to revenue generating opportunities.

7. Development of a skills matrix and long term staffing plans to identify redundancies, vacancies, and impact of attrition.

8. [MCFLMosFB] [EMP] and [MCFLMosFB] retired volunteer policies.

9. [MCFLMosFB] [EMP] Benefits and Retirement Plans

10. [MCFLMosFB] managed volunteer programs.

11. [MCFLMosFB] Vehicle and Capital Equipment Plan

# Efficiency – A General Discussion

Efficiency is a single term that indicates the relationship between expended resources and realized benefit. A simple example is the miles per gallon rating of a vehicle. When the miles traveled per gallon of fuel of one vehicle are greater than that of another vehicle, a common assumption is that the first vehicle is more efficient than the second vehicle. However, the rate at which a vehicle expends fuel does not consider the consequence of ownership and operation. For instance, if the second vehicle is less expensive, more reliable and carries a larger payload, then deploying the second vehicle may be a more efficient solution in terms of overall cost and capability. Understanding that efficiency can be an incongruous concept under the best of circumstances is problematic with respect to quantifying all matters related to [MC] functions; however, if certain elements that contribute towards an assessment of efficiency are viewed qualitatively as well as quantitatively, then descriptive statements that reliability indicate tendencies toward efficiencies can be made.

The notion of an efficient [MC] is ambiguous and rare; but there are some descriptive elements that would serve to indicate if a [GVBMNT] trends towards being efficient. We begin by establishing the singular truth of [B] which is [MCRev] = [MCExp] and adding the goals:

[1] [MC] reserves-on-hand is greater than or equal to Estimated Emergency Reserve Required [MC] Debt, current value held equal to 0

[2] [MCRLE] is minimized,

[3] Ad Valorem Tax Millage Rate is minimized

[4] Automated Processes associated with the Municipal Corporation is maximized

[5] [MC] [EMP]s is optimized

[COFFEE]'s charter was sufficiently broad to allow analysis of financial records, processes/procedures, and methods for the purpose of promoting transparency in [GVBMNT], accountability by agents of the [GVBMNT], and the expenditure of minimum resources with the expectation of maximum benefit. However, [COFFEE]'s charter is limited to presenting information and interpretations of that information so that the elected officials and authorized agents of the [GVBMNT] can make informed decisions as to spending revenues and operational practices and policies. If the [CC] and the public could be provided the following information, the research effort would permit other groups to focus on single departments and interrelated practices regarding [B]s, staffing, planning, and practices.

1.  A comprehensive accounting of all real estate holdings, their current market value, outstanding mortgage, potential taxable revenue, and annual maintenance cost.
2.  A comprehensive list of all capital equipment, current value, anticipated date of replacement, and replacement cost.
3.  A comprehensive list of all non-capital inventories, current value, anticipated date of replacement, and replacement cost.
4.  A comprehensive list of all services provided by the [MC], the statutory requirements of each service, the skill sets required performing each service, and the time-burden of each service.
5.  A comparative assessment of the cost of goods and services provided by [MCFLMosFB] with respect to wages.
6.  A model to provide for long term planning of [MCRev] and [MCExp].

Much of the study was conducted via numerical analysis of hard data as well as interviews with staff and citizens to gain an appreciation of the human factor. Both numerical analysis and human factors must be considered when rendering a decision as to what is best for a community.

It is noteworthy to give voice to the fact that [COFFEE] is not a regulatory or policymaking body. Though empowered with extensive access to records, facilities and personnel, [COFFEE]'s contribution is limited only to reporting its findings. If done right, the way forward will be obvious to those who have the authority and power to implement changes and to decide what actions should be considered. It is also appropriate to make clear that an effort such as [COFFEE] is an ongoing collaboration and not a single event that concludes with a final report. Changes in a [MCFLMosFB]'s demographics manifest a change in the [MCFLMosFB]'s needs, values, and capabilities. It is prudent to have an ongoing effort that examines how well stuff have been done in the past, what are the requirements for [MCFLMosFB] to be successful now, and what do we believe [MCFLMosFB] will require in order to be successful and sustainable in the future.

To honestly and completely undertake and support an endeavor such as [COFFEE], requires extreme courage to accept the [REALITY] that becomes apparent and faith in the talent and motivation of those who dedicate their professional lives to [MCFLMosFB]. In parallel, we must acknowledge gratitude to those [MCFLMosFB] citizens who volunteered their time and expertise to study [MCFLMosFB] dynamics to present efficiency findings in a respectful, unbiased, factual, and thorough manner.

If done properly, the initial [COFFEE] study establishes a benchmark, foundation, and direction for future and ongoing efforts. Over the course of one or two [B] cycles, there would exist a sufficient body of information to develop metrics that can be periodically and efficiently analyzed and reported with the overall goal of being able to respond to changes in the regulatory and economic paradigms.

It is irrefutable that every community is governed by an organization that represents the collective values of that community. In the case of forming [COFFEE], and the subsequent study and reports, one could assume that at present, the community wants to do everything it can to create an open, inclusive, respectful, creative, productive, safe, and fiscally responsible [MC]. Because this is the first time that [MCFLMosFB] has ever done this exact thing, it can be argued that the collective values have changed. What remains to be seen is whether such a change manifests lasting improvements or was just something to allow politicians to brag about or criticize during election season. It is with the sincerest hope that [COFFEE] YR12 is the beginning of something that will only get better and bring the community together so that competing interests become common goals.

# [MCFLMosFB]

[MCFLMosFB] has a population of approximately 10,109 people, has a reported 09 Median Household Income of $48,220 and covers an area of 4.3 sq mi (11.1 km2), consisting of 2.9 square miles of land and 1.4 square miles of water. [MCFLMosFB] charter dictates a council/manager form of [GVBMNT].

[MCFLMosFB] [EMP] equals approximately 129 people, full time and part time (permanent & temporary),

[MCFLMosFB] volunteers equal approximately 80 citizens to meet its service requirements.

[B] varies between $10 and $15 million

[MCFLMosFB] employee salary average equals $44, 614

Ad Valorem Tax Millage Rate FY11/12 was 8.5285 mils, which is expected to generate just under $5M or 56% of the $8.8M General Fund [B]. It is expected that the millage rate will be adjusted upward this fiscal year in response to a furthering decline in property values.

Aggregate revenues to [MCFLMosFB] are derived from several sources including

1.  Direct taxes based on property value;
2.  Service based fees and licenses;

3. Revenue sharing from [GovFLMos], [GVBMNTFL], and [USFG] agencies;
4. [GovFLMos], [GVBMNTFL], and [USFG] grants;
5. Contributions and donations from private citizens.

Of the aforementioned revenue sources, the authority of [MCFLMosFB] to establish rates and therefore forecast revenues is limited to the direct taxes levied on citizens, residents and businesses through items 1 and 2 above. The amounts associated with items 3 through 5 are determined beyond the sphere of controllability of [MCFLMosFB] and, as often as not, come with expectations as to how that [USD] is spent. In all cases, the discretion to which [MCFLMosFB] has with respect to the distribution of [MCFLMosFB] revenues is constrained by the following parameters:

- Regulatory Requirements
- Contractual Requirements
- Community Values.

In the last decade, the distribution of [MCFLMosFB] revenues has resulted in the appearance that one or more of the aforementioned parameters have been exceeded to some degree. At the time of this report, [CRA] is attracting interest for the manner in which its financial matters were handled, [MC] debt, current value held is more than one order of magnitude larger than it was a decade ago, Ad Valorem Tax Millage Rate is greater than 80% of the current legal limit, [MCFLMosFB] [EMP] has been reduced by almost 30% while experiencing pay freezes for the last three (3) consecutive years, tooling and infrastructure required to effectively run [MCFLMosFB] is in need of upgrade and repair, [B] amendments tend to respond to shortfalls in [MCFLMosFB] revenues and increased [MCFLMosFB] expenses, and the [MCFLMosFB] reserves is deemed to be in decline and approaching levels that warrant serious consideration.

The financial planning of [MCFLMosFB] is primarily done by [CM] with support of [MCFLMosFB] Boards and [MCFLMosFB] [EMP]. The [B] process that is observable by the general public and approved by the five (5) elected [CC] members is limited to the next fiscal year and [B] amendments within the current fiscal year. Considered and detailed analysis of future and long-term requirements is not an activity that is conducted in a manner that promotes a collective understanding by everybody with a vested interest in the community. In summary, everybody gets to see a high-level glimpse of the present but only a few, if any, have any visibility of what is on the horizon. The net result of such a process is that uninformed [MCFLMosFB] expends the time and energy of [CM] and [MCFLMosFB] [EMP]s through questions and accusations that compel a defensive approach on the part of the [CM] and [MCFLMosFB] [EMP]. Such expenditures consume limited resources and tend to produce little, if any, tangible improvement to [MCFLMosFB] finances, its infrastructure, or the safety and security of [MCFLMosFB] citizens.

Consideration of the idea of efficiency with respect to a community, it would seem that, in the absence of any data, a commitment by every [MCFLMosFB] citizens to exert energy towards helping [MCFLMosFB] create a model community that is safe, inclusive, and secure, would reduce the extent to which negative elements are introduced into their community. It would also seem that a [MC] that can trust and rely on citizens to help out and that can be called upon for services without an expectation of reward or compensation, would go a long way towards fixing all of the stuff that need to be fixed and creating an environment of true ownership of their [MC]. The good news is that [MCFLMosFB] has both dedicated volunteers and [MCFLMosFB] [EMP]s who welcome and rely on volunteer assistance. However, only a small percentage of the total pool of talent and capability is engaged in an initiative that requires the participation of everyone who has a vested interest in [MCFLMosFB].

# General [GVBMNT]

Overhead costs for general [GVBMNT] operations were a [COFFEE] focus area. Trends of [MCFLMosFB] expenses indicate the following escalating costs:

- Retiree and COBRA Insurance benefits escalating at a rate of about 8%/year
- Retirement contributions escalated 19% over 5 years
- Banking fees increased by 8X … $871 to FY10/11 costs of $6,712 (efficiency target)
- Postage averages $11,420/year (efficiency target)

# [MCRev]

[MCRev] was an area of focus for [COFFEE]. [MCRev] FY11 is at a 5-year low. [MCRev] Grant - money handed down from [USFG], [GVBMNTFL], and [GovFLMos] came in just over $3M, while the 5-year cost of the grant-writing services contract for the same period was $276K. Court fines/fees income is off by 61%--down to just $70K from $116K just 5 years ago. Recreation department program activity fees are up 20% ($406K), but costs of the recreation department remains an item for further study.

# 10-Year Spending History

Of note—and perhaps interest—is the fact that the [CRA] funds transfer value over the life of its existence is very nearly equal to the sum of its FY11 debt. [CRA] will not pay off its $5-million debt until the end of FY26 and will amass $1,898,636 in interest payments over the remaining period of the loan. This debt was not incurred by voter referendum; [CRA] board approved the debt at a public meeting. [GVBMNTFL] Statutes currently authorize [CRA] such powers; but these powers exclude direct voter input.

# [MCFLMosFB] Personnel Policies

[MCFLMosFB] Personnel Policies adopted by [MCFLMosFB] Ordinance 435 on 15 Apr 87 (amended by [MCFLMosFB] Ordinance 40 times over the years) is the governing policy on personnel management. It applies to all [MCFLMosFB] [EMP] and does not include [CM], [CA], [MCFLMosFB] boards and [CC]. [COFFEE] examined this document in detail and observed the items listed below. It is [COFFEE]'s recommendation that [CC] consider the observations so that a meaningful recommendation could be made to [CM] regarding the current disposition of published policy and actual practice.

1. This document would be more effective if it applied to [MCFLMosFB] [EMP] and [MCFLMosFB] volunteers—no exceptions or exemptions.
2. There is no clear delineation between "the [MC]" and "the [CM]" regarding personnel actions. If these terms are used interchangeably, it is both nebulous and confusing.
3. The "Work Week" definition should be incorporated into a general "Pay Period" definition. Pay periods define how overtime is calculated.

4. Paragraph 3.07: Public Release of information, Paragraph A is not written as a policy.

5. The holiday pay sections are overly complex and may need to be revised.

6. Annual leave earning levels may need to be revised to more closely mirror civilian sector jobs.

7. Paragraph 9.03B effectively awards extra time off for good attendance. This appears to be inefficient, if not paradoxical.

8. Paragraph 9.04B accrual rules are not applied to all [MCFLMosFB] [EMP] without waiver. It is suggested that this matter be considered for potential adjustment.

9. Paragraph 9.06, Payment for Unused Leave:

    a. [COFFEE] fails to recognize any efficiency in allowing [EMP]s to sell back annual leave. It is [COFFEE]'s suggestion that this matter be considered for realignment with commercial sector employment.

    b. The sick leave accrual rate is high; [COFFEE] recommends that [CC] and [CM] consider realigning this with commercial sector employment.

    c. Sick leave payout should cease and the maximum accrual should be lower. [COFFEE] recommends consideration of an alternative approach that may include the idea of increasing the sick leave donation levels in lieu of the excessive accrual and payout of sick leave options.

10. Recommend tuition reimbursement guidance remove payment for a "C" grade or lower.

11. Recommend Vision Care insurance be available for [MCFLMosFB] [EMP] (with contribution) versus the plan currently in effect in Paragraph 14.03, B, (2).

12. Paragraph 17.03 offenses needs clarification on who makes the determination of what "group" an offense falls under; [COFFEE] recommends streamlining this list for ease of use and clarity.

# [MC] Pension Obligations

Annual [MC] Pension obligations for [MC] [EMP]s have increased to $742,000 from $470,000 from fiscal year ended 09/30/09 to 09/30/11, which equates to a 58% increase. The General [EMP]s' annual pension costs have increased from $289,000 to $395,000 from the fiscal year ended 09/30/09 to 09/30/11 and equates to a 37% increase. Additionally, the future unfunded obligation for the Police and Fire pension stands at $4.5 million and General [EMP] pension unfunded balance is $1.9 million. One can state that a prior year's overall economic downturn in the equities markets was a significant contributing factor; decreasing property values exacerbated the situation further. The issue is not to discuss the causes, even though they must recognize history and remember to examine the potentials disciplined and/or undisciplined past steps of funding, but rather to find future solutions to the funding of such pension obligations. It is time to recognize that there are many variables to future funding of such obligations and/or potential future examination of adjustments to such funding requirements. It is [COFFEE]'s observation that further and immediate examination of such costs, and not delay discussion nor jump to quick short term solutions that only yield short term results would be prudent. There has been an initiative by [CC], led by (the late) [FicChaEighteen], to address the police and fire pension fund with a proposed transfer to [GSoF] System. It has been observed during a previous [CC] meeting this option does not appear to be beneficial. [COFFEE] suggests further and rigorous examination of all angles of future pension obligations. As mentioned in a previous section, Other Post-Employment Benefits (OPEB) and other unfunded benefits are of great concern and are interrelated. [COFFEE] recommends comprehensive planning and examination of pension commitments remain a management (and on-going) priority.

# Departmental Studies

Throughout the study, [COFFEE] members met individually and in pairs with representatives of the various departments. Additionally, each of the department heads provided unsolicited information regarding the services, staffing, and responsibilities. The subsections that follow are summaries of [COFFEE]'s findings with respect to the departments. Specific areas and issues are handled individually in the section of this report that follows the Departmental Studies. Of significant note is information provided by [CM] showing the impact of allowing [EMP]s (who are under the old [MC] employment system) to retire. If all if five (5) eligible [EMP]s retired, the net pension savings estimate to [MCFLMosFB] in the first year would be $141,639. The first year savings to [MCFLMosFB] for salary (and benefits) would be approximately $209,000.

The five (5) members were polled last year and indicated a general unwillingness to retire early due to the penalties associated with early retirement. The same five were polled this year—with the understanding the early retirement penalty would be reduced to 3 percent from the current 6.7 percent—and indicated they would consider that option. The full impact of this option would have to be examined by the actuary to determine the full cost and efficiency of this course of action.

## Financial Administration of [FLMosFB]

Financial administration of [FLMosFB] ensures that [MCFLMosFB] is adhering to law; is the processor of all business transactions with [MCFLMosFB]; and the custodian of all records. All of the responsibilities and the vast majority of the activities associated with this department are governed by state law. There is some latitude with respect to process; however, it is generally true that any changes in this department with respect to the principal mission would be mandated by the state and not at the discretion of the local community.

With the aforementioned statement in mind, the individuals in this department have taken on additional responsibilities to respond to the needs of the local community. In some cases, such as IT, the department has personnel principally designated with no regulatory responsibility and in all cases, individuals perform functions well beyond the minimum requirements of their position in order to perform their duties as efficiently as possible and to respond to the ongoing demands of an evolving community.

[COFFEE] learned that the staffs' knowledge and commitment to the critical elements of their role is substantial. It was also learned that each individual maintains a passion for his/her profession and a commitment to [PubServ]. Every individual interviewed was forthcoming and helpful.

[COFFEE] learned that the people in the department may be lacking the resources to truly be efficient by their standards and that the department members strive to get better at their jobs each and every day. However, they are all asymptotically approaching a boundary that can only be moved with increased resources in the form of man-hours, technical ability, and technology. After evaluation of the information provided and interviews with the staff, [COFFEE] identified the following conditions:

- ❑ Services formerly provided by 3rd party contractors supporting [MCFLMosFB] are no longer being provided and there now exists both a knowledge and capability vacuum.
- ❑ Software packages used by this department are not compatible with computer technology that is currently sold.

❑ Computer resources – servers and workstations are comprised of technologies spanning three generations.

It is [COFFEE]'s considered opinion that "doing nothing" is not an option, and that a commitment by the community is absolutely necessary. This commitment would be in the following areas:

❑ Software purchases and development
❑ Research less costly banking and payroll support options
❑ Purchases of new computers, file servers, and transport/routing/switching equipment
❑ Data Entry and other administrative support

[MCFLMosFB] volunteers, [MCFLMosFB] contractors, [MCFLMosFB] full-time [EMP] and [MCFLMosFB] part-time [EMP], may provide the aforementioned items that do not require a purchase of any kind. Those items that do require the purchase of software or hardware may be provided by donations, grants, or [B]. Review of past [B]s indicates a general decline in consideration of the technology and services needs of this department. It is [COFFEE]'s suggestion that the needs of financial administration of [FLMosFB] be brought to the forefront for public discussion, and that the community be afforded the opportunity to implement a solution.

## Building and Zoning Department

[MCFLMosFB] Building and Zoning Department serves five (5) basic and necessary functions for the [MCFLMosFB].

1. Ensures all permitted construction activity is performed by licensed contractors and in accordance with all applicable building codes and zoning regulations.

2. Provides ongoing monitoring and enforcement of existing structures to ensure that they are compliant with applicable building codes and zoning regulations.
3. Is the principal certification authority for the disposition of damaged structures and disaster recovery?
4. Are the principal keeper and distributor of relevant records to insurance companies, real estate agents and general contractors?
5. Administers the National Flood Insurance Program and Flood Plain Management

Of the services provided, the law requires virtually all of them. Some of these services generate revenue for [MCFLMosFB], but the amount of revenue is relatively small when compared to Ad Valorem Tax Revenue and revenue sharing with the County and State. In interviews with [MCFLMosFB] Building and Zoning Department staff, [COFFEE] has arrived at the following understandings:

1. The level of staffing compelled cross-utilization of individuals in [PW] FLMosFB] to aid in disaster recovery.
2. Leverage technology to save, recall, and manage historical records of [PW] or leverage existing capabilities of the County and State.
3. The few members remaining in the department are knowledgeable, professional, dedicated and are ever mindful of the regulatory and practical responsibilities of their functions.

Any discussion as to improving their efficiency would be dominated by the practical benefits of investing in technology that would permit them to reduce their inventory of hard copy records and allow for electronically searchable documents. Initial inquiries into the matter clearly indicate that a number of solutions are available and that an investment range of eight to twenty thousand dollars will likely be required to improve records management. It is [COFFEE]'s suggestion that this matter be given additional study so that appropriate options can be presented for public discussion and potential inclusion in the financial planning process.

## [FD]

[FD] is one of two departments that regularly respond to 911 Emergency calls from [MCFLMosFB] citizens and businesses. The criticality of the service this department provides can be quantified to a degree when the conversation is limited to protecting property but cannot be reasonably quantified when potential loss of life is considered. [FD] responds to about 1,200 total emergency response calls per year. Of those calls, over 90 percent are of an emergency medical assistance nature and not related to fire. The individuals assigned to this department are led by an experienced and dedicated professional in both the skill sets required to perform most, if not all, of the tasks required of the department as well the tasks required of a department head with fiduciary responsibility. The department regularly receives awards and recognition for the service it provides and the manner in which it provides those services. Without exception, [FD] is one [FD] that [MCFLMosFB] citizens are justified in being extremely proud of and grateful to have.

However, [FD] does have its detractors who have voiced concern over the percentage of the annual [B] allotted to the department, the manner in which the department's vehicles are used, and the perceived preferential treatment the department receives with respect to the purchase of new equipment. In deference to those who believe an alternative approach to providing emergency services is in order, [COFFEE] has included a narrative of how other local communities are getting the job done. However, other than to say that additional study is required before a responsible recommendation can be put forth, [COFFEE] is not advocating any single approach to Fire and EMS services.

A neighboring community, [FDMCFLMosIndia] leverages a "blended" [FD] structure. [FDMCFLMosIndia], made up of six paid firefighters, the Fire Chief and fifteen active volunteers, provides fire prevention and fire suppression programs. [FDMCFLMosIndia], staffed with paramedics and certified Emergency Medical Technicians, also provides first response advanced life support (ALS) to medical emergencies. The total FY11 annual [B] for this type of service was $729,708—that figure is nearly $1.1-million less that the FY11 [B] for [FD]. [MCFLMosIndia] firehouse is manned 24 hours a day, seven days a week with one (1) Paramedic and one (1) EMT and a reserve of fourteen (14) on-call volunteer firefighters. The Fire Chief is on duty 7:30AM to 4:30PM Monday through Friday and on call after hours. All firefighter/paramedics and firefighter/EMTs are certified fire inspectors and the Chief holds a certificate as an Instructor II. Like [MCFLMosFB], nearly 90% of their annual calls were for emergency medical services or other calls—only 7% were related to fires (FY10 data). Their average response time was 2 minutes and 39 seconds for over 1,400 annual calls for service.

Given the nature of services needed by [MCFLMosFB], [COFFEE] feels a blended [FD] may produce substantial savings to the [MC] with no degradation of level of services. A volunteer fire cadre—supported by paid, 24/7 EMT staff and leadership—offers the least intrusive solution to the current [B] growth. Overall, the [FD] [B] is up 11% over the past five years—largely due to increases in benefits such as tuition reimbursement (up $24K {268%} from last year) and [EMP] health plans (up 21% over the past 5 years). One area of concern to the general public is the response time for the Mosquito County Ambulance Service. The Service is required to transport patients to medical treatment facilities. If [FD] maintained the First Responder capability to respond, assess, and stabilize patients, the level of transport service would still be the same. [FD] is unable to transport patients at all; it seems sensible to staff the fire services based on the general needs of [MCFLMosFB] citizens maintaining a full-up capability to respond to an occasional fire call where the EMTs could be dual-hatted firefighters versus firefighters being dual-hatted EMTs. Maintaining just a volunteer force cadre of firefighters may be an acceptable solution.

Through site visits, public discussions, data analysis, and private discussions, [COFFEE] was able to discover only one issue that rose to the surface in which we feel competent to bring forward in this report. All investigation or study of other matters produced results in which there was a plausible, justifiable, and reasonable argument for the particular condition of an issue or measurable parameter. It is [COFFEE]'s current perception that [FD] is extremely well run and the attention to detail by the leadership is such that the [FD] is always looking for and implementing ways to maximize the benefits of the ever increasing demands of the community in an environment of decreasing funding.

One item [COFFEE] is prepared to comment on at the time of this report is the absence of a publicly available [B] plan that is sufficiently detailed to educate the average [MCFLMosFB] citizens on all of the various revenue streams serviced by the this department and the expenses incurred by this department in both the near and long term. [COFFEE] suggests that the periodic publication of the [FD]'s long term revenue and expenses be considered in order to educate the public at large of the contribution to the community and requirements from the community for the contributions to continue.

# [PD]

[PD] is entrusted with the task of ensuring that the state of the community remains secure and safe according to the expectations of their community. The individuals assigned to this department are expected to prevent and solve crimes, arrest criminals, and provide the [MCFLMosFB] citizens and populace a level of protection and personal freedom. There are many private [MCFLMosFB] citizens and [OwnBus]s in the community who are grateful for the service [PD] provides and the manner in which it provides. There are very few [MCFLMosFB] citizens and [OwnBus]s who can fully appreciate the responsibilities that their police officers have sworn to meet and limitations they are forced to perform within; their general assessment is that [PD] is one that the community can trust and be proud of, and that any effort to assist [PD] Chief in studying the department and identifying specific measures to improve performance and reduce costs should be conducted by individuals who have the requisite clearances, credentials, and official authorizations.

[MCFLMosFB] provided materials show a 00/01 [PD] personnel count of 48 total [EMP]s and a 11/12 personnel count of 45 [EMP]s. Personnel counts include full-time, part-time-permanent (PPT), and part-time temporary (TPT) personnel. While the change in number of [EMP]s over a period of twelve years is slight, the type (full time vs. part time) of [EMP] warrants discussion. In FY01, the [PD] had 24 full-time [EMP]s; that number in FY12 is 29—a 21% increase over 12 years. The 4-person increase coincides with a decrease in the size of the TPT and PPT personnel; this transition and other costs effectively doubled [PD] personnel costs from $1.3M in FY01 to $2.6M in FY12.

[PD] is currently comprised of 21 sworn law enforcement officers, 8 regular full time civilian personnel, and 15 permanent or temporary part time civilian support personnel (including dispatchers)—a total of 44 full and part-time personnel. The 21 sworn law enforcement officers represent a 2.1-per-capita force, but the rank structure of the sworn-officers corps may warrant a closer examination to compare its structure with similarly manned departments.

Currently, [PD] is pursuing two personnel realignment initiatives that will yield cost saving results on an annual basis. The first (completed) successful initiative resulted in annual future salary savings of $30,000; the second initiative is in process and similar results (savings) are expected. Other ongoing operations initiatives include consistent review of overtime issues, achievement of a 60% paperless environment in one year, scanning archived paper documentation of which volunteers are utilized and 1/15 completion in a 5-month period. A plan is underway to reduce the copiers used by [PD] to just one unit by modifying a room to allow access (24/7) to the copier without compromising confidential material. This should result in a reduction of $264 per month in operations/lease costs. Currently, and on a continuous basis, building lights and air conditioning cost containment is maintained through simple monitoring initiatives. Due to training initiatives, there are many times when one officer attends a training class and subsequently returns to the department to train the department.

There are six officers certified/utilized to train department police personnel. There are ongoing and future long-term initiatives the department is researching and considering for implementation. [PD] leverages on-line training, examines new technology, and other opportunities on a continuous basis.

[COFFEE] recognizes that [PD] will be in the process to complete triennial accreditation beginning in July of 12. It is important to insure this department can focus on actions necessary to ensure recertification is accomplished. This process occurs every 3 years and benefits both [MCFLMosFB] citizens and [PD].

[CapEq] replacement planning requires further focus. The [PD] chief stated the [PD] plan for vehicle replacement "worked out to 2 vehicles per year" but offered no further elaboration. Vehicle maintenance and fuel usage data provided by the [PW] indicates that police vehicles are very low in fuel efficiency—only 9-10 MPG (with the exception of motorcycles that are very fuel efficient)—and are used as assigned vehicles for certain staff members to commute to/from their places of residence. Acquisition and use of police vehicles should be an area for increased focus—Mosquito County Sheriff's office (MCSO) began acquiring more fuel-efficient vehicles in 08 to counter burgeoning fuel costs. MCSO deputies are allowed to commute with the MCSO cruisers—it is seen as a crime deterrent—but those deputies who live outside the county are required to pay for a certain amount of fuel out of their own pockets. [PD] officer contributions such as this may be an acceptable alternative to ceasing the practice of using [PD] vehicles as commuting vehicles outside of the [MCFLMosFB] Limits.

Overtime is a significant expense in [PD]. The purpose and level of overtime may require closer examination to gauge the effectiveness of staffing levels. Retirement contributions doubled from FY07 to FY11 from $211K to $455K; this is an area that may require focused examination. [PD] expenses are up 22.5% over the represented 5 years.

## [PW]

[PW] is responsible for virtually everything that is driven on, walked on, and played on that is not owned by a private citizens or a company. Included in this responsibility are storm water, structures, lighting, vehicle maintenance, and many other functions necessary for [MCFLMosFB] citizens to be able to, and want to, live in [MCFLMosFB]. In addition to the day-to-day maintenance of public areas and [MCFLMosFB] vehicles, it is the [PW]'s responsibility to get [MCFLMosFB] "up and running" after a natural disaster such as a hurricane.

The breadth and depth of skills required to be successful are difficult for an average citizens to understand and well beyond the [B] allocations for [PW] full-time employees and [PW] part-time employees. It is through [PW] Head's own admission that current staffing and funding levels mandate choosing between the immediate and the important on a daily basis. Through limited site visits, [COFFEE] meetings, and informal discussion, [COFFEE] has come to understand that the [PW] operates in a proactive (within resource limits) operational and reactive mode. A resource-supported vision coupled with continued flexibility with existing personnel will meet existing level-of-service needs, but there will be challenges during surge or emergency conditions.

Efforts by [COFFEE] members to better understand planning and resource allocation of [PW] have not been fully successful due to limitations of time and resources as well as the breadth and depth of department responsibilities. However, it is not unfair or disrespectful to put forth that by and large, [PW] is run in a manner that is analogous to a service station that responds to the needs of the day, while also attempting to perform scheduled day-to-day activities.

Of the issues learned during [COFFEE]'s inaugural study, eight (8) elements became apparent to [COFFEE]:

1. [B] and Planning is stymied by limitations on resources for [PW] preventive and beautification functions. [PW] could benefit from a focused volunteer corps to

augment and address shortfalls in manual labor sources. It is [COFFEE]'s suggestion that [PW] Head, of [MCFLMosFB] be provided assistance to build and manage this function.

2. Equipment requirements and utilization have not been communicated to [COFFEE] in such a manner that [COFFEE] can assess the efficacy to which equipment is purchased, leased, rented, or deployed. Due to capital [B] constraints, identified equipment needs have been put on hold. Needs have been identified through [B] process on previous occasions. It is [COFFEE]'s suggestion that the issue of equipment requirements and utilization be further studied.

3. The [PW] employs 16 full time and two part time [EMP]s to address administration, grounds maintenance, roads & drainage maintenance, facilities maintenance, vehicle maintenance and janitorial services for community center, gym, [PD], City Hall, and community Center. It is [COFFEE]'s suggestion that the issue of Recreational Facility maintenance be considered for further study and the costs associated with maintenance be included in fee structures.

4. Many of the services provided by [PW] are repetitive and sufficiently defined to implement a competitive cost analysis and Request for Bid process in an effort to migrate resource allocation of [PW] [EMP] from the repetitive and mundane to those efforts left unattended because of limited resources. [PW] currently utilizes many public/private partnerships to accomplish its mission. However, there are many instances where this may not be feasible for reasons of cost or logistics. That is not to say that, going forward, more of these opportunities will be not be explored. It is [COFFEE]'s suggestion that [PW] Head consider soliciting competitive bids for defined tasks

in order to perform an unbiased cost-based analysis of resource utilization.

5. There are numerous maintenance projects that are not being engaged because of the staffing and [B] limitations of [PW] Head. [PW] Head would welcome capable volunteers who can work un-supervised to accomplish tasks that have been identified as low priority due to higher priority demands and needs. It is [COFFEE]'s suggestion that [PW] Head identify and define all projects that may be performed by managed volunteers and that the [MCFLMosFB] put forth a "Call for Service" to allow volunteers to help with projects ranging from pressure washing, painting, landscaping, and any other project that could be reasonably performed by volunteers.

6. There does not appear to exist a defined and regulated volunteer force that would augment staffing before, during, and after a natural disaster. During these times, for many would-be volunteers, personal considerations may impede availability. The nature of the work involved following an even may limit volunteer involvement for safety and liability reasons. It is [COFFEE]'s suggestion that if such a force exists, then its existence and the requirements to join need to be made public. If such a force does not exist, then it is [COFFEE]'s suggestion that one be formed.

7. Vehicle maintenance costs have doubled in the last 5 years as indicated in the data. What isn't reflected is that during the period there was a shifting of cost centers from contract maintenance to in-house. [COFFEE] does not have the combined costs of both contract and in-house maintenance costs over the 10-year period.

8. An aging fleet and a vehicle-to-[EMP] ratio of over 1 vehicle for every 2 [EMP]s and a 33% rise in fuel costs suggest a focused study of fleet requirements is prudent.

# [RecMCFLMosFB]

[RecMCFLMosFB], like all of the other departments mentioned in this report, is codified in the [MCFLMosFB] Code but provides no services essential to the regulatory or financial requirements of [MCFLMosFB]. However, [RecMCFLMosFB] is a testament to the community's commitment to an active and engaged life. It serves as a hub in the center of a wheel comprised of residents of [MCFLMosFB] and neighboring communities. [RecMCFLMosFB] sponsors a number of programs that appeal to virtually all age groups and a wide variety of interests. It is difficult to argue that [MCFLMosFB] needs [RecMCFLMosFB] in the same way it needs [PD], [FD], [PW], Building and Zoning [MCFLMosFB], or Administration of [MCFLMosFB], however, the community is better because it has it.

With that understood, [COFFEE]'s study revealed a number of concerns that warrant further study and investigation. [RecMCFLMosFB] spends approximately $3 for every $2 it brings in as revenue. Furthermore, interviews and questionnaires regarding fees and "product portfolio" indicate that:

1. Premium services are being offered at significantly discounted prices;
2. Contracted instructors are receiving as much as 89% of the total revenues for classes offered;
3. There is little or no consideration given to the cost of facilities and facility maintenance when reporting the financial performance of a program

Furthermore, some of the services being offered by [RecMCFLMosFB] are also being offered by businesses in [MCFLMosFB] and other Barrier Island communities.

[RecMCFLMosFB] runs an annual deficit of $275K to $300K. Two (2) primary reasons for the shortage are the department salaries/benefit cost of over forty percent (40%) and the percentage paid to the instructors to run the classes.

There are approximately twenty (20) different classes offered by the [RecMCFLMosFB] in the fall, 38 in Winter/Spring, and 78 in summer. The instructor percentage fee/pay varies from 89% to 75%.

The percentage is dependent on when the class started with the [MC]. The current trend is to reduce the instructor fee percentage.

The monthly rate being paid by the student is extremely low. The Instructors are knowledgeable skilled and professional. Because the [RecMCFLMosFB] class instructor is getting such a high percentage rate of the total revenues from the [RecMCFLMosFB], he/she can keep the student rate low. This results in the [MCFLMosFB] tax-payer subsidizing instructor fees for attendees (a number of whom are not residents of their municipality). [COFFEE] acknowledges the intrinsic value these quality-of-life programs bring to the community. The [RecMCFLMosFB] does not keep accurate records of in-[MCFLMosFB] or out-of-[MCFLMosFB] participation in individual classes.

To help offset the loss of revenue to [MCFLMosFB] the instructor percentage could be lowered and the student fee could be increased. Another possible solution would be to charge a flat lease/rental fee to the Instructor. This lease rate would be calculated based on actual cost/expense that the [MCFLMosFB] incurs for that facility space—including the costs for staffing the [RecMCFLMosFB]. This method would at least insure [MCFLMosFB] is able to cover their expenses and help reduce or eliminate the cost deficit.

Recreation [B]: The 10/11 total salary [B] was $322K (48%) of the $720K total [B]. Instructor fees amounted to $323K (45%).

These services provide a level of quality of life that must be considered in this report. The use of these facilities is open to both residents and non-residents of [MCFLMosFB]. Determining the best way to recover costs for these facilities requires additional study.

The [COFFEE] concludes that additional study is warranted for the purpose optimizing the cost analysis and accounting of the various programs, fee structures, terms & conditions of contracted instructors, and the product portfolio.

# Specific and Miscellaneous Issues

The subsections that follow speak to specific issues that were either pursued by [COFFEE] or were brought to their attention. Due to the virtual randomness of the issues, they are presented in alphabetical order.

## Vehicle or Car Allowances (s)

[CM] currently receives a monthly [MC] [EMP]s Vehicle or Car Allowances payment of $450 that is treated as income, which works out to be $5,400 per year. The [CM]'s one-way commute from his home to City Hall is .8 miles with an estimated average of 4.8 miles per business day and an additional mileage to [GovFLMos] Complex is approximately 24 miles round trip two to three times per month yielding an estimated total annual mileage attributed to normal business activity of approximately 2,280 miles resulting in an estimated compensation per mile of $2.36 per mile of business related travel. The current federal standard for mileage reimbursement is $0.555 per mile. Therefore [CM] is effectively being reimbursed over three (3) times the federal standard (consideration that reimbursement is a taxed benefit). It is [COFFEE]'s impression that the [CM]'s [MC] [EMP]s Vehicle or Car Allowances be considered for public discussion and possible adjustment.

## Cell Phone Subsidy

[MCFLMosFB] offers selected individuals a monthly [MC] [EMP]s Cell Phone Subsidy . In interviews and observation indicate that such a subsidy is motivated to enhance an [EMP]'s relationship with his employers, cost effectively respond to a lack of a [MC] wide trunking radio system, allow for a single contact number 24/7, and provide an alternative means of communication in the event of a loss of landline telephone.

Analysis indicates that the policy is not consistent with respect to getting reimbursed for having a cell phone. In some cases [MC] [EMP]s Cell Phone Subsidy is far less than what some commercial companies provide and is more in other cases. During interviews with [MCFLMosFB] [EMP], [COFFEE] learned that more than one [MCFLMosFB] [EMP] regularly uses the cell phone to conduct business on behalf of [MCFLMosFB] and receives no [MC] [EMP]s at all. It would seem that a case-by-case decision as to the "who and how much" question associated with [MC] [EMP]s Cell Phone Subsidy feeds a potential concern for favoritism. Furthermore, since some [MCFLMosFB] [EMP] who do receive a Cell Phone Subsidy are at their desk or in their office far more often than not, a case could be made to shorten the list of positions that warrant a Cell Phone Subsidy. The wage structure for senior [MC] [EMP]s is such that offering [MC] [EMP]s Cell Phone Subsidy seems more than generous. It is

[COFFEE]'s suggestion that [MC] [EMP]s Cell Phone Subsidy be taken up in a public forum for the purpose of simplifying the policy and potentially Total [MC] [EMP]s Cell Phone Subsidy .

## Cost Accounting for Outsourcing

The extent to which [MCFLMosFB] [EMP]s provide services to [MCFLMosFB] citizens is well beyond what can be accurately reflected in a balance sheet. Such a statement is true each and every day and even more so when the [MC] is recovering from a natural disaster or responding to one of the various emergencies that involve [MCFLMosFB] citizens. However, it would be irresponsible to neglect or ignore cost accounting practices completely under the assumption that all services are being provided in the most cost effective manner possible. It is with this notion in mind that additional study and consideration be given to well defined repetitive processes so that competitive bidding be considered. It is not this [COFFEE]'s suggestion that large-scale outsourcing is a solution or an improvement. It is this [COFFEE]'s suggestion that a limited initiative for well defined and repetitive activities be considered in order to allow specialists to provide services more efficiently than the generalists that the [MC] must keep on staff. Examples of possible repetitive services that may potentially be outsourced are tree-trimming and mowing.

## Credit Cards

Visa® Credit cards are made available to each sitting members of [CC], the [CM], and Department Heads of [MCFLMosFB]. Interviews and volunteered statements indicate that some of the individuals issued these cards use them infrequently, if at all. Accounts and store credit cards are issued [MCFLMosFB] personnel for business related expenses in order to reduce the administrative burden of purchase orders. Store-specific accounts and credit cards garner discounts on merchandise. [COFFEE] recognizes that it is common to be issued a "company credit card" if there is a likelihood that an [EMP] travels or regularly incurs expenses in the course of their professional duties; however, [COFFEE] was tasked to identify any areas where potential efficiencies could be gained.

[COFFEE] reviewed the [MCFLMosFB]'s credit card process and found efficiencies in using the system along with a greater accountability for transactions. Cards are used appropriately and facilitate local-area purchases saving time in the process. The cards are insured (no charge) for fraud and the number and control of the cards appears sufficient to thwart inadvertent or unauthorized use.

## Cross Training, Internships, and Leadership Development

[COFFEE] has learned through interviews, public discussion, and observation that every [MCFLMosFB] [EMP], regardless of job title performs multiple necessary functions throughout the course of their day, week, etc. The aforementioned statement becomes more evident in times of hardship such as responding to impending storms. Over the years, because of necessity, required skills (and in some cases certifications) are shared amongst multiple individuals within a single department and among multiple departments. [COFFEE] became aware of a few examples but recognizes the actual extent to which [MCFLMosFB] [EMP] are cross-trained is much greater. However, there is no formality associated with communicating to the general public all of the skills required to run [MCFLMosFB] and a matrix that identifies how all [MCFLMosFB] [EMP] match up. It was [COFFEE]'s initial hope that such a matrix could be developed within the time allotted, but that initiative was de-emphasized by other activities and consideration of the time constraints. In a perfect world, such a matrix would exist so that there is no delay or confusion as to who can be called upon in time of need and the impact of an individual's absence. It is [COFFEE]'s suggestion that further study into the creation of a skills matrix be supported such that vacancies are clearly identified and understood as well as unjustifiable redundancies.

In past, [MCFLMosFB] has been a prime training opportunity for individuals starting their careers in [PubServ]. [COFFEE] was told numerous stories of the role [MCFLMosFB] played in the education and training of individuals who went off and are enjoying success plying the skills they learned here in the cities they now work. These stories included compensated and uncompensated personnel. [MCFLMosFB] has done a good thing by investing in future generations. [COFFEE] is aware of one current [MCFLMosFB] [EMP] that is in a senior leadership position who began his career as an intern with [MCFLMosFB].

[MCFLMosFB] [EMP] retention and development was a principal topic discussed at one of the public meetings, in which everyone in attendance had the opportunity to contribute, was that at present there is no defined program for developing the talent needed for the long term success of [MCFLMosFB]. Any loss of a mid to senior level [EMP] leaves a vacuum that some departments have no real plan to deal with; on that same note, there is no program to develop the next generation of junior, mid, or senior level personnel.

One example is the fact that [CM] has faithfully served [MCFLMosFB] for 26+ years. In most public sector jobs, the thirty-year point is considered the optimum point to retire. [COFFEE] has yet to understand what [MCFLMosFB]'s plan is to respond to the [CM]'s retirement. Another example is the recent resignation of the Assistant Director of [PW] [FLMosFB] and the ripple effect that vacancy has had on [PW] [FLMosFB]. In public discussions with [CM], it has been made known that the staff's age is such that many of the senior positions could readily become vacant through retirement within the next five years. [COFFEE] suggests that further study of this matter to be prepared for resignations, retirements, or other events that result in the loss of a [MCFLMosFB] [EMP].

## Data Sharing

It is [COFFEE]'s understanding that data provided by [MCFLMosFB] be in a format that does not allow unauthorized changes to the content, and that all data provided to [MCFLMosFB] citizens and the various boards is maintained by [MCFLMosFB] so that a "true original" is maintained for public record. During the course of [COFFEE]'s inaugural study, several requests were made by [COFFEE] members for the data to be provided in electronic or "soft" copy in its native format (Word, Excel, PowerPoint, etc.) to the exclusion of all other formats where possible. Consistently, and with few exceptions, virtually of the data provided to [COFFEE] was in paper form or in electronic image such that analysis or inclusion in this and subsequent reports required manually re-typing the information. This approach presented a huge impediment to progress and significantly increased the potential for errors. In conversations with the [MCFLMosFB] City Clerk and [CA], [COFFEE] learned that is was acceptable for [MCFLMosFB] to provide information in its native format as long as [MCFLMosFB] maintained a copy of the original data. Yet, data provided after this clarification was still in either hard copy of image format. It is [COFFEE]'s suggestion that the issue of making data available to the citizenry in a format that readily facilitates incorporation into a study such as this or analysis be publicly discussed for clarification and implementation. The benefits of such an initiative would reduce the steps taken for publication, create a more fluid exchange of ideas, and contribute to the creation of an environment that welcomes [MCFLMosFB] citizens' involvement.

It was the original intent of [COFFEE] to provide [CC] with an academic work in which the original data was provided along with the assessment and any conclusions so that any reader could reference the information that contributed to the assessment. Because the vast majority of the information had to be retyped in order to be included and that [COFFEE] was subjected to an aggressive schedule, much of this data has not been included in this report and may be found on the [MCFLMosFB]'s website, www.[MCFLMosFB].org.

## [CitSys]

During public discussion, site visits, and interviews, [COFFEE] became aware that traffic citations were being issued using paper form factor and that, in addition to the extensive processing time, migrating towards an electronic system is going to be mandated by the [GVBMNTFL] in YR14. The issues associated with the current method are both resource intensive and error-prone. Migrating to [CitSys] will reduce both the time per traffic stop, and errors associated with transcribing hand-written documents.

One of the [COFFEE] members focused on [CitSys] in order to better understand [CitSys] and provide assistance in preparing a package that could be considered by [CC]. Since the effort began, [COFFEE] has learned that multiple solutions are available and that there is also a wide range of investment requirements ($150K – $300K) associated with each option. [COFFEE] believes that a well-managed grant effort might be available to offset the [MCFLMosFB]'s outlay. [COFFEE] is not prepared to suggest any specific approach at this time but is confident in suggesting that the matter be studied further in close consultation with [FD] chief and IT Specialist so that the appropriate technical solution can be presented for public discussion and potential implementation.

## E-Commerce, Fee Payment with Credit/Debit Cards

At present [COFFEE] is unaware of [MCFLMosFB] conducting fee-based business with private citizens and business in a form other than cash or check. It has been proposed by numerous citizens and [MCFLMosFB] [EMP]s that it may streamline business processes and potentially improves [MCFLMosFB] revenues if the [MCFLMosFB] were to implement credit card and debit card-processing capability at all venues where fees are charged. [COFFEE] is insufficiently qualified to speak to the merits of this proposal but suggest the matter be considered for further study in order to make a sound business based decision.

## Compensation and Benefits

[MC] [EMP]s Compensation and Benefits requires specific examination. Portions of this report point towards areas of potential efficiencies and realignment with industry and federal [GVBMNT] standards.

## Special Skills Incentive Pay

During the course of data gathering and interviews, [COFFEE] learned that two [MCPWFP]s receive an annual taxable payment of $250 as special skills incentive pay. One [MCPWFP] receives payment for masonry skills and another [MCPWFP] receives it for horticulture skills. These two [MCPWFP]s receive salaries of approximately $41,000 and $38,000 per year respectively which works out to an hourly wage of $19.80 per hour and $18.40 per hour respectively.

The breadth of services to be expected of [MCPWFP] is adequately covered in the standard pay range. Furthermore, [MCPWFP] are generalist by necessity and it is not unreasonable to expect personnel who have been on the job for a reported 15 years to develop the skills necessary to fully satisfy the intent of their employment.

## Special Skills Incentive Pay [PD]

Two of the four Special Skills Incentive Pay payments that are in addition to normal compensation are mandated by [GVBMNTFL]. Given the special nature of the responsibilities and community expectation with respect to the performance of [PD] and the conduct of individual Police officer [MC]s, combined with the fact that Police officer [MC]'s compensation is the result of collective bargaining, [COFFEE] respectfully declines from making any commentary regarding compensation packages. However, every member of [COFFEE] is grateful for the professionalism and diligence of Police Officers of [MC].

Educational Incentives are mandated by Department of Law Enforcement. A Police officer of [MC] will receive $30 monthly for a two-year Associate's Degree and $80 monthly for a four-year Bachelor's Degree per month or equivalent.

Salary Incentive is state mandated by Department of Law Enforcement for specific advanced training courses that enhance an officer's knowledge, skills, and abilities for the job performed.

Combination of Education and Training can be up to $130 per month for Advanced Training Courses and Education.

The Corporal Incentive is an appointed position by [PD] chief and is based on having eighteen (18) months as a sworn Police Officer, satisfactory evaluations, and designates this individual to serve as a Shift Supervisor during the absence of a Patrol Sergeant.

## Special Skills Incentive Pay [FD]

Individual members of [FD] receive payment above their normal salary for various certifications. Unlike [PD], some of these incentives (educational incentives) are funded by [GVBMNTFL] and have no impact on the expenses funded by [MCFLMosFB] other than the administrative cost of processing the funds. Unlike [PD], certain incentives are made available at the discretion of [CM] in consultation with the [CC].

As a result of a [MCFLMosFB] study in the mid-90s, firefighters now receive Driver/Officer pay up to 10% of their base pay instead of raising base pay. These stipends are paid to all ranks—including [FD] chief, Fire Commander, and Fire Captains. During an interview with [FD] chief, he acknowledged that senior personnel rarely (if ever) drive the fire trucks. Using FY11 payroll data, the value of Special Skills Incentive Pay [FD] paid to the 5 personnel alone totals $32K—over half of the total amount ($66K) paid to all firefighters. In order for these personnel to qualify for Special Skills Incentive Pay [FD], they must complete certification testing — the cost of which is paid for by the [MCFLMosFB].

[COFFEE] observed that Special Skills Incentive Pay [FD] for Driver/Officer paid to senior firefighter personnel warrant further examination and action.

## [MC] Facility Utilization

[MCFLMosFB] owns and/or maintains facilities that fall into three (3) basic categories:

1. [GVBMNT] Support (to include storage and parking)
2. General Utility (pump stations, electrical and communications equipment shelters)
3. Community Use (parks, gymnasiums, meeting rooms)

All of these facilities impact [B] with respect to the cost of maintenance and repair, and the loss of Ad Valorem Tax Revenue because the property is not taxable. However, some of these facilities are available for revenue generating services such as basketball leagues and parties.

Facilities are generally in good repair, but the organization, use, safety, and cleanliness of certain facilities calls into question the efficiency of their use. [MCFLMosFB] stores records at multiple locations using [PW] facilities, [PD] facility, Recreation Department [MCFLMosFB], and others. A concerted effort to digitally scan, relocate, and store these documents would provide more facility space to the community. General house-keeping of [PW] facilities is in order to eliminate unneeded items, hazardous chemicals, and general clutter.

It is [COFFEE]'s considered opinion that additional study is required to characterize [MCFLMosFB] facility utilization in terms of which facilities are utilized, the terms and conditions to which those facilities may be utilized, and the potential for enhancing the revenue stream associated with [MCFLMosFB] facilities.

## Financial Planning

There has been no long-term financial plan presented to [COFFEE] or the general public as of the time of this report. There have been numerous public statements made by [CM] to respond to specific issues, but a clear comprehensive plan, which details [MCRev] and [MCExp] expectations, does not appear to exist. Detailed and long-term financial planning, including demographic trending and consideration of future scenarios, is not evident in current practices. [CM] has given clear indication that such effort would be extremely valuable to planning and has obtained volunteer support to create and implement such a system for use in the [B] process. It is [COFFEE]'s hope that comprehensive long-term business planning will become standard procedure in the near future.

## Financial Reporting

By and large, the financial reporting process currently in place prevents ongoing opportunities to competently revise spending plans in response to changes to revenue expectations and communicate those changes in a meaningful way to [CC] and [GenPub]. The net effect is the perception that few people know the actual financial status of [MCFLMosFB]. When combined with the reporting of the most recent financial statement, there is a growing perception that if anyone does have a complete picture of [MCFLMosFB]'s financial condition it is not being effectively managed. [COFFEE] makes no statements as to the validity of such perceptions but reports that all efforts to consolidate financial data into a single coherent message have proven to be unsuccessful as of the time of this report. The aforementioned statements compel the suggestion that a periodic reporting of [MCFLMosFB] revenues and [MCFLMosFB] expenses be considered. The periodicity needs to be regular and more frequent than semi-annually. In public discussions with [CM], there seemed to be some hesitation to report monthly and virtually no hesitation as to implementing a bi-monthly reporting schedule. For the initiative to address the concerns previously mentioned, a report that shows a comparative analysis of planned vs. actual and revised expectations for the remainder of the fiscal year would be a solid starting point. It is therefore [COFFEE]'s suggestion that the issue of bi-monthly reporting on the financial performance of [MCFLMosFB] be considered for public discussion and potential adoption as standard process.

## [GVBMNT] form

A [GVBMNT] form has to be filled out anytime a [MCFLMosFB] citizens or [OwnBus] does business with [MCFLMosFB]. One question that could be asked is whether there are any forms that could be processed on line. Virtually of the forms are available on line but must be submitted in hard copy to the appropriate department. Some of these forms require a signature, some require either a notarized or a witnessed signature and some require [USD] in order to be processed. In terms of deciding which of these forms could be processed on line, one has to either revise the signature requirements or implement an acceptable electronic signature process. If [USD] is to be exchanged, then a business plan to justify implementation of on-line payment processes is appropriate. It is [COFFEE]'s suggestion that the issue of converting all business processes to on-line be studied to ascertain the appropriateness of such a transition.

# [MCRLE]

The Financial Statement for [MCFLMosFB] for fiscal year ending September 30, YR11 listed total [MCRLE] of $14,566,371. Using data provided by City Hall, these holdings represent approximately 2.2% of the total value of all property in [MCFLMosFB]. Though not excessive at first glance, it is appropriate to note that any migration of public lands to private ownership will generate approximately $8,500 in Ad Valorem Tax Revenue to the General fund per $1,000,000 value. It is [COFFEE]'s suggestion that additional effort be made to clarify the [MCRLE] in order to identify opportunities to enhance [MCRev] or Reduce [MCExp].

## [MC] Recreational Department
## Services and Revenues

Cost accounting practices for the various programs and services offered by [RecFLMosFB] indicate little, or no consideration for the value of the facilities provided by [MCFLMosFB]. More study is required to better understand the issue. The cost of goods sold by [RecFLMosFB] weighs heavily in favor of the 3rd party vendors providing instructor services. There is indication that current arrangements are to the detriment of [RecFLMosFB]. The method to which [RecFLMosFB] fees are set is not based on a business base price point analysis. More effort is required to assess the efficacy of user-based fees and identify opportunities to improve gross revenues.

## Record Management System (RMS)
## and Silent Dispatching

Silent Dispatching- This term relates to the process of using mobile computing technology to communicate routine, non-urgent information to dispatch via a touch screen computer in the response vehicle. This technology will improve the efficiencies of the dispatcher by reducing non-critical radio communication to the dispatchers, and allowing them to be focus on other critical task without interruptions. RMS facilitates dispatchers during increased dispatch activity and is a significant enhancement for both [PD] and [FD]. Police officers [MC] will be able to log their response (on-scene time) without talking on the radio, allowing the dispatcher to be fully engaged in the [PD] operation.

A records management system (RMS) is an agency-wide system that provides for the storage, retrieval, retention, manipulation, archiving, and viewing of information, records, documents, or files pertaining to law enforcement operations. RMS covers the entire life span of records development—from the initial generation to its completion. An effective RMS allows single entry of data, while supporting multiple reporting mechanisms. RMS enables an integrated and centralized police records management system for preserving data integrity and enhancing departmental efficiency. With this integrated system for police records management, the police department can update, share, and access critical data via one centralized database, enhancing communication and improving the efficiency of processes. This organized information can be easily transmitted car-to-car, dispatcher to car, and then to the State and/or Federal agencies. Some of this information will soon require mandatory electronic reporting. This unfunded mandate is currently not possible without a new or upgraded RMS. It should also be noted that [PD] is the only agency in the county that does not currently have RMS with wireless connectivity to patrol cars.

Upgrading or replacing the current 12 year old (RMS) has numerous benefits to the police department but the cost of acquisition must be weighed. A significant benefit is officer safety such as the ability to know if a car is stolen or potentially operated by a person who is wanted PRIOR to approaching the vehicle is much safer. Other benefits are:

- Provide real time information to dispatchers and officers electronically
- Better manage staffing requirements by shifts, locations and day of the week
- Provide information to [CC] and citizens
- Provide an investigator resource
- Reduced time spent on report writing and traffic stops
- Provide a history of department activity
- Increasing the time spent on community policing
- Doing business and residential checks

## Vehicle Usage

[MCFLMosFB] owns and leases a variety of vehicles. [COFFEE] was presented multiple lists of vehicle information, but consolidating the list in terms of what is owned, what is leased, the terms of the lease, the cost associated with each vehicle, etc. was well beyond what [COFFEE] could accomplish in the limited time [COFFEE] had prior to this report. Furthermore, any intelligent discussion as to the extent to which those vehicles are deployed was beyond their grasp within the time frame. It is therefore [COFFEE]'s suggestion that further study into optimizing the size, management, and deployment of [MCFLMosFB] Vehicle fleet.

## Vehicle Maintenance

[COFFEE] recommends a departmental or independent study of this level of service. Spot checks of maintenance records indicate either more detailed documentation and recording of specific actions be recorded, or that specific actions exceed reasonable parameters for time expended versus maintenance action completed.

## Information Technology (IT) Infrastructure

[MCFLMosFB] Information Technology Infrastructure is estimated by expert testimony to be approximately 10 years behind the times. Software, PCs, and servers are of antiquated capacity and function with an ineffective variety of operating systems. Upgrading server systems will increase the efficiency of the transparent [FB] initiative and be more compatible for interdepartmental communications. No long-term IT improvement plan exists; [B] imperatives over the past few years superseded the focus on this infrastructure component. [MCFLMosFB] Information Technology Infrastructure is showing its age.

Half of the hardware is 6-7 years old (though some of the hardware is "spare" computers due to staff reductions). They are replaced as the [B] allows, but often must be kept running several years longer than their recommended lifespan.

Investment in [MCFLMosFB] Information Technology Infrastructure may produce long-term efficiencies.

Many of their department software packages (Police, Fire, Recreation, and Accounting) have been with the same company since YR00, so only version upgrades have been implemented. In that time, we've progressed from Windows NT-based PCs and servers, through Windows XP, and are now beginning to install Windows 7 computers. However, several of the department software packages require expensive upgrades to work on Windows 7 and their [B] hasn't allowed us to make these upgrades. Most department heads would like to replace their software, but are constrained by [B] and data conversion issues.

## Software

Because of their limited [B]s for general software purchases, most users are running MS office 00, though a small number are using MS office 07 and 10. The same [B] constraints have required employees to run other software as long as they can. Most users have been running the same software for years, even a decade or more. Certainly, some users could benefit from additional training. However, the training would be either for their specific department software ([PD], [FD], Accounting [MCFLMosFB]) or older versions of software (Office, etc). So for example, there would no benefit to provide training on office 10, since most users don't have access to this software.

Most users have been working with the same software for many years; in some cases, over a decade. The [MC]'s information Systems Specialist provides troubleshooting and training as needed for most software. Additional training could benefit some [EMP]s, but as indicated above, this training would more likely be for specific department software or older software packages. [CM] has hired few new [MCFLMosFB] [EMP] over the last several years; these [MCFLMosFB] [EMP] are provided software training either by IT or fellow [EMP]s (as needed). Since staff reductions outpace new hires, the need for formal software training is presently limited.

## Concluding Remarks

[COFFEE]'s initial charter was broad enough before the work started. Every response to a question yielded another question. At the time of this report, there are still more questions than answers but that doesn't mean there is nothing we can do right now to start improving the financial condition of [MCFLMosFB] and educating the community as to their challenges and opportunities. There are several small steps that are suggested in this report. Some will yield immediate results; others will require more time and effort. These small steps will have only a minor impact on the overall long-term results. There are some larger steps that [COFFEE] hopes will be taken, but these steps require courage, discipline, and total honesty with ourselves and everyone involved. Otherwise, long-term success and unity of [MCFLMosFB] will be an accident—if it happens at all—and not a deliberate and unified effort.

- ❑ The development and communication of ongoing, detailed financial planning that speaks to the regulatory requirements of [MCFLMosFB] will go a long way towards migrating away from being perceived as reactionary and will promote public involvement.
- ❑ A systematic approach towards defining the needs of [MCFLMosFB] in terms that facilitates and promotes volunteerism. It is true that [MCFLMosFB] has a proud history of volunteerism, but [COFFEE] has learned that there is much more that private citizens can do if they knew it needed to be done and there was someone from

[MCFLMosFB] to manage the effort and ensure it was done safely and correctly.

❑ Development and implementation of a volunteer force to respond to the increased workload requirements associated with natural disasters and public events.

❑ Getting the message out that [MCFLMosFB] is one community and inviting everyone to be a part of it.

Efforts similar to [COFFEE] have yielded temporary results for the better, and we are seeing today that a few long-term effects have caused as many, if not more, problems than were solved. It is [COFFEE]'s belief that an ongoing effort that continuously seeks to improve both the performance of [MCFLMosFB] and the manner in which [MCFLMosFB] is studied. The idea of restructuring [COFFEE] to reduce the formality and constraints would encourage a more fluid exchange of information and facilitate a more efficient improvement process. The idea of keeping this effort going and allowing new people to come in and let others step down so that every citizens is given the opportunity to learn how [MCFLMosFB] works would seem to be a good thing, but as [COFFEE] is only fact finding committee and has no decision authority, it is just a suggestion.

It is [COFFEE]'s hope that this report is just another step in a series of steps that will bring the community together with a common vision and sense of purpose. The names of [COFFEE] members are in public record but are not listed in this report because there were so many contributors that were not official [COFFEE] members, listing them all would be inefficient. Therefore, it is best that we list no single individual. This report was a combined effort of private citizens and [PubServ]s. In some cases, the direct contributions of individuals do not appear in this report, but every effort was made to capture the intent of their message. If the contribution was sent through [MCFLMosFB] city clerk, it is part of public record and can most likely be found on [MCFLMosFB]'s website. To the extent that the specific verbiage is interpreted as it was intended, keep in mind that everybody involved in this effort was and is committed to doing what can be done to make [MCFLMosFB] better, and that a negative interpretation is likely the wrong interpretation. Though there are some within this community who may never learn that this report exists, it is not unreasonable to assign authorship to the dedicated [PubServ]s and interested [MCFLMosFB] citizens.

# I Just Can't Do It Anymore

There was a time when [TGTDTT] could not understand what it meant to be alive for twenty-six years, and today [TGTDTT] has a hard time imagining what it means to have the same job for twenty-six years. [TGTDTT] is not talking about working for the same employer and moving up in the company, [TGTDTT] is talking about getting hired by someone on one day and given one job title and staying employed by those exact same people keeping the exact same job title for twenty-six years. [FicChaTwentyFour] did it and now [FicChaTwentyFour] wants a change.

For almost three decades, [FicChaTwentyFour] knew exactly who to please and how to please them. With the election of [FicChaTen] and [FicChaThirty], the published [COFFEE] Report and the appointment of [FicChaTwelve] to [CC], [FicChaTwentyFour] had decided if [FicChaTwentyFour] was going to have to learn a whole new list of people to please and what it is going to take to please them, [FicChaTwentyFour] might as well do it someplace new.

[TGTDTT] did not want to see [FicChaTwentyFour] go because [FicChaTwentyFour] was the one guy in town who knew how to run [MCFLMosFB] better than anyone else. [TGTDTT] conceded that stuff was changing and [FicChaTwentyFour] is close to retirement, but let's get a few years to make the transition while [MCFLMosFB] implement the [COFFEE] way of doing stuff.

Privately and publicly [TGTDTT] asked [FicChaTwentyFour] to reconsider. [TGTDTT] stopped short of begging and refused to use the "sense of duty to the community" argument because it was offensive to [TGTDTT] and [TGTDTT] suspected it would be offensive to [FicChaTwentyFour].

"I just can't do it anymore." was all [FicChaTwentyFour] would say.

[CC] named a park after [FicChaTwentyFour] and after about a year [FicChaTwentyFour] picked up another [CM] gig in south [GSoF].

[TGTDTT]'s stories about [FicChaTwentyFour] are intended to be humorous, but many of them are at [FicChaTwentyFour]'s expense. For instance, [TGTDTT] learned how to make [FicChaTwentyFour]'s leg shake and [FicChaTwentyFour]'s eyes get really big. At first [TGTDTT] didn't believe [TGTDTT] was actually causing the reaction so [TGTDTT] began testing the idea. Sure enough, [FicChaTwentyFour]'s eyes would get big and [FicChaTwentyFour]'s leg would start to shake. As [TGTDTT] learned stuff that would cause the phenomena, [TGTDTT] added it to the list of stuff [TGTDTT] didn't really need to say around [FicChaTwentyFour] because it freaked [FicChaTwentyFour] out.

In [TGTDTT]'s earliest meeting with [FicChaTwentyFour], [TGTDTT] was trying to unravel the various [USD] streams to complete a section of a report for capital improvement that [FD] chief and [TGTDTT] were working on. Every time [TGTDTT] came back to wanting a formal description of all [MCFLMosFB] revenues and what they could be used for, [FicChaTwentyFour]'s eyes would get big and the leg would begin to dance.

[FicChaTwentyFour] and [TGTDTT] collaborated somewhat in getting [MCFLMosFB] [EMP] to like [COFFEE].

In the beginning of the whole thing, there were not only [MCFLMosFB] [EMP]s but other [MCFLMosFB] citizens who thought [COFFEE] was just plain bitter. Being one of the people who had literally written the book on [COFFEE], [TGTDTT] worked with [FicChaTwentyFour] to get the word out that their agenda was about understanding and reporting to those who have the power to implement change. [COFFEE] was concerned with process and cost; the stuff that any outside consultant would research.

By the time the report was released, [FicChaTwentyFour] and [TGTDTT] had collectively obtained a virtual 100% buy-in on all of the facts recorded in the report. Furthermore, all department heads of [MCFLMosFB] had begun to immediately respond to all of the stuff that was within their power to improve. When the next [B] cycle came to a head, every department head at [MCFLMosFB] was able to provide a thorough detailing of the funds necessary to complete their mission and a list of specific initiatives department head [MCFLMosFB] had put in place to optimize the way in which [MCFLMosFB] did business.

[TGTDTT] honestly thought good was being done and that stuff would settle down.

But [ELCTN11] had been the catalyst of several individual and collective solar-flares in the community. [FicChaTwentyFour] had nowhere he could turn for counsel that [FicChaTwentyFour] could trust except [FicChaTwentyFour]'s wife and kids.

[FicChaTwentyFour] still had time on his contract so [FicChaTwentyFour] leaving now would require a delicate touch if it were to be handled correctly. [FicChaTwentyFour] handled it brilliantly.

As [TGTDTT] mentioned, [CC] named a park after [FicChaTwentyFour]. [CC] also let [FicChaTwentyFour] retire now with the benefits package that was not supposed to kick in for another three years.

After [FicChaTwentyFour] left, it was discovered by forensic accountants that for over a decade [FicChaTwentyFour] had been contributing to a tax-free retirement program that [FicChaTwentyFour] was not eligible for as a [CM] under contract. Nothing will come from that because after [ELCTN12] there is no political will to persue it.

[FicChaTwentyFour] is a decent guy whom [TGTDTT] likes and respects. But that respect and affection does not come with a global seal of approval for all the actions and decisions [FicChaTwentyFour] has made or taken.

For instance, [TGTDTT] takes issue with the fact that [FicChaTwentyFour] withheld valuable information that would have prevented all of the arguments regarding [MCFLMosFB] finances. If there was ever a guy who made you convinced that he was hiding something that had to do with [MCFLMosFB] finances, it was [FicChaTwentyFour].

[FicChaTwentyFour] is very similar to Meyer Lansky in that Meyer had an impeccable reputation for fairness and honesty and absolute discretion in all business matters. But no one ever knew anywhere near as much about where all the money was than Meyer. The difference between the two is that Meyer was better at making you believe the reputation was justified.

# [FicChaTwelve] [CC] [ELCTN12]

## August 04, 12

(BeginTrans [FBResMailGrp])

There will be another (of many) [B] fiscal year 12-13 meetings [TSCMuniCom] 6PM on Wednesday, 8 August. This is where [USD] goes and when you can have the most significant impact on your wallet (and the wallets of others) along with conserving the services you deem important in [MCFLMosFB].

[CC] will also discuss the award of a contract for landscape improvements.

PLEASE NOTE: Since this is [B] fiscal year 12-13 meeting and not [CC] meeting, there will be no opportunity for [CitComm]. At the beginning of the meeting, however, [CC] [FB], Mayor may provide a few opportunities during [B] fiscal year 12-13 discussions for people to speak 3-minute maximum duration on the items of [B] fiscal year 12-13 discussed.

[FicChaTwelve] was not present for [CCMFLMosFB] meeting, so [CC] member [FicChaTen] put together these notes.

Here's what happened at last night's [CC] meeting

1. The old Pizza Hut building is being purchased and potential owner is asking for an appeal

to the current code fine liens of over $100k imposed on previous owner, otherwise his business plans to fix up the property and move into it are not executable. It was the sense of [CC] that an appeal by the purchaser for a lien reduction as allowed by [MCFLMosFB] Code 2-361 would be favorably reviewed in order to get this property improved and back on the tax rolls.

2. [MCFLMosFB] quarterly newsletter: Three [MCFLMosFB] citizens have been working with the [CMFLMosFB] newsletter to revive the publication and mitigate the cost to taxpayers via Advertisements from local businesses. The small group requested [CC] to approve a top limit of $2200 to allow the publication of 5000 copies of an 8 page inaugural edition in mid-September to allow for candidate reviews. Passed.

3. Annual Storm water Utility Assessment for FY13. Passed. Discussion revolved around the often-made-point by [CC] that a City-wide Capital Improvement Plan needs to be completed and this sort of activity must be included. This would allow [MCFLMosFB] to know what its following year requirement will be versus merely collecting the same amount of tax money as the previous year. As our projects are completed and debt paid down, our requirements should decrease to maintenance of the systems and our tax requirement should decrease, as well.

3. Ordinance 1053: Mid-year Amendment to [B] Fiscal year 11-12]. Accounting adjustments were made. Passed.

4. Discuss/take action on the types of signs that are regulated by city code moratorium will be discussed at 16 August meeting. Free Speech sings are allowed on private property...the

Libertarian in me applauds this and believes they will be self-regulating via personal integrity, neighbors and friends. As long as signs are placed such that safety is not an issue (e.g. blocking street views, etc), there should be no restrictions.

5. Discuss/take action on: Grant writer request for proposals. [CC] directed [CM] to modify request for proposal to make this a "pay as we need it" approach and to encourage multiple offers to approach [MCFLMosFB] with potential upcoming grants. [CC] will be the final decision authority regarding which grants to pursue and our decisions will be based on: our needs, our ability/willingness to match funds, and our ability/willingness to pay the long term "tail" associated with grants.

6. Discuss general procedures for request for proposal qualifications. Information only.

7. Discuss/take action on request for proposal for cleaning of community center. [CC] directed [MCFLMosFB] manager to proceed with this RFP (w/ preference for local vendors). At same time, [CC] asked that another requisition for proposal be prepared for potentially contracting out cleaning services for all [MCFLMosFB] facilities, as often economies of scale can be gained by offering larger pieces of work. [CC] also requested the same effort be accomplished for potentially contracting out grounds services. Once proposals are received, [MCFLMosFB] will compare contract costs to having to maintain maintenance fleets and personnel.

8. Discuss/take action on search for a permanent city manager. In a 3-1 vote, [CC] decided to appoint a [MCFLMosFB] citizens' committee to conduct the search versus spending $20k or

more to hire a head hunter. The committee will advertise for [CMFLMosFB] candidates, collect applications/resumes, review them, cull the applicant pool over several iterations, and submit their final five for [CC] interviews and selection. [CC] members will provide their appointees' names at the 8 August special [B] fiscal year 12-13 meeting and request the first briefing from the committee at the 15 August regular meeting (looking for timelines, etc).

[FicChaTen]   Picking a died-in-the-wool [CM], trained as [CM] and steeped in that line of thinking will only get us more of the same. Cities around our country are in dire straits due to poor business practices in city management, yet they continue to hire the same sort of [CM] to replace the [CM] they have just fired or lost. They continue to have the same problems and wonder why.

I am making a push for our requirements/ desires to include more business-oriented professional qualifications and demonstrated ability. I think we need out-of-the-standard-[CM]-box thinking to help us continue to gain efficiencies in [MCFLMosFB].

9. Discuss/take action on request for proposal for professional auditing services. [CC] stated its frustration that this request for proposal hadn't been acted upon as directed some time ago. Due to the delay, [MCFLMosFB]'s current auditor will accomplish this year's audit. In

the meantime, state law requires [MCFLMosFB] to appoint an Auditor Selection Committee from which will flow the request for proposal. [CC] members will make their appointments (one per member) at the 8 August meeting.

[FicChaTen] please stay engaged. [B] fiscal year 12-13 time is upon us and any Fundamental changes will require your ideas and support. I am encouraged by what I am seeing in the early stages of this year's process, but we need to ensure maximize efficiencies while maintaining appropriate [GVBMNT] service.

[FicChaTen] thanks for your continued support.

[CC] member [FicChaTen]

(EndTrans [FBResMailGrp])


(BeginTrans [FBResMailGrp])

Sunday, August 12, 12 11:18 AM
Subject: Recent [MCFLMosFB] Mailing

You may have received an unsigned letter in your mailbox recently regarding [B] fiscal year 12-13 decisions. [FicChaTwelve] evaluated the veracity of the information; [CC] member [FicChaTen] composed a response.

If you would like to see [FicChaTen]'s response, please let [FicChaTwelve] know and [FicChaTwelve] will forward it to you.

[FicChaTwelve]

(EndTrans) [FBResMailGrp])

| | |
|---|---|
| [TGTDTT] | What on earth would compel you to give that poorly written incoherent rant any additional press? |
| [FicChaTwelve] | The whole purpose of [FBResMailGrp] is to get information out and clear up misinformation (or responses to it). [FicChaTen]'s mail group is limited, but the mailing was not. I simply let others see what was said, and that there are at least two sides to every story. |
| [TGTDTT] | There is a vacuum out there and the numb nuts are filling it will stupidity. Your saying that it might be stupid doesn't address the lack of well-informed discussion on the key issues to be addressed. In fact, you and the other [CC] members are letting everyone else frame the debate. |
| [FicChaTwelve] | I didn't send [FicChaTen]'s response to everyone . . . only those who asked to see it. |
| [TGTDTT] | It's not just that. [FicChaThirty]'s complaints that the policies and procedures have not been revised does not change the policies and procedures, and none of you are asking for the level of detail required to allow community involvement in helping making things any better. |
| [FicChaTwelve] | I understand what you are telling me and you are right, things do seem a little stuck in the mud right now. |

[TGTDTT]

I know you were appointed to [CC] by [CC] and did not run for election. There are some that believe you are going to run for election. Should you decide to run, my hope is that the other candidates are clearly weaker, even less informed, and posses even less leadership skills than what I am seeing right now.

[FicChaTwelve]

I don't sense the support to pursue an elected position. I use intellect to decide, and I speak from the heart. Those qualities are mutually defeating in politics.

[TGTDTT]

If this stings, it is meant to. If it doesn't, then I have to live with my lapse in judgment.

[FicChaTwelve]

You're right . . . that did sting.

[TGTDTT]

Leaving City Hall this afternoon after a pleasant and productive meeting with the interim [CM] to discuss [B] fiscal year 12-13 and activities that would serve to bring [MCFLMosFB] together as a single community, I took time to notice the breeze, the sun, and the smile on [FicChaTwentyNine] as she said hello to me in the breezeway.

On the way home I thought about a good friend of mine who is also a dedicated public servant and thought he might enjoy a cold and delicious beverage when he got home this evening. So I stopped by the store picked up a six-pack and dropped them off at his house on the way to my home. Though apparently disconnected notions - [B] fiscal year 12-13, the weather, a pleasant smile, and a cold beer for a friend, they are intrinsically connected to me living in [MCFLMosFB] and being a part of the community. My part is small and virtually insignificant. There are others who play a much bigger role in the community and contribute far more positive energy than I do, but every little bit of positive influence matters.

There are those who say that there is a great deal of work that needs to be done and they are right. There are those who say that [MCFLMosFB] is a great place to live and that we need to protect our way of life. Those people are also right.

Today I went to a meeting that I was invited to in order to find a way for me to be of service in the community. After the meeting was over, a fellow [MCFLMosFB] citizen was happy to see me for no other reason than she likes me. On the way home, I was able to ensure that my friend knows that I appreciate the sacrifices he makes in the service of our fair community with the hope that it brings a smile to his face when the frosty suds is brought to his lips. Now, with a smile on my face, I look forward to seeing what wonderful opportunities for me to enjoy myself and bring joy to others will occur.

I owe the wonder of this day to [FicChaTen] and [FicChaTwelve]. Had they not inspired me, none of what I described would have happened and I probably would have just driven home after work and turned on the TV.

[FicChaTwelve]     Thank you for pointing out the simple things in life. You sound like the kind of articles that would be nice to read in [MCFLMosFB] quarterly newsletter!

(EndDialogue)


(BeginTrans) [FBResMailGrp])

August 16, 12

My apologies for the late notice.

There will be a Town Hall meeting tonight (Thursday) at 6PM at the [TSCMuniCom] across the breezeway from City Hall. Topics will include recent information regarding Recreation Department [MCFLMosFB] cost and discussion of those specific facilities with attendees. As always, there will be ample time for open and interactive discussion.

I hope you can make it!

[CC] candidate [FicChaTwelve]

(EndTrans [FBResMailGrp])

(Begin [FicChaTwelve] [CC] campaign meeting)

Friday, August 17, 12 6:01 PM
Subject: [FicChaTwelve] for [CC]
[FicChaTwelve][TGTDTT]

[TGTDTT]    Tomorrow morning when you wake up, there will be 80 days until the election.

Before you start talking to people, you might want to hone your narrative a bit and be ready to address the following:

Why are you running?

Why do you think people should vote for you?

What do you hope to accomplish during your term and does it help me, the average citizen?

How do you intend to go about accomplishing the things you set out to accomplish?

Why should I even care about voting for anyone running for [CC]?

What are the top three challenges facing [MCFLMosFB]?

What is your plan to address the top three (3) challenges facing [MCFLMosFB]?

Who supports you?

Tell me about your run-in with the law as well as why those things should not disqualify you from office?

Who are your detractors, and why do you think they would prefer you not get elected?

Who else is running, and why are as good, if not better than they are?

For each of the other candidates, what good things do you think they will do for [MCFLMosFB]?

For each of the other candidates, what do you think they will do that is not good for [MCFLMosFB]?

How do you intend to demonstrate to the electorate that you are the superior choice without telling anyone that you are?

I honestly believe you need help to win this election. I believe that your weaknesses can be exploited such that you will be seen as the weakest of candidates. I also believe we can turn those weaknesses into strengths.

[FicChaTwelve]    You are a very good friend!

[TGTDTT]          Whether I have a role in your campaign is entirely up to you. I know that you talk to others who can offer good counsel and I will not be offended in any way if my only role is to vote for you. Understand that this is a finish line that you might cross with a whole bunch of people but the burden for making it happen is yours alone.

[FicChaTwelve]     There is no one in [MCFLMosFB] that I would rather explain my answers to each of these questions to than you. I want you to have a BIG role in listening to my responses and running me through the gauntlet.

(End [FicChaTwelve] [CC] campaign meeting)


(Begin [FicChaTwelve] [CC] campaign meeting)

Saturday, August 18, 12 6:26 PM

Subject: How to be the guy without telling anyone that you are the guy. Walking the walk.

[FicChaTwelve][FicChaThirteen][TGTDTT]

[TGTDTT]     79 days until the election. Only a couple dozen at most know you are a [CC] candidate. Once you tell the world, the one thing you can count on is that the majority will not understand why or realize why you deserve their support. My preliminary thoughts as to a methodical approach to ensuring everyone knows that you are running and can understand at least one reason why you deserve their support. Some of the ideas may not work for you because everyone has their own style; however, some of the ideas might inspire thought and be helpful.

My first hypothesis is that the person who best understands and can articulate the issues are the most persuasive. Therefore my first suggestion is that we proactively get the word out that you have an understanding of the issues. You have to be the most competent and professional person while at the same time empathetic, genuine, and approachable.

[FicChaThirteen]:     Well you don't ask for very much.

[TGTDTT]     Public Speaking Engagements

"Leadership and the role you play in solving the problems of today and tomorrow" is a 20 minute talk to young people - schools, cub scouts, athletic teams, civic clubs, etc. that inspires the next generation to get informed and involved. At no point do you talk about your running for [CC] but you talk about the rewards and need to become a part of [MCFLMosFB].

"The Path to Financial Security" is a 15 to 30 minute talk that outlines the current overall financial state of [MCFLMosFB] and presents the various paths that could be taken to mitigate debt, increase reserves, and ensure the quality of life in [MCFLMosFB]. This talk is more towards adults and should be based on fact, present options, and communicate that you want to work with people to implement new ideas that can be measured and tested so that things that work are continued and things that don't are modified or abandoned.

"[MCFLMosFB] - 12 to 32" is a one hour talk that presents the various changes in the demographics and the anticipated needs of the community.

"[MCFLMosFB] - Criticism and Praise" is a 15 to 30 minute talk that openly discusses what is really good about [MCFLMosFB] and the areas that would benefit from new ideas.

[FicChaTwelve]

If you would like to look for opportunities for me to speak publicly, I will make myself available. I am certainly comfortable with who I am, who I'll represent, and the way I'll represent them. Again, it will be a closed pie-hole and open ears…and a deep desire to return "unity to community" in [MCFLMosFB]!

[TGTDTT]

Meeting the people - Round 1

Go to every home and business in [MCFLMosFB] at least once to introduce yourself. Tell whomever answers the door that you are running for [CC] and why. Let them know about your web site, any upcoming events, and leave them a pamphlet that invites them to support you and be involved in the future of [MCFLMosFB].

Meeting the people - Round 2

More selective than Round 1 that allows for the people to spend some quality time talking about things. One on one Q&A.

[FBWC] Candidate Forum 12 - you know the drill on this

You need all of the data that [FicChaTen] had for his campaign. How we get it, I don't know but we need it.

Public appearances at every restaurant in [MCFLMosFB], every event we can find out about.

We need to hold coffees, barbeques, and anything else we can think of.

Founder's Day Parade

Those are my thoughts so far.

[FicChaTwelve]

You have got to be the most organized person I know. Without a doubt, the path to success will be engaging with people in their own familiar surroundings, talking about their specific needs and questions, and being the person with two big ears and a closed pie-hole. The 79 days ahead will (early on) be spent getting the word out to key conduits and donors; but the final 45 will be literally going door-to-door to shake hands, listen, respond, and convince as many people as possible that their future will be more secure with my representation.

[TGTDTT]

It seems to me that [FicChaTwelve]'s first public act is to tell everyone that he is running for [CC], the things that he done since being appointed and what he intends to do if elected. But until someone else makes it an issue, he should stay focused on why he is a good choice for being on [CC].

The reason I say this is that it has already been made public in more ways than one and he has already experienced the support of [MCFLMosFB] when people have tried to use it against him.

If it is brought up, [FicChaTwelve] can present the incident as one of life's turning moments that made all the difference in his life. As a military man who put his life on the line for his country, it is easy to forget that he is just a man who is also a father with responsibilities. That reckless driving ticket was the key incident that compelled him to take a hard long look at life so that he could learn the lessons and be the person that deserves the [LOVE] and respect of his family and friends. Since then, [FicChaTwelve] has rededicated his life to his family and friends and focused some of that positive energy towards helping [MCFLMosFB] become more of a community that can weather any storm on the horizon . . . . or something like that.

[FicChaTwelve]    . . . that was PERFECT! and it is true!

[FicChaTen]    I concur. [FicChaTwelve] will have my complete attention. As an inoculators what do you think about being up front w DUI/reckless driving thing?? Maybe "I learned about life from that" early piece . . . just to get it out if the way and immediately on to policy issues?? I think Cahn Pallack is going to assist as much as he can.

[TGTDTT]

[FicChaTwelve] told me he was running for [CC]. If that is what he has chosen to do, I want him to win. But I don't think it will be easy and I do think that the successful approach is going to be dramatically different than [FicChaTen]'s campaign. [FicChaTwelve] believes we can bring [MCFLMosFB] together. I believe the way to do that is for him to talk about really cool things to young people who can't vote yet because they will go home and tell their parents about this great guy who talked to them about leadership and civic involvement, etc. I also believe [FicChaTwelve] needs to talk about serious things to the people who can vote - The path to fiscal security - populating the 100+ acres to the north, fixing the non-conforming lot problem, optimizing government expenses, increasing the business base, etc.

[TGTDTT]

[FicChaTwelve] needs to talk to everybody about getting involved in [MCFLMosFB], which means I want him to give a few talks to young people about leadership and how being a part of the community is rewarding. But I lack any contacts to get him in front of a football team, little league team, high school classroom, etc. Any ideas as to who we could talk to get [FicChaTwelve] in front of multiple groups of young people - including Social Studies or Civics classrooms?

[FicChaEleven]    The same question regarding his speaking to adults.

[TGTDTT]    I was also thinking that a Liberty Catalyst interview and subsequent positive mailer about electing one of the good guys might be something to consider.

[FicChaEleven]    Phone lists, address lists, etc?

[TGTDTT]    I know [FicChaTen] is busy, but we owe it [FicChaTwelve] to do what we can to ensure he accomplishes his goal.

[FicChaTwelve]    It sounds great! I've been working on the questions you wrote and have good responses to each (well . . . one response is a question . . . but it will have to do!)

[FicChaTwelve]    I will be back this weekend.

[TGTDTT]    Getting my head around the tone and tenor led me to the text that follows. If it is good text, let's find a way to get it out there. If it is bad text, let's replace it with something better and then get it out there. But the idea of getting people to start talking about why [FicChaTwelve] should get a full term based on who is he is and what he has been a part of in the short time he has been on [CC] seems to make sense to me . . .

[FicChaTwelve] is already there and is doing a good job. Give him the chance to continue the work.

1. Bring [MCFLMosFB] [EMP] policies, salaries, retirement, and health benefits in line with today's economy
2. Optimize processes and procedures so that people look forward to doing business with [MCFLMosFB]
3. Expand the current volunteer effort in [MCFLMosFB] to reduce the demands on the General Fund and increase community involvement
4. Reduce the obstacles to developing the annexed acreage to the north and the non-conforming lots in [MCFLMosFB]
5. Ensure the voice of every citizens is heard and that everyone feels welcomed to be a part of [MCFLMosFB]

[FicChaTwelve] was called to service when he was appointed to [CC] when [FicChaEighteen], a legend in [MCFLMosFB], passed away. [FicChaTwelve] has been considerate, competent, respectful, and honest with all those he has done business with. It wasn't his intention to continue beyond his appointed term, but now that progress is being made towards improving the financial health of [MCFLMosFB] and the inclusion of all our [MCFLMosFB] citizens, [FicChaTwelve] feels he owes it to the community to continue on and asking for your support.

There may be those who choose to raise past misunderstandings in an attempt to confuse people, but since [FicChaTwelve] has been on [CC], [MCFLMosFB] citizen's support of [MCFLMosFB]

[GVBMNT] has improved and the cost of [GVBMNT] is being reduced. The bottom line is that [FicChaTwelve]'s participation is making [MCFLMosFB] a better place to live. Please join me in my support of [FicChaTwelve] for [CC]. It will be a decision you that you can take pride in.

[FicChaTwelve]    This is great advice for the walk-arounds and for stumping as you say. All points are salient and the two people running are responsible for the journey that got us where we are. I just need to deliver that message in a positive way that leaves people questioning why they'd want to revert back to those days without leaving opposing candidates with black eyes.

Thanks for all the assistance . . . I appreciate it greatly!

[TGTDTT]    Now that we know who all is in the race, the theme has to be all of the good things the newcomers have done and all of the things the newcomers will do next term. Present the message in such a way as to inspire people to support your vision as well as let them know that your vision is one that will bring the most long-term good to [MCFLMosFB].

[FicChaTen]    The single most comprehensive detailed [B] fiscal year 12-13 review has produced savings that will permit an actual reduction in the tax rate of our homes without compromising services. Two of the candidates are on record as recommending Ad Valorem Tax Millage Rate increases in the past and had no knowledge as to how that money was going to be spent.

[TGTDTT]

[CC] is making progress in the transition of [MCFLMosFB] real estate that serves no purpose and cost taxpayers for the upkeep. Two of the people running for [CC] never thought the non-conforming lots and undeveloped [MCFLMosFB] real estate was ever anything to be serious about.

There are other specifics but you get the point that every single problem [CC] is solving can be directly attributed to all three of the people now running for [CC]. You were not elected, but in the short time you have been there, things that really help [MCFLMosFB] are getting done.

[FicChaEleven]

If we were to take some time to write your 30 second pitch and your 5 minute stump speech so you can get out and start meeting people and letting them know that what we have now is what [MCFLMosFB] needs right now.

[TGTDTT]

I want to put the same message to [FicChaFourteen] but I don't know where he is on all of this.

(End [FicChaTwelve] [CC] campaign meeting) August 19, 12

(BeginTrans [FBResMailGrp])

Greetings,

[CC] meeting is scheduled for this Wednesday at 6PM.

Have a blessed Sunday!

[CCMFLMosFB] candidate [FicChaTwelve]

(EndTrans [FBResMailGrp])


(Begin [FicChaTwelve] [CC] campaign meeting)

Wednesday, August 29, 12 11:38 AM

Subject: The history of [MCFLMosFB] - Trends and paradigms

[FicChaTwelve][TGTDTT]

| | |
|---|---|
| [FicChaTwelve] | Do you think a Town Hall meeting where we show the video and talk about it would be worthwhile? I'd like to come by in the morning and watch it (or take it to watch)-give me a call when you're up. |
| [TGTDTT] | There might be some value in understanding [MCFLMosFB] from its birth to its current manifestation. |
| [FicChaTwelve] | As I mentioned on the phone I watched the video - Living in [MCFLMosFB] that was put out to celebrate 50 years of [MCFLMosFB]. |
| [TGTDTT] | [MCFLMosFB] was chartered in order to prevent the construction of a beach |

side mobile home park (See Ordinance #1). From that point on, virtually every facility, activity, and event was the result of volunteer efforts. The founders of [MCFLMosFB] put in their own money to make something happen.

[FicChaTwelve]

Over time, and I don't know why, the mechanism for funding pet projects transitioned from the private sector to [MCFLMosFB]'s [B] that was funded by Ad Valorem Tax Revenue. It is now consensus that [MCFLMosFB] finances fund [OptProj].

[TGTDTT]

What is interesting is that none of the people who lay claim to being instrumental to [MCFLMosFB] are even mentioned in the video. The only exception is a brief "Happy Birthday" message from [FicChaTwentySix] because he was [CC] [FB], Mayor at the time of the celebration.

[FicChaTwelve]

To suggest that everyone see the video might not be a bad idea. To suggest a public showing of the video, or at least the portion that deals with [MCFLMosFB] (the middle of it to the end) might also be a good idea.

[TGTDTT]

The message is that real volunteerism is not just being a [MCFLMosFB] member but it is rolling up your sleeves and doing some work as well as reaching into your wallet to fund the projects you believe should be funded. This [MCFLMosFB] was founded on real volunteerism and when people talk about protecting our way of life, if they are not including reaching into their own wallets or picking up a shovel as part of the effort, then it is just empty rhetoric.

(End [FicChaTwelve] [CC] campaign meeting)

(BeginTrans [FBResMailGrp])

August 30, 12

There will be a [MCFLMosFB] [CC] meeting starting at 6PM at City Hall. On the agenda:

1) Public Hearing on proposed [B] fiscal year 12-13, including [MCFLMosFB] Ordinance 0001060 that reduces our millage rate to 0.5% below the rollback rate (lower taxes) and [MCFLMosFB] Ordinance 0001061 to adopt [B] fiscal year 12-13.
2) Ordinance 1058 imposing a moratorium on [MCFLMosFB] sign code seeks to impose a moratorium on the enforcement of [MCFLMosFB]'s sign code on certain types of signs.
3) Public Hearing of amendments to [MCFLMosFB]'s Comprehensive Plan.
4) Resolution 921 vacating and abandoning a portion of the east end of the canal

Please come out to a very important meeting!

[CCMFLMosFB] candidate [FicChaTwelve]

(EndTrans) [FBResMailGrp])

(BeginTrans [FBResMailGrp])

September 6, 12

[CC] meeting was a 4-hour session with [CitComm] being delayed until after 9PM due to giving [MCFLMosFB]'s Comprehensive Plan and [B] [CRA] fiscal year 12-13 items priority on the agenda.

[B] [CRA] fiscal year 12-13 was approved (first reading) with a 2% reduction in our millage rate...the lowest of all the major municipalities in the county. The [B] [CRA] fiscal year 12-13 was included in the approval even though [CRA] board has not finalized the [B] [CRA] fiscal year 12-13. That will happen on the 13 Sep meeting.

[MCFLMosFB]'s Comprehensive Plan was sent back for more revisions. [CC] member [FicChaTen] and others felt the language is too restrictive to give [MCFLMosFB] leeway in the decision process.

The sign moratorium went back to [MCFLMosFB] Planning and Zoning Board for more clarifications. It was generally felt that the language in the moratorium was too broad in some areas.

Some [MCFLMosFB] citizens expressed concerns that they had not had access to the draft [B] [CRA] fiscal year 12-13 or enough time to review it. The draft [B] [CRA] fiscal year 12-13 was available on [MCFLMosFB] Webpage and at the Library, but it was pointed out that [MCFLMosFB] could use other means to get the word out on items of importance (like this) such as Facebook.

The next (and final) reading of [B] [CRA] fiscal year 12-13 will be on 19 September.

I was enthused by seeing new faces and inputs at [CC] meeting last night! Keep coming out-it's important!

[CCMFLMosFB] candidate [FicChaTwelve]

(EndTrans [FBResMailGrp])


(BeginTrans [FBResMailGrp])

September 12, 12

There will be a Special [CC] meeting at City Hall [TSCMuniCom] 5:30PM. The single subject of the meeting is the [MCFLMosFB] quarterly newsletter. It appears someone feels listing the candidates who are running for [CC] [FB], Mayor and [CC] member on November 6th is against [GVBMNTFL] law.

There will also be a [CRA] meeting where they will discuss the [B] [CRA] fiscal year 12-13, the new [CRA] Plan talk to a representative from the bank that holds our "you-can't-pay-it-back-early-[CRA] -loan" and [CRA] Business See you there!

[CCMFLMosFB] candidate [FicChaTwelve]

(EndTrans [FBResMailGrp])


(BeginTrans) [FBResMailGrp])

September 18, 12

Tomorrow night is the final reading of [B] fiscal year 12-13 that delivers:

    2% reduction in Ad Valorem Tax Millage Rate
    0.5% REAL reduction in Ad Valorem Tax
    0% reduction in [MCFLMosFB] service levels and
        capability

100% of what you expected (in a positive way) after November 8th 11

Some may dispute these statistics- statistics are just numbers. You have tax bills you can review.

Of interesting and important note, our value of property went UP 1.5%.

Now comes some commentary: how did this happen? Because [MCFLMosFB] citizens (volunteers & appointees) devoted time and expertise to understand [B] [CRA] fiscal year 12-13, team with [MCFLMosFB] [EMP], and balance community needs in a way that presented viable, cost-saving ideas. That ATTITUDE buoyed the value of living in [MCFLMosFB]…the value of our space…the value of our homes…and what defines us as a [MCFLMosFB]!

[MCFLMosFB] received kudos from [FlaTo] editor's Lessons for [USFG] (end commentary)

Please come to the meeting. This is your final opportunity to provide input on the proposed plan to spend YOUR tax dollars.

[CCMFLMosFB] candidate [FicChaTwelve]

(EndTrans [FBResMailGrp])


(BeginTrans [FBResMailGrp])

September 20, 12

Greetings

I'm not sure where to start here, but let's start with good news: [B] [CRA] fiscal year 12-13 passed on its second reading. We have an official tax rate cut-it's not a lot, but it's a statement.

There was debate regarding what minimum qualifications should be required for permanent [MCFLMosFB] [CM]. On the one hand, requiring an advanced (Master's degree) in a limited range of specialties (Public Administration was one of them); or on the other hand, accepting a lower-level degree and evaluating experience as equivalent to advanced education. After a vote, the formerly described requirement held.

The hired auditor cited several "red flag" transfers of funds in [B] [MCFLMosFB] Fiscal year 11-12 but was non-specific as to what they might portend. A review of [MCFLMosFB] debt growth over the past 14 years is not pretty…$376,113 in 1998 and $9,622.000 in 10. . . (here comes the commentary) indicating we were living beyond our means.

[CC] voted to go with a "business casual" dress standard for Fall/Winter months and polo shirts for Spring/Summer.

[CC] approved the [JLACFL] response letter. This should close our issue with the [CRA] and the [JLACFL].

[CC] [FB], Mayor remarked on [FlaTo] editor's article citing [MCFLMosFB] as an example for [USFG].

Thank you for the great turnout last night. It was a pretty short meeting (3 hours) … civility is still challenging us, but we can work on that!

Best Regards,
[CCMFLMosFB] candidate [FicChaTwelve]

(EndTrans [FBResMailGrp])

(Begin [FicChaTwelve] [CC] campaign Meeting)

Monday, September 24, 12 9:55 PM

Subject: Batting 1000% - House Visits for Conservatives
in [MCFLMosFB]

[FicChaTen][FicChaTwelve][FicChaFourteen][FicChaFifteen]
[JoeBob][TGTDTT]

[JoeBob]

I found people at home at 3 houses on xxxxxxx Ave. this evening. I made sure they understood the conservative versus lib fight. They will all vote what I call the Tea Party Line.

111 xxxxxxx Ave.: [FCx], a conservative Christ-follower. Wants [FicChaTwelve], [FicChaFourteen] and [FicChaFifteen] signs put up ASAP. [FCxx] is active in conservative politics and communicates with Mr. Posie. She already knew the major issues.

222 xxxxxxx Ave.: [FCxxx]. Nice guy. Very conservative views. Wants all 3 signs as well.

333 xxxxxxx Ave.: nnnn. Strong Conservative and will vote for the 3 above. [FCxxxx] says he works for a [GVBMNT] agency and it's probably not a good idea to have the signs in his yard. I said no problem – let me know if you change your mind.

But of these 3 homes I visited, all will vote to keep the libs out. We don't want the [PD] and [FD] paid out of borrowed monies ([CRA]). We [LOVE] the [PD] [MC] and [FD] but we don't want more than we can afford. We don't want waste. We want [MCFLMosFB] debt reduction. We want to be more like [MCFLMosIHB] from a financial standpoint. It's pretty simple really. [MCFLMosFB] citizens don't like hearing they each owe $1750.00 toward [MCFLMosFB] debt due to the fiscal malfeasance of the previous [CC]s. I make sure they know it. Then I make sure they know that the town next door has a $5M surplus. That alone will make most [MCFLMosFB] voters want to vote the conservative line and keep the libs out.

I will visit more homes tomorrow and get back to you with more addresses for signs. I leave for dog training tomorrow at 6:30 (for my beautiful Rottie) but I may catch some [MCFLMosFB] voter before that time. I intend to see that xxxxxxx Ave. is plastered with the right signs. Door to door, face to face, (a friendly face), can make that happen. [FicChaFourteen] said you all have plans to visit hundreds of homes. That is a sure way to win – because you have the moral high road. If you have numerous workers like me to help you, each worker could just cover a portion of 1 street and the good guys could win 80%

of the votes. So I volunteer to personally speak to every homeowner on xxxxxxx Avenue. It is also a good way to meet neighbors. It is important that the names [FicChaTwelve], [FicChaFourteen] and [FicChaFifteen] are ingrained in their minds. If I meet a lib, it will be a brief but friendly visit – not a problem, no arguments. You need an overwhelming show of support to put a good lid on this small vocal minority.

[FicChaTen]

Outstanding!!! You are a patriot and great guy. That is EXACTLY how we and the nation, hopefully wins our [MCFLMosFB] back (in our case, improves on what we have already started . . . but in our nation's case, sadly, restart what our Founders intended).

[FicChaTen]

[FicChaTwelve], [FicChaFourteen], [FicChaFifteen]. I suggest you GET YOUR SIGN to [JoeBob]'s neighbors ASAP!! His plan is exquisite in its simplicity and we need to execute it [MCFLMosFB]-wide.

[FicChaTwelve]

[JoeBob], Thank you for the effort you are putting forth. I think the idea of street campaigns is GREAT. I will drop off signs at 111 and 222 xxxxxxx. I'm going to try to get a street campaign going on xxxxxxx Court right now. [TGTDTT] has been hitting the streets in my area and doing well. This may be the exact countermeasure to the misinformation. [JoeBob], can I put you in touch with some other [MCFLMosFB] voters as interest grows?

[FicChaTen]

Though you are going to some doors as part of your campaign, we should coordinate 'street' champions to take "the message" to their [MCFLMosFB] voter neighbors. I suggest we sit down this weekend and determine true champions of the small [GVBMNT] cause that we are aware of on as many streets as possible. Then each of us can target them to carry the message (with signs) to their [MCFLMosFB] voter neighbors. My house, 12:00 on Saturday works for me if it does for you. I think we have [MCFLMosFB] street map still from last year's campaign . . . we will start with major thoroughfares.

[FicChaTen]

As we have discussed, "the message" has to be short/succinct: in 10 short months, new [CC] has PROVED Efficient Government IS POSSIBLE. Even through continuing flak from [GOB], via multiple coordinated efforts to increase transparency, accountability and efficiency, we have been able to deliver [B] fiscal year 12-13 that for the first time in [MCFLMosFB]'s history provided a real Ad Valorem Tax Millage Rate (not just fuzzy math Roll Back Rate mumbo jumbo), while INCREASING our dangerously depleted [MCFLMosFB] reserves about 2100% (that past [CC]s have raided to pay for [OptProj] and never replenished even in the 'good times'), INCREASED debt paydown ([CRA] payback), and found efficiencies that cut departmental [B] fiscal year 12-13s by 7.1% . . . OBTW, did all of that while MAINTAINING [MCFLMosFB] service levels and capability! Please internalize those talking points and use them freely.

[FicChaTen]

Wouldn't say this part right now (may scare off fence sitters) . . . but just think what we will be able to do when we right-size services! Heck, just the [FD] chief technical efficiency we encouraged him to delve into will save 3 firefighters starting next year!

[FicChaTwelve]

Thank you for the continued support... you are a friend through-and-through, but more importantly you see well into the future and know what we're doing now is tough...but will make sure that past promises are kept and future expectations are met down the road!

[TGTDTT]

Brochures have distributed on xxxxxxx Drive and xxxxxxx Court. I will bring by the walking sheets and the remaining brochures. The recent emails you have included me on lead me to believe that the risk of duplicate effort is sufficiently high and the best course of action is to allow you the opportunity to collect your thoughts and direct my efforts in accordance with your plan.

[TGTDTT]  I don't exactly know how best to express my thoughts, nor am I prepared to express any opinions as to my impressions of what I have seen so far of this campaign.

[FicChaTwelve]  You're wrong. You actually are part of a no-kidding grassroots effort that may be even more effective than the (admittedly) hard door-to-door that is currently the effective norm in [MCFLMosFB]. I'm mostly hurt...and partially stunned...that you'd hang up your hat on what is clearly a successful contact campaign.

[TGTDTT]  What I will offer is that a well run, disciplined, and organized effort that facilitates the candidate articulating his or her argument to as many voters as possible will probably yield the best results possible under the circumstances.

If you have such an effort, it has not been made apparent to me and it would be counter-productive to duplicate efforts. It would also seem that given what little I am aware of, there is little opportunity to best understand the results on November 6th.

[FicChaTwelve]  Your effort and [JoeBob]'s effort don't have to overlap . . . they really should be synergy (although I kind of wrinkle my nose at that term). What you are doing personally is WAY more important to me as your friend than it is in reaching a campaign victory. I respectfully ask that you reconsider bowing out.

Hang with me bro I've been down this road before and know how the ups and downs go!

[FicChaTen]   We are on the right side of history and principle, gentlemen . . . God Bless and good hunting.

(End [FicChaTwelve] [CC] campaign meeting)


(BeginTrans [FBResMailGrp])

September 29, 12

I am honored to report the endorsement of Mel Area Association of Realtors on my campaign for [CC].

I interviewed with their board along with a number of other political candidates.

Their kind words of endorsement and encouragement mean a great deal to me.

Let's keep progress on point!

[CC] candidate [FicChaTwelve]

(EndTrans [FBResMailGrp])

(BeginTrans [FBResMailGrp])

October 4, 12

Last night was a positively-charged atmosphere with [MCFLMosFB] citizens information-sharing, questions, and helpful suggestions! This is great!

The [FBLC] donated an awesome handicap chair for beach access. The chair will be stored at [MCFLMosFB] Fire Station 01 if you need to use it.

[CC] approved the bid results for the new cleaning contract at [MCFLMosFB] Community Center. [CC] approved the plans for La Ol Beach Club Reception Center Upgrade … (opinion) it will really look nice along A1A!

Ordinance 1058 imposing a moratorium on [MCFLMosFB] sign code passed the first reading. It must now go to [CRA] board for their approval and then back to [CC] for second-reading passage.

The non-conforming dock issue was sent back to [MCFLMosFB] Planning and Zoning Board for more refinement.

There were two really good [CitComm] s I want to share:

1) [MCFLMosFB] recreational area S. Island needs a new pontoon boat (24-foot minimum) and motor so [MCFLMosFB] volunteers can get over to the island to clear invasive plants and clean up trails. We need some folks to put together a BIG team to at least do the trail and invasive plants (Australian Pine and Brazilian Pepper) clean-up.

2) It was suggested that a quarterly financial report be presented to [CM] and [CC]. [CC] agreed this should start immediately.

There was a LOT of discussion about the [MCFLMosFB] quarterly newsletter—particularly on the fact that Aluminum can recycling efforts were inadvertently replaced by an illustration. I recommend you listen/watch the YouTube version to hear everything that was said, but the [MCFLMosFB] quarterly newsletter is here to stay!

[CC] approved to increase the hours of a [MCFLMosFB] Volunteer Services Coordinator to take on the tasks of [MCFLMosFB] Volunteer Services Coordinator and [MCFLMosFB] Special Events Coordinator. [CC] gave a deadline of 45 days for Recreation Department Head of [MCFLMosFB] to come back with its annual plan for events.

Due to time constraints and level of detail in Ordinance 1062 and Ordinance 1063 they were tabled so folks could depart to watch Presidential Election Debate and there you have it. Feel free to give me a shout if you have questions!

[CC] candidate [FicChaTwelve]

(EndTrans [FBResMailGrp])

(Begin [FicChaTwelve] [FCCFLMosFB] campaign meeting)
Thursday, October 04, 12 8:41 AM

Subject: Quick Comment

[FicChaTen][FicChaEleven][FicChaTwelve][FicChaThirteen][FicChaFourteen][FicChaNineteen]

| | |
|---|---|
| [FicChaTwelve] | [FicChaNineteen], I've started a "Rumors" list on my website. I hope to get [TGTDTT] to update the link so it |

drops down as a menu selection under "The Latest" tab. I already addressed [RecFLMosFB] and [MCFLMosFB] quarterly newsletter rumors.

[FicChaNineteen]  talk to [FicChaSixteen] . . . .he heard [FicChaTwentySix] [FicChaTwentyOne] & [FicChaTwoBee] out in the lobby when he went out . . . saying oh we pulled a fast one over on them . . . he THINKS that is going to be their new campaign against ya'll . . . "[CC] wants to outsource the [MCFLMosFB] quarterly newsletter"

[FicChaNineteen]  the nerve of them. Also [FicChaTwentySix] is starting his PROPAGANDA AGAIN of how ya'll want to cut the [RecFLMosFB] so [FicChaEleven], can you send a letter to xxxx & xxxx xxxxxxxxx xxx xxxxxx RD that her main point yesterday was about the [RecFLMosFB]. Shouldn't there be something in the letter how as [CC] [FB], Mayor [FicChaTwentySix] didn't do his homework & gave our [PD] & [FD] away to [PelCo] . . . with no tax relief money from [PelCo] . . . better yet . . . put the newspaper article in the letter . . . .it came out in [FlaTo] around Aug . . . or so of 05/06 . . . when [FicChaTwentySix] was campaigning . . .

[FicChaTwelve]  [FicChaThirteen] told me she was the one who was going to "swear to the veracity" of [FC02C]'s [PD] complaint that night at Street Festival and was the one who "accompanied and comforted" [FC02C] when she put on her charade at IAP when I was there. [MCFLMosFB] politics is great… [MCFLMosFB] politics is great… [MCFLMosFB] politics is great…

[FicChaNineteen]

Found out tonight that [FicChaTwoBee] advocates outsourcing the [MCFLMosFB] quarterly newsletter. [FicChaTwoBee] is [FC02C]'s best friend & the [CRA] television director. [FicChaThirteen] & I saw that [FicChaTwoBee] was a [FicChaTwentySix] [FicChaTwentyOne] girl . . . .

[FicChaNineteen]

Please see the letter from [CMFLMosFB] newsletter [FicChaOneA]. A few days ago a resident of xxxxxx Ave obtained, via a public records request all the email addresses of [MCFLMosFB] citizens who signed up to be on distribution for an electronic copy of the [MCFLMosFB] quarterly newsletter publication. It was the ONLY request for this information received by [MCFLMosFB]. As required by law, [MCFLMosFB] provided the email information.

Today, those email addresses received derogatory information about a candidate for [CC] election. The "from" email address looked like a very "official source" but it is not. I am sending this out to the [FBResMailGrp] to ensure widest dissemination of this alert.

(End [FicChaTwelve] [CC] campaign meeting)

[MCFLMosFB] Correspondence

October 4, 12

Dear Residents:

It has come to the attention of [MCFLMosFB] that a group email was sent out recently to residents who signed up to receive the [MCFLMosFB] quarterly newsletter. This email was not sent by, or on behalf of, [MCFLMosFB]. All [MCFLMosFB] emails end with @fujiwharabeach.org.

It was generated by a private individual with no sanction from or by [MCFLMosFB]. This was not sent from a [MCFLMosFB] email address.

If you choose, you may be able to block future emails from the originator of the private email (contact@fujiwharabeachupdates. com). Please contact [MCFLMosFB] city clerk at {[MCFLMosFB] CClk@fujiwharabeach.org or [MCFLMosFB] Information Systems Specialist at [MCFLMosFB]IIS@fujiwharabeach.org for any future concerns you may need addressed on this issue. We apologize for any confusion.

Respectfully,
[CMFLMosFB] newsletter [FicChaOneA]


(EndTrans [MCFLMosFB] correspondence

(Begin [FicChaTwelve] [FCCFLMosFB] campaign press release)

"A Case for the New Guy" By [TGTDTT]

This November, the voters of [MCFLMosFB] have the opportunity to place three (3) relatively new people on [CC]. The other three candidates previously held seats on [CC] as recently as five years ago and in one case, over a decade age. Realizing that most [MCFLMosFB} voters do not have a first-hand personal relationship with all of the candidates, myself included, the decision as to who we vote for is largely based on analyzing the odds as to what will likely yield the best outcome for [MCFLMosFB]. When I considered the question as to my vote this election, the following factors guided my thinking.

1.  Generationaly, the "new" candidates, all of which are accomplished professionals and committed to [PubServ], see the world as it is now and are accustomed to using modern approaches and tools to analyzing problems and developing solutions.
2.  Based on what I have learned from all of the public statements made by the candidates, the "new" candidates believe strongly in the active participation of [MCFLMosFB] citizens to bring about positive change where the "not new" candidates have positioned themselves as serving a niche demographic or as an independent that knows what is best for us.
3.  The three "new" candidates run on a campaign that speaks to the issues [MCFLMosFB] is facing and discussing the various positive measures to address those issues. The "not new" candidates demonstrate they have neither an appreciation for the issues [MCFLMosFB] is facing nor any solutions to proffer. Instead, the "not new" candidates enlist the support of anonymous authors in a "fear and

smear campaign" which is perhaps an attempt to bring forth the worst in [MFCU] behavior instead of appealing to our sensibilities.

I am a [MCFLMosFB] citizens, a [MCFLMosFB] voter, and both a [OwnProp] and [OwnBus] in [MCFLMosFB]. In the fifteen years I lived in [MCFLMosFB], I made friends and built a good life for my family. It is my personal belief that those who treat people with respect are better [PubServ]s than those who malign others. I am convinced that those who demonstrate an understanding of specific issues that we face tend to make better decisions than those who turn a blind eye to the matter or push it off as being someone else's responsibility. And last, but not least, there is no value in returning to office those who have raised our taxes, put [MCFLMosFB] in debt, and made us vulnerable to legal action.

Nobody is perfect. Most of us are good people who want what is best for our families, friends, neighbors, and [MCFLMosFB]. In my travels and meetings with [FicChaTwelve], [FicChaFourteen], and [FicChaFifteen], it clear to me that they are good people and share the values that will make [MCFLMosFB] and all [MCFLMosFB] citizens happier and healthier. After seeing the public behavior of [FicChaTwenty], reviewing the performance of [FicChaTwentySix] and [FicChaTwentySeven], and reading the anonymous letters and blog postings of their supporters, it is difficult to believe that allowing them to be on [CC] will make anything better.

Please do your homework when deciding who to vote for in this election. Understand that [FicChaTwenty], [FicChaTwentySix], and [FicChaTwentySeven] have all actively lobbied to raise Ad Valorem Tax Millage Rate and use funds [OptProj]. [FicChaTwelve] and [FicChaFourteen] have reduced the Ad

Valorem Tax Millage Rate and inspired [MCFLMosFB] to improve practices without reducing [MCFLMosFB] service levels and capability. [FicChaFifteen] is an educated, intelligent, and decent person whose professional life has been finding sensible solutions for complex managerial and technical problems. When I think about who I want making decisions affecting my life, [FicChaTwelve], [FicChaFourteen], and [FicChaFifteen] seem a far better, common-sense choice.

CC: [MCFLMosFB] quarterly newsletter, [FBResMailGrp], [FlaTo], Hometown News

(End [FicChaTwelve] [FCCFLMosFB] campaign press release)

# [FBWC] Candidate Forum 12

(BeginTrans [MCFLMosFB] update)

Wednesday, October 03, 12 10:56 PM
Subject: [CC] candidate Update
Greetings to you [MCFLMosFB] citizens:

This is a message to share some revealing information with you and it has to do with a sitting [CC] member who is running for re-election – [FicChaFourteen].

In reading the [MCFLMosFB] quarterly newsletter that was just published and mailed, [FicChaFourteen] had a couple of quotes in his candidate piece: "I take my responsibilities seriously to make decisions for [MCFLMosFB]. . ."

Another quote "Rest assured, [MCFLMosFB] is in good hands and I hope to continue. . ."

There are a few things people need to know about [FicChaFourteen]: One would expect a [CC] member, after taking the oath of office, would set the highest ethical, honesty and behavior standards. Outlined below are factual items outlining [FicChaFourteen]'s violations and evasions of those standards. All of these occurred while [FicChaFourteen] has been a sitting [CC] member in his current term! Here is a summary of some of [FicChaFourteen] violations:

[FicChaFourteen] is habitually delinquent in paying his [MCFLMosFB] Business Tax for the business he conducts from his residence. (Sec. 58-93 and 96) Was delinquent in paying his [GovFLMos] Business Tax. (Fined 3/16/12)

[FicChaFourteen] has allowed his [GovFLMos] Contractors License to lapse and continued to do business without valid licensing.

[FicChaFourteen] was caught contracting without a license on March 15th 12 and issued a $250 citation by The County. (Operated without a license for 6 ½ months before being caught (8/31/11 to 3/15/12.)

[FicChaFourteen], during that same time, operated as a contractor without a valid certificate of insurance as required by law.

[FicChaFourteen] filed his 11 Florida Corporation Report and fees one year late on March 15th 12, the same date he filed the 12 Annual Report, which was required in order to renew his Contractors License.

[FicChaFourteen] defrauded [MCFLMosFB] of permit fees by installing windows in his home without a building permit as required by Florida Building Code and [MCFLMosFB] Code.

[FicChaFourteen] on July 27th 11, again attempted to defraud [MCFLMosFB] of permit fees when he and a licensed certified general contractor were caught installing sliding glass doors at his residence without a building permit.

Documentation on each of the above violations is on file with [MCFLMosFB] city clerk.

Do you think [FicChaFourteen] understands and respects the oath of office he took?

Is competent to manage [MCFLMosFB] Business?

Should be making decisions that affect over 10,000 [MCFLMosFB] citizens including you?

These are not just accusations . . . [MCFLMosFB] city clerk has documentation on each of the infractions listed above. Honesty and Integrity by our elected officials is a MUST!

[FicChaFourteen] has never addressed the infractions that he has committed during the period he has been a sitting [CC] member. [FicChaFourteen] has never denied any of them, [FicChaFourteen] has never explained any of them, [FicChaFourteen] has never apologized for any of them and when

[FicChaFourteen] was confronted with them at a [CC] meeting [FicChaFourteen] proudly gestured to those present that [FicChaFourteen] is the one being described.

Thanks for taking the time to read this!

(End Trans [MCFLMosFB] update)


(BeginTrans [FBResMailGrp])

There are two political forums scheduled this month, both on different dates at [TSCMuniCom]. Both will begin at 7PM.

16 October: [FBWC] Candidate Forum 12 hosted by the [MosConCoa] and moderated by [MicBil], Talk Radio Professional at Clear Channel Radio.

23 October: [FBWC] Candidate Forum 12 hosted by the [FBWC] (a moderator has been selected but not identified).

All candidates for [CC] [FB], Mayor and [CC] member are invited to attend. [FicChaTwelve] sent an affirmative RSVP to both events. [FicChaTwelve] hopes you try to attend both, too!

Best Regards,
[CC] candidate [FicChaTwelve]

(End Trans [FBResMailGrp])


(Begin [FicChaTwenty] [MCLMosFB] campaign meeting)

Thursday, October 08, 12 8:41 AM
Subject: [FBWC] Candidate Forum 12

[FicChaTwenty][FicChaTwentyOne][FicChaTwentyTwo]
[FicChaTwentyThree][FicChaTwentySix][FicChaTwentySeven]
[FicChaTwoBee][FC02C]

[FicChaTwenty]    Hi, Everyone.

There is some confusion regarding the [CC] candidate forum. Here's what's happening. A local Tea Party group has scheduled a forum for [CC] candidates at our [TSCMuniCom] on Tuesday, October 16. The sponsoring group is [MosConCoa], with [WhiRob] supposedly the man in charge. [MosConCoa] does not appear to be registered anywhere, but [WhiRob] is shown as the registered agent and chairperson of the [LCF], the Tea Party group that spent thousands of dollars on [CC] Election 11 last November (resulting in the election of [FicChaTen] and [FicChaThirty]) and is spending more large sums this year to get [FicChaTwelve] and [FicChaFourteen] elected. Their forum was arranged by [FicChaEleven] and it is being moderated by the uber-biased [MicBil] (it's hard to use any part of the word "moderate" in any sentence with "[MicBil]")! It doesn't take a rocket scientist to recognize the purpose and inevitable outcome of this outside group's forum.

[MCFLMosFB]'s traditional candidates forum sponsored by the [FBWC] since around 1975 will be held at the [TSCMuniCom] on Tuesday, October 23, at 7 pm. (This forum had already been scheduled when [FicChaTen] scheduled [FBWC] Candidate Forum 12 ahead of this one undoubtedly to steal [FBWC]'s thunder.) Out of respect to the [FBWC] and their tireless efforts each election year to host an impartial forum, this is the forum that [FicChaTwentySeven], [FicChaTwentySix], and I will be participating in.

Please help get the word out that [FBWC] Candidate Forum 12 is the effort of an outside group once again trying to impose its agenda on [MCFLMosFB]. [FBWC] Candidate Forum 12 is not a legitimate, unbiased forum.

Please also help get the word out that our traditional [MCFLMosFB] forum will, as always, be presented by the [FBWC] on October 23 at 7 pm at the [TSCMuniCom].

Candidates [FicChaTwenty], [FicChaTwentySix], and [FicChaTwentySeven] will attend [FBWC] Candidate Forum 12 but will not attend [FBWC] Candidate Forum 12

```
(End [FicChaTwenty] [MCFLMosFB] campaign meeting)
```

Monday, October 08, YR12 3:25 PM

[FicChaTen][FicChaEleven][FicChaTwelve][FicChaThirteen][FicChaNineteen]

Subject: Candidate Forum

[FicChaTwelve]        Looks like [FicChaFiftyOne] just got an e-ear full!!

[FicChaTwelve]        Look what she wrote . . . and then what [FicChaFiftyTwo] said in response!

```
[FicChaFiftyOne] wrote:

Dear friends of [MCFLMosFB]:

Over the past year, many changes have been happening
to our town. Our [CM] has left after 27 years of
excellent  service.  Professional  Fire  Firefighters
of  [MCFLMosFB]  have  felt  the  need  to  form  a  union
```

for the first time to protect their jobs since the incorporation of [MCFLMosFB].

Several of our long-time [EMP]s are looking for other positions or early retirement and the [FD] head, [MCFLMosFB] has had officers leave. The face of [MCFLMosFB] is changing, and not for the better.

As a former [CC] member, I have heard myself and other members of past [CC]s and [MCFLMosFB] [EMP]s being accused of everything from misappropriations of funds, fiscal irresponsibility and mismanagement from the current [CC]. Every year [MCFLMosFB] goes through an internal audit and an external audit by a private company.

[MCFLMosFB] records are also reviewed by the County, the State of Florida and because we received some Federal funding, records are reviewed by them also. In the history of [MCFLMosFB], NO fiscal mismanagement has every occurred by anyone.

There is a standard called "Best Practices" established by these governing bodies for all [GVBMNT] agencies to follow. So, whatever the "best practices" that were in place were the rules [MCFLMosFB] followed. This current [CC] has been looking for a "smoking gun," even hiring an expensive forensic auditor (with your tax dollars), to prove this theory.

They have found nothing! The results have been that [MCFLMosFB] followed the "Best Practices" that were in place at the time.

This current [CC] has stated that they want to hire a person to handle [MCFLMosFB] events by funding the position through the [CRA]. These are the same traditions that have been in place for over 37 years, and "handled" by volunteers. [FBWC] is a non-profit service organization that spends every dollar they raise to help others, mostly in this community. Our Founder's Day/Marketplace is one item [CC] wants to replace. It appears that the next, is the [FBWC] annual hosting of a non-partisan political forum. Every election, these volunteers provide an unbiased environment where the candidates can come and meet our citizens, present their ideas and answer questions in a polite civil arena.

[FicChaEleven] has decided this is not enough, she has taken it upon herself, with the assistance of the [LCF], to provide a separate event. The [LCF], a libertarian group that has formed a political PAC, has brought its funds from outside our [MCFLMosFB] to help influence our elections. This is not the unbiased forum that we, as Residents, have received from the [FBWC].

The Conservative Coalition is funded and run by the [LCF]. [MicBil], is by no means a non-partisan person, but rather a main participate in this group.

Fair and balanced, I think not.

[FicChaFiftyOne]

Proud resident of [MCFLMosFB]


(Begin Reply)

[FicChaTwelve] [FicChaFiftyOne] [FicChaFiftyTwo]
Monday, October 08, 12 12:22 PM
Subject: Re: candidate Forum

I do not know from where you got my email address.

I assume it was legally obtained, but legal does not equate to 'desired.'

REMOVE ME FROM any FUTURE MAILINGS.

DELETE MY ADDRESS.

DO not GIVE IT to ANYONE ELSE.

GIVE THESE INSTRUCTIONS to WHOMEVER YOU GOT MY ADDRESS
FROM and to ANYONE YOU MAY HAVE ALREADY TRANSFERRED
IT TO.

Yes, I =do= accuse prior [CC]s of irresponsibility
and mismanagement.

One has to look only at the monstrously increased
debt and unfunded (impossible to pay) liabilities
to prove that.

And the mismanagement through 'illegal' use of
[CRA] funds even adds to the clear conclusion of
mismanagement, if not malfeasance. At the very least,
previous [CC]s did not exercise due diligence. Of
that, there is no question whatsoever.

Do not fail to comply with my instructions above. You
do not have my permission to use my address for any
purposes whatsoever. If such permission was implicit
in its existence at other places, that permission
is now explicitly withdrawn.

(End Reply)


(BeginTrans [FBResMailGrp])

October 9, 12

Received word that [CC] candidates [FicChaTwenty],
[FicChaTwentySix], and [FicChaTwentySeven] will not

attend the 16 October [FBWC] Candidate Forum 12 Forum. [FicChaTwentySix] said he has been "a long supporter of [FBWC] and believes this local organization should receive the utmost in community support".

I'm not sure why these candidates can't attend two forums (a week apart) and it seems almost unbelievable that all THREE of these candidates can't attend BOTH forums. I (for one) plan to be at both . . . and look forward to questions regarding [MCFLMosFB] and its future.

Please pass the word to your friends and neighbors in [MCFLMosFB] that TWO forums gives you TWICE the opportunity to hear the candidates' positions on a variety of topics.

Best Regards,
[CC] candidate [FicChaTwelve]

(EndTrans [FBResMailGrp])


(BeginTrans [FBResMailGrp])

October 14, 12

Our upbeat campaign message continues to resonate with voters across [MCFLMosFB]. Our weekend contact with Residents at hundreds of homes returned great ideas, resounding support, and a clear message: We [LOVE] your positive campaign and we are grateful for [CC] achievements.

November 6th is fast approaching...please encourage everyone you know to come out and vote...it's really that important!

All the best,
[CC] candidate [FicChaTwelve]

(EndTrans [FBResMailGrp])

(BeginTrans [FBResMailGrp])

October 15, 12

Greetings [FBResMailGrp]!

The first of two candidate forums will be held tomorrow night at [TSCMuniCom] at 7PM at City Hall.

[MicBil] will moderate the forum. All [CC] candidates for mayor and [CC] were invited to attend. There will be plenty of seating and of course it's free and open to the public.

I know the Presidential Debate starts at 9PM, but this will conclude in plenty of time for you to go home for the debate.

Hope to see you there!
[CC] candidate [FicChaTwelve]

(EndTrans [FBResMailGrp])

## October 16, YR12

| | |
|---|---|
| Producer: | Cue Theme Music. Go to Camera 1 |
| Your Host: | Welcome to [FBWC] Candidate Forum 12. Tonight we come to you from [TSCMuniCom] where, for the first time in the history of [MCFLMosFB], an alternative or additional moderated forum is being offered to the people. This forum is brought to you by [LCF]. Let's turn the program over to this evening's moderator, talk show radio personality [MicBil]. |

[MicBil]

Good evening everyone. It is my sincere pleasure and honor to be facilitating tonight's conversation with those seeking elected office and the good people that will be voting for them.

The fact that all of you in the auditorium audience see six chairs and only three candidates is something I hope everybody takes a moment to think about. What does it say about the people who want your vote but are not willing to take the time to tell you why they deserve it.

We do have three of the six candidates seeking seats on [CC] with us this evening. Let's just go down the line and introduce yourself to the audience.

[FicChaTwelve]

Hello everybody. I'm [FicChaTwelve] and running to retain my seat on [CC]. Most of you know that I was appointed to [CC] five months ago after the unfortunate passing of [FicChaEighteen]. It was never my intent to seek public office and I had no intention of running in this election until I looked around and there was no one else standing up for what I think is important. Important to me and every person in this audience.

[FicChaFourteen]

Uh hello. Good Evening. As I am sure all of you know, I'm [FicChaFourteen] and I am seeking re-election to [CC]. In the first two years of my first term, I was a lone voice that spoke to deaf ears. I have felt better about my service to the community in this last year than I ever thought possible. With the exception of a few people that have acted like jackasses, the job a [CC] member is almost fun.

[FicChaFifteen]

Good Evening. I am [FicChaFifteen] and I am running for Mayor. My wife and I moved to this community after leaving [USN], and I am a program manager of several multi-million dollar federal defense contracts. The issues before [MCFLMosFB] can be as technical as the programs I manage already. My decision to run for [CC] [FB], Mayor is based on the fact that [MCFLMosFB] could use some young and proven brainpower.

[MicBil]

Thank you. Let's ease into the single issue that you will fight for if elected to [CC].

[FicChaTwelve]

That's easy. The single issue is transparency. We cannot expect to do anything together as a community until the community can at least see what is going on. There is not a single other thing that we must do that would not be done better if everyone knew all of the facts and was invited to be a part of the solution. This is especially true for questions concerning Recreation Departments, Police Departments, Newsletters, Disaster Recovery, City [EMP] Pension Commitments, and so much more.

In my travels throughout this city, going door to door to meet with as many people as possible, I have become all too aware of a few things that full transparency would relax. The first is the constant questioning of why something was done. The second is the cry of how it got that way. The third is: What is the best thing to do to make things better?

I served [USAF] for 24 years and rose to the rank of Command Master Sergeant. There were times when I was directly responsible for mission success, which always included saving lives. There were times when my job was to make sure the generals had all of the information needed to plan successful missions and save lives. During those magnificent years in which I traveled the world, met the love of my life, and raised three magnificent children, there is one lesson that has served me well in my military, professional, and personal lives. That lesson is to be absolutely honest and forthcoming with everyone who has a personal stake in the outcome of a decision so that there are no surprises.

[FicChaFourteen]

The single issue I will fight for is civility in how we treat each other. I am so sick of people acting like immature little babies. When I am visiting my customers, I have over nine hundred customers, they tell me that they are sick of it too. These stupid immature people need to stop stealing signs, writing anonymous letters, threatening people. It makes me sick.

[FicChaFifteen]

I am in a constant pursuit of optimum processes that produce the desired or expected result in the most cost effective manner possible. Right now, the long term and the short term planning boards do not meet at or near the same time, which results in significant delays in processing requests. A home owner or a land developer could wait six months to a year in a decision that could have gotten the same approvals in a much shorter period of time. Changing the meeting times or anything about how the boards operate can only be done by leadership on the [CC].

[MicBil]

Do you have anything you would like to add [FicChaTwenty]? How about you [FicChaTwentySix]? What do ya say there [FicChaTwentySeven]? Nothing? That's right. The three of you can't answer the question in front of these fine people because you aren't here.

Sorry about that folks. Just couldn't help myself. Back to the task at hand. So [FicChaTwelve], [FicChaFourteen], and [FicChaFifteen], please name one municipal ordinance that you are willing to expend political capital to overturn.

[FicChaTwelve]        Huh?

[FicChaFourteen]      Could you repeat the question?

[FicChaFifteen]       Overturned completely? None come to mind. There are several that I wished had not been passed, but they were spending bills and that money is gone.

[MicBil]              Moving right along. There seems to be some confusion, well not confusion so much, as that every single person you ask has a different answer, about the annexed property to the north. What is your take on that matter?

[FicChaTwelve]        The decision to annex that property was not thought out at all. The only thing that did come out of it was the release of grant funds to pay for police and fire for a period of three years. That was almost ten years ago. So for seven years, the taxpayers of this city have been paying for the police and fire protection of about 150 acres of land that we have no control over the land's use. That property is controlled by [USAF] and they have no compelling reason to relinquish that control or to adjust their decisions regarding permissible usage.

[FicChaFourteen]      None of my customers, and I have over 900, understand why the heck the city annexed that property. I say we build a convention center and business complex to attract people and businesses.

[FicChaFifteen]

I have not really studied that question, but I concur that the general lack of agreement indicates an overall lack of understanding of what we should do next.

[MicBil]

Sounds good. Now it will come as no surprise to those of you in the audience that regularly listen to my show that I have reservations about any government office that is not constitutionally mandated and serves as just another expense to be paid by the taxpayer. These reservations include Economic Development Councils or Committees and Redevelopment Zones, more specifically, Community Redevelopment Agencies known as CRA's. My Question to the three of you that had the courage to be here tonight, Ah. Did it again. Sorry. Sorry. My question is "What is your understanding of the current situation in your CRA and what actions, if any, are you going to take?"

[FicChaTwelve]

Thank you for that question. I have been working to have the best answer any one could ever have to that question since YR07. In trying to understand the situation, I aroused a snake pit. Two of those snakes visited my employer with a story that I was using company resources to harass city [EMP]s and that my harassment was causing the [EMP]s to fear going to work or walking to their car. Two other snakes made sure the police knew when my car was within city limits and where it was located. Those same snakes made sure the on-duty officers would engage me in the hopes that I could be arrested or at least ticketed. As it turns out, they got lucky but not for the reasons they thought and it turned out to be all about nothing. There was another incident where one of the snakes is making public accusations that I accosted her or approached her in a threatening manner. All of these snakes that I am telling you about have a direct connection to [CRA]. All I have done is request information and forward that information to those who have expressed an interest. So I have lost my job, been arrested, and have had a second set of charges dropped because I made a series of public records requests. Ladies and gentlemen, take a good long look at the people who currently control [CRA] and jog your memory as to who used to control [CRA]. I had to find a new job and defend myself against false charges for asking [FicChaTwenty], [FicChaTwentySix], and their appointees a question. Are these the people you want on your [CC]? As it turns out, these snakes had good reason to be concerned.

The evidence showed a pretty creative interpretation of the rules concerning the distribution of [CRA] revenues. So after much discussion and actions between everybody who had any say so in the matter, [MCFLMosFB] is in the process of paying [CRA] an amount that will shut everybody up except the people who don't think the money should be paid back at all.

[FicChaFourteen]   I think were on the right track.

[FicChaFifteen]   The repayment matter is one that could have been decided either way. It is still unclear that a preponderance of evidence shows that the solution being implemented is the optimum solution. Financially, these matters always represent a financial loss due to the cost of defending your decision. In this case, the decision should not have been made and now we know why. In this case, the money in question ranges from 1.2 to 3 million [USD] and legal expense being incurred by the tax payer represent about 0.01% of the money to be paid back. If elected, the decisions I make will consider how much of your money am I willing to hand over to attorneys as well as how much of my own money I might have to give an attorney.

[MicBil]   Very good answer [FicChaFifteen], Longwinded as always [FicChaFourteen], and [FicChaTwelve] . . . don't be afraid to elaborate or just go off on some ridiculous tangent.

When I lived here, one of the topics that was being discussed then and is still being discussed is your fire and police departments. What say you [FicChaFourteen]?

[FicChaFourteen]    Huh. Me? I thought [FicChaTwelve] goes first. You caught me off guard. Okay, police, fire, yeah.

Let me just start by saying that I am extremely proud of our fire and police departments. Those people do an outstanding job. The idea of going back to a volunteer [FD] has been floated ever since the city implemented a professional [FD]. So far, no one has come up with a clear answer to that question so we will keep what we have until something better comes along.

[FicChaFifteen]    I don't believe there is serious effort behind either going to a volunteer [FD] or a contracted [FD] because no one really understands what the impact is.

[FicChaTwelve]    Where is the harm in asking if we can do something we are doing now in a smarter way? Why does simply asking the question cause people to draw meritless conclusions? The answer to both those questions is 'Fear'. Fear is the spawn of [EGO]. [EGO] is junk food to the human spirit and such must either be consumed or abandoned before truth can be revealed in all its glory and brilliance.

I ask my wife how she is doing every day. Most days she replies with a "Fine", some days she replies "Great!" Every now and then, especially during the holiday season, my birthday, and our wedding anniversary, she says "What? Nothing. Why do you want to know?"

So when I hear someone trying to avoid a simple question, my mind turns to all of the possibilities that my wife has chosen from in the past and will choose in the future. But then I remember that the question was about something else. Like the city's budget or if we are breaking the law.

My point is that if everything is out in the open and discussed in a calm rational way, then all questions are readily answered and everyone understands the answer. I realize that I am willing to give up being surprised about the good stuff if it means never being surprised by the bad stuff. What stuff you might ask. Well, the pensions and retirement benefits for the police officers, fire fighters, and city [EMP]s. These things are promises that elected officials have made. But they are also operational processes that require maintenance, renewal, revision, and in some cases, being discarded. The role of the elected official is to respect the promises of those who have held office previously and the needs of today. The role of the politician is to tell you that I love everything you love and dislike everything you dislike. If you elect me, I will make you proud. The role of the person who actually gets elected is to keep count of how many people have caught on to the fact that I was so full of crap during the campaign and really did not know what I was talking about.

[MicBil]

Note to self. Never ask [FicChaTwelve] an open-ended question ever again. It's getting late so let's say our goodbyes to the good people in the auditorium here with us tonight and the good people who have tuned in to see the broadcast of this discussion later this evening. I say we let [FicChaFifteen] be the first this time.

[FicChaFifteen]

My friends, family, co-workers have all known something for a long time that some of you are just now finding out. That is that I am a terrible public speaker. If the author of this book wasn't editing out all of my uhms and "you know"'s, the reader would know as well. But with that being said, do you really care that I come across as lost in thought? Are you not comforted that I am thinking at all.

I came from some place else and I haven't lived here all that long. Big deal. I have a big heart and a smart brain. I have to make really good decisions and communicate them in a really good way because I hate fighting. Everything about running a municipal corporation is based on two plus two equaling four. I don't see a lot of reason to get upset about that. If you vote for me, I will always tell you that two plus two is four if you ask me.

[FicChaFourteen]   I am out there every day talking to people. Some of you have seen me. I really care about what is going on and I make sure that your voice is represented on the [CC].

[FicChaTwelve]   I am here this evening telling anyone and everyone about a lesson I learned that has saved countless lives and kept my marriage as wonderful as it is. I love you sweetheart.

There is part of me that believes that the other members of the current council wanted me to teach that lesson to others. Which is why I was appointed [COFFEE] Chairperson and then to [CC] after [FicChaEighteen] passed away. A vote for me is the choice that you want that lesson taught to as many people as possible and practiced by as many people as possible.

[MicBil]   [FicChaTwelve], are you wearing an ear piece?

[FicChaTwelve]   No. Why"

[MicBil]   You really are starting to sound a great deal like [TGTDTT] and it is kind of freaking me out.

And it is on that note that I will call this forum to a close. To the candidates that showed up this evening and on my radio show this morning, I say thank you. Nobody knew what questions I was going to ask this evening but me. Every question I asked gave each participant the same opportunity to answer in the best way they know how. Everybody heard the questions and everybody heard the answers.

To everybody in the auditorium here tonight, please accept my thanks for the respect you showed the candidates and each other.

And a special thanks to [WhiRob] and [LCF] for making this all happen. Good night.

|  |  |
|---|---|
| Your Host: | Well folks, that is all the time we have. A special thank you to candidates for their riveting answers and [MicBil] for asking the riveting questions. I don't know what was so special about his questions. I could have aked those questions. I would have asked better questions. I'll show them. |
| Producer: | Dude. Get back on script. |
| Your Host: | Our sponsor this evening was [FBLC]. I do hope you enjoyed tonight's show. |

And remember, we let you know WHAT TO THINK ABOUT and WHAT TO THINK ABOUT what you think, so YOU DON'T HAVE TO. Good night. Aaaaaand, we're out.

Producer:            Do you want to explain that little whatever that was that just happened.

Your Host:           I just figure if [FBWC] thinks I am numero uno in their book, who does [FBLC] think they are bringing in [MicBil].

Producer:            What does the Fujiwhara Beach Lions Club have to do with any of this?

Your Host:           Well that is just fine. It will be my turn at the podium this time next week. I'll show this town how to really ask a serious question.

# [FBWC] Candidate Forum 12

(BeginTrans [FBResMailGrp])

October 17, 12

There are lots of interesting items on the agenda tonight; so if you can attend, please do! City Hall . . .PM.

Our contract auditors will present their response to our independent auditor's compliance findings

There will be discussion about the Storm water Utility Fund

[CA] will discuss the releasing of private email addresses you provided to [MCFLMosFB]

The second reading takes place of Ordinance 1058 imposing a moratorium on [MCFLMosFB] sign code imposing a moratorium on sign code enforcement (if/when it passes, the moratorium goes into effect)

There will be presentation on the operating cost s of the Community Center…there might be discussion on this one

There will be a Skate & Dog Park update (discussing cost s, liability, etc.)

Ordinance 1062 will come up for its first reading. This ordinance defines how [MCFLMosFB] goes out for bids (RFPs) for contracts

We'll discuss our Fiscal Year (FY) 4th Quarter [B] fiscal year 12-13 Amendment—this sort of closes out the books on our FY12 [B] fiscal year 12-13 year

[CCMFLMosFB] candidate [FicChaTwelve]

(EndTrans [FBResMailGrp])

(BeginTrans)

(BeginTrans [FBResMailGrp])

October 18, 12

If you have campaign signs out in your yards (or your neighbors do), please pass the word to bring them in for Halloween night. Past campaigns experienced a 25% loss rate on signs during this single event.

[CCMFLMosFB] candidate [FicChaTwelve]

(EndTrans [FBResMailGrp])

(BeginTrans [FBResMailGrp])

October 19, 12

Greetings [FBResMailGrp],
Wednesday's meeting concluded around 9:30PM.

Contract Auditors presented their response to our independent auditor's compliance findings. They basically said that the way the retirement funds were reported wasn't necessarily the best way to do it, there wasn't anything improper.

The [MCFLMosFB] quarterly newsletter email address was a lawful public records release. The only way to protect email addresses you provide to [MCFLMosFB] would be to have a 3rd party maintain the email addresses and send out electronic copies from there (much like what [FicChaTwelve] does with this [FBResMailGrp]).

Ordinance 1058 imposing a moratorium on [MCFLMosFB] sign code passed and it goes into effect immediately. You still have to get a permit for your signs, but there is no fee.

The costs of the community Center were discussed at length. [PW] Head, [MCFLMosFB] is going to recalculate based on hours used...more to follow.

Lots of folks commented on the Dog Park and Skate Park. It was agreed to keep both parks monitored for the next six months and to have [COFFEE] research options and present them to [CC].

Ordinance 1062 was scrapped. This ordinance was supposed to establish a local business preference process.

The Rec Department is trying to get another 24-foot pontoon boat and motor. The cost is going to be somewhere between $6,000 and $9,000...however, this cost was not planned for in [B] fiscal year 12-13. The boat is used to ferry folks to [MCFLMosFB] recreational area S. Island on weekends to perform trail maintenance and invasive species removal. If you know of someone who has a pontoon boat they'd like to donate, let me know!

[CCMFLMosFB] candidate [FicChaTwelve]

(EndTrans [FBResMailGrp])

(Begin [FicChaTwelve] MCFLMosFB] campaign meeting)

Subject: candidate Forum

Monday, October 22, 12 10:22 AM

[FicChaTen][FicChaEleven][FicChaTwelve][FicChaThirteen]
[FicChaFourteen][FicChaFifteen][FicChaThirtyOne]Cahn
Pollock

| | |
|---|---|
| Cahn Pollock | (On his cell phone) Thanks for the clarification. If they said [LCF] made a contribution, then, that would be an outright lie and an elections violation. |
| [FicChaEleven] | As far as I can tell, the only person who has said the [LCF] is contributing [USD] to the candidates is [FicChaTwentyThree]. The candidates have only said they are contributing to the election. That could mean anything I would think and becomes – he meant-she meant. Going down that road would distract from the message and confuse the issue. It would move the focus from where [MCFLMosFB] is today and why. |
| Cahn Pollock | My two cents: trying to demonize some conservative committee in a mostly Republican [MCFLMosFB] is a non-starter. So, don't give the cabal's rants a second thought. |

| | |
|---|---|
| [FicChaEleven] | If we let them know that it is bothersome or worries people they will hit it hard. It will probably be something that they use in a last minute mailer. |
| [FicChaFifteen] | So, I think any mailer should redirect the focus back to what is the real issue here. Our debt, saving [MCFLMosFB], keeping the ability to continue the services everyone loves, being fiscally responsible, being environmentally sound, and protecting [EMP]'s jobs and pensions . . . |
| Cahn Pollock | Just my opinion but they are looking for justification to go negative on you guys that is not character based because so far that has not worked. One response to the Conservative Coalition being an outside group is it is an entity that is made up of 3 groups and a number of the members of two of these groups are [MCFLMosFB] citizens. The coalition simply sponsored the event. The forum did not support or promote their beliefs or agenda. Most of the audience was comprised of [MCFLMosFB] citizens. Do not allow them to turn this into an election issue. Keep hammering that they did not show up. What does that say about them? Who cares who sponsored it or how many forums there were? |
| Cahn Pollock | Another point is the [FBWC] is composed of approximately 69 members with 2/3 [MCFLMosFB] citizens and 1/3 non-Residents. 12 of the 69 members according |

to my handbook are honorary members with 11 of them living in FB. So why is that organization so much more legitimate as an [FB] only org? Just because of the name? Again, they are looking for something to make people run away from you guys because they are not getting the support they need based on their record.

[FicChaEleven]   Need to stay friendly, positive, confident, and welcoming tomorrow night.

[FicChaThirteen]   Just show how [MCFLMosFB] is in a tough spot and you guys have the right skills, experience, and desire to get us back on the right track. If they try to tie the [LCF] in somehow in a question at the forum, it is easy for you guys. They have not contributed to your campaign and you are a [CC] candidate who was invited to a forum to meet [MCFLMosFB] voters you are asking to vote for you and answer their questions so you felt it important to be there. Since you represent everyone in [MCFLMosFB] and feel you need to be responsive to the [MCFLMosFB] voter's NEEDS and not YOUR OWN, you will appear whenever you are invited, and regardless of who is inviting you. You think that is important. If the citizens feel they need more than one opportunity to hear your views then that should be the driving factor not who has provided that opportunity.

| | |
|---|---|
| [FicChaEleven] | Do not let them control the dialogue or force you guys off your message. |
| Cahn Pollock | Decide what you want to get across or present and then tailor your answers to do that. Like [FicChaEleven] said, answer the question succinctly and then provide the info that benefits you. Make them go on the defensive. [FicChaTwenty] will get irate and be her normal unlikable self, [FicChaTwentySeven] will be at a loss, and [FicChaTwentySix] will be the only one who has a chance of not totally imploding. Keep him trying to keep up with you guys and he will not have the chance to stick to just the script they have been working on. He is not quick on his feet when extemporaneously speaking. |

(BeginTrans [FBResMailGrp])

Greeting [FBResMailGrp],

The second political forum, [FBWC] Candidate Forum 12, will be held at City Hall at 7PM tomorrow night. All candidates who are running for [GVBMNTFL], [GovFLMos], and [MCFLMosFB] elections were invited.

I'll be there…and I hope you make it, too!

[CCMFLMosFB] candidate [FicChaTwelve]

(EndTrans [FBResMailGrp])

(BeginTrans)

Fellow [MCFLMosFB]ers-

[FBWC] Candidate Forum 12 will occur tomorrow night at 7PM at [TSCMuniCom].

This will be the third and final mass opportunity to listen to your candidates and question them on positions (the WCCR-AM interviews and the first FB political forum being the first two). Hopefully, [FicChaTwentySix], [FicChaTwentySeven] and [FicChaTwenty] will show up for the first time to speak with us.

[CC] member [FicChaTen]

(EndTrans)

(BeginTrans [FBResMailGrp])

October 23, 12

[FBWC] Candidate Forum 12 is tonight at 7PM at [TSCMuniCom].

If you can, please bring a non-perishable food item to donate for their World Food Day Drive.

[CC] candidate [FicChaTwelve]

(EndTrans [FBResMailGrp])

[FBWCMbr]:     Hello. Ladies and Gentlemen - Could I have your attention for a moment before we get started?

[FBWC] invited candidates running in [USFG], [GVBMNTFL], and

[GovFLMos] elections as well as [CC] and almost all of the candidates accepted. Therefore we are going to have sessions. The first session will be [CC]. The second session will be [GovFLMos] and the third session will be the remaining two candidates who are running for [GVBMNTFL] and [USFG] offices.

[FicChaTwelve]: (Speaking into a microphone on stage to the crowd) Good evening good people. Show of hands. How many of you have already made up your minds?

Most of the hands in the audience go up.

[FicChaTwelve]: (Still speaking into the microphone) Yep. That is what I thought. Well, I do hope you enjoy the show.

Producer: Cue Theme Music. Go to Camera 1

Your Host: Welcome to [FBWC] Candidate Forum 12. This year, there are four candidates vying to fill two [CC] seats and two candidates running for Mayor. One candidate is seeking re-election, one candidate was appointed to [CC] and is asking the voters to keep him there, three of the candidates are either former [CC] members or Mayor, or both, and one of the candidate's is a first timer. Let's meet the candidates.

[FicChaTwelve] Good Evening. I'm [FicChaTwelve] and I am a [CC] candidate.

| | |
|---|---|
| Crowd: | Hi [FicChaTwelve]. |
| [FicChaTwelve] | I come to you today as a man whose wickedness has been broken. Like you, I am not perfect. None of us are. And that includes everybody else up on this stage. I can tell you that I believe I am different from at least two of my distinguished colleagues on which I currently share the stage in that I know that I have things to learn and I will admit that I do not know something. That is why my voice has to include your voice. Asymptotically, we approach a full brain. I would no sooner make a decision for you than I would flap my arms in an effort to stop the wind. |
| | As crazy as it sounds, this is what everybody in this room is trying to choose between. One choice is people who will make decisions for us. The other choice is people who will make decisions with us. |
| | Three of the candidates sharing this stage with me decided that we needed to create another layer of government that is empowered to incur debt that is not approved by the taxpayers but is the taxpayer's responsibility to pay back. |
| Your Host: | Thank [FicChaTwelve] but your time is up. |
| [FicChaTwelve]: | Relax there Skippy. As I was saying, the stage has six people on it. Three of the |

people know what is best for you. Three of the people know that working together brings out the best in people. If you want to know who is who, just take a look at their faces right now. Three people look a little pissed off, two people are trying not to laugh, and I am the one talking. So now go vote.

[FicChaTwenty]

"There is no debt except the Rec Center" and "The [CRA] debt is not really debt". [FicChaTwentySix] says more development will save [MCFLMosFB]. I have had it up to here with you and your TEA Party fanatics trying to rip this city apart. A city that I love and have given so much of my time and energy into making it a model community that we can all be proud of.

Your Host:

[FicChaTwenty]. Ma'am. It is not your turn yet.

[FicChaTwenty]

Put a sock in it. Before you people came here, life was just fine. Now you think you know what is best for my city. Well I don't think you do. I don't think any of you do. [FicChaTwelve], [FicChaFourteen], and this new kid have no idea how to behave and represent my city with dignity. Instead, you three go around trying to embarrass us. You and your Tea Party carpetbaggers have made life hellish for the good employees of my city.

[FicChaFourteen]    That is so wrong. What is it with you and [FicChaTwentySix] trying to keep everything a secret? The two of you have been behind every effort to prevent the publishing of public documents.

[FicChaTwentySix]    Hold on just a second. Don't you try and lump me in with [FicChaTwenty] like we are of one mind or something. Every decision I have made on behalf of the city has been with the intent of making this city a safer place to live where fewer people fall down.

[FicChaFifteen]    Good Evening. I am [FicChaFifteen] and I am running for Mayor. My wife and I moved to this community after leaving [USN] and I am a program manager of several multi-million dollar federal defense contracts. The issues before [MCFLMosFB] can be as technical as the programs I manage already but usually are not. My decision to run for Mayor is based on the fact that [MCFLMosFB] could use some young and proven brain power.

[FicChaTwentySeven]    (Reading from note card) I see the biggest challenge facing our city is budgeting for services and infrastructure repairs. My priorities will be to maintain quality of life and the city services our residents want, find additional sources of revenue to help fund those services, increase our tax base to lower property taxes, and create a business-friendly environment to attract new environmentally clean businesses. My other priorities include strategic budget planning, and taking the necessary steps to insure that funds are available for repairs to the infrastructure of the city for now and the future. To accomplish these goals, I would appreciate your vote on Nov. 6.

Your Host: Well okay then. What do say we move on to the audience questions where every member of the audience had the chance to complete a question card. The questions asked will be selected totally at "random". So the first question from a member of our audience that all the candidates must answer is, "What is your favorite thing about [FB]?"

[FicChaFourteen] I have had the honor of being one of your elected representatives the past three years. I take my responsibility seriously to make decisions for our [MCFLMosFB] that will affect all of us in the short and long terms. Economic times are tough and all the members of the sitting [CC] work very hard every day to insure the stability of our [MCFLMosFB]. Great strides have been made by the current council to implement efficiencies, streamline costs, and encourage new ideas and faces to participate in [MCFLMosFB]'s governance. Due to these efforts, next year's budget will include a reduced tax rate, increased debt pay down, and a large amount of cash being added to the dangerously dwindled reserve fund. We are moving forward to insure the long-term growth and sustainability of [MCFLMosFB]. Rest assured, YOUR [MCFLMosFB] is in good hands and I hope to continue on this path of stability and prosperity for our community.

[FicChaFifteen]

Since 1960 the population of [MCFLMosFB] has grown from 800 to over 10,000. We enjoy high quality services and we need to plan and budget as we grow. [MCFLMosFB] finances have not been managed efficiently to include under funded pensions and mismanaged debt. [CC] has been cleaning up [MCFLMosFB] books and incorporating efficiencies, but much work remains. I will use my knowledge of government and business to lead the next Council to put our [MCFLMosFB] on solid financial ground.

My qualifications include an MBA and Project Management experience. In council meetings I have demonstrated how technology makes government more open, efficient and accessible. I will put my 25 years in the U.S. Navy and corporate world to work for [MCFLMosFB].

My wife of 21 years and three talented kids provide me the motivation to ensure our [MCFLMosFB] is fiscally healthy for years to come. I promise a commitment to ethical leadership and teamwork – where residents are encouraged to share their vision and business owners feel welcome.

[FicChaTwenty]

The importance of November's [CC] elections cannot be overstated, because the fundamental nature of my [MCFLMosFB] is at stake. Voters will decide whether to restore the progressive [MCFLMosFB] which brought us all here or continue along the path started by [CC] majority this year to change who we are. While some changes are necessary to deal with economic realities caused by the struggling economy, I believe that tearing the place apart is not the solution. Looking forward, we need to resolve our fiscal challenges, encourage business growth in our [MCFLMosFB]'s north end, plan for needed capital projects, and ensure that [MCFLMosFB] [EMP]s have the resources and training to ably perform their jobs. We must rebuild our [MCFLMosFB]'s reputation, honor [MCFLMosFB] agreements with other agencies, respect our [MCFLMosFB] [EMP]s, welcome experienced [MCFLMosFB] volunteers, and preserve our quality of life. More than ever, [MCFLMosFB] needs forward-thinking, knowledgeable, [MCFLMosFB]-friendly leadership. Through two decades of [MCFLMosFB] leadership positions (including [CC]), I believe I've demonstrated the ability needed to help restore my [MCFLMosFB].

[FicChaTwentySix] I am grateful for all that [MCFLMosFB] has become in its short 50 years. For the past several months, I have spoken with residents regarding their vision for the future and what they believe the goal of [CC] should be. My focus on Council will be:

Restoring a sense of community with a focus upon conservation, preservation, recreation, and public safety. [CC] must encourage [MCFLMosFB] citizen participation in order to ensure a promising heritage for future generations.

Ensuring [MCFLMosFB] services remain viable and effective and that we have the essential resources to meet resident needs. We have the best resident-focused services in the county and clearly retaining those are priority for you.

Establishing a smart economic growth plan for [MCFLMosFB]. The only way to lessen resident tax burden is to restore economic viability to the City. We must implement a plan to address the vacant land and store front that is paralyzing our [MCFLMosFB] economy.

[FicChaTwentySeven] (Reading from note card) Over fifty years ago, my family moved to [MCFLMosFB], and I attended [MCFLMosFB] schools. I married here and our three sons also attended our schools. My wife and I chose to stay here because of the quality of life our [MCFLMosFB] provides.

Over the years, my involvement with [MCFLMosFB] has been extensive, with many years of participation with [MCFLMosFB] Little League (President, board member, coach), [MCFLMosFB] HS baseball (assistant coach), and several [MCFLMosFB] boards (including [CC]).

My priorities will be to maintain the [MCFLMosFB] services our residents want, find additional sources of revenue to help fund those services, increase our tax base to keep everyone's property taxes as low as possible, create a business-friendly environment to attract new environmentally-clean businesses, make plans for funding and completing infrastructure maintenance and upgrades which cannot be delayed much longer, and pursue grants to cover a large portion of these [COST s.

[FicChaTwelve] I believe in the value of community unity, teamwork, and the contributions of volunteers. My contributions started by creating an email group of people who wanted to be kept abreast of [MCFLMosFB] business that led to our current transparency level. I led [COFFEE] that produced a score of spending efficiency recommendations.

In just 5 months as interim [CC] member, I helped usher in a lower millage rate with no impact on jobs or services, increased our strategic reserves by 2,700%, helped solve the [CRA] issue, and helped introduce technology to efficiently get information to our residents. I want to sustain our level of services by conserving the resources that fund the intensity of those services. I will examine additional revenue opportunities, but will weigh the benefits and the impact to the [MCFLMosFB] in the long-term. I know the value of tax dollars and ways to conserve them. My wife and I have a vested interest in our [MCFLMosFB]'s success!

Your Host:

Well folks, that is all the time we have. A special thank you to candidates for their riveting answers. Our sponsor this evening was [FBWC]. I do hope you enjoyed tonight's show.

And remember, we let you know WHAT TO THINK ABOUT and WHAT TO THINK ABOUT what you think, so YOU DON'T HAVE TO. Good night. Aaaaaand, we're out.

[FBWCMbr]: Okay. Would the candidates for [CC] please exit the stage and would the candidates for [GovFLMos] please take seats on the stage. I said [CC] please exit the stage and would [GovFLMos] please take your places on stage. I swear this is like herding cats.

# [FicChaTwelve] [CC]
# [ELCTN12] Final Push

---

(Begin [FicChaTwelve] MCFLMosFB] campaign meeting)

Subject: [FBWC] Candidate Forum 12 Debrief
Wednesday, October 24, 12 7:43 AM

[FicChaTen], [FicChaEleven], [FicChaTwelve],
[FicChaThirteen], [FicChaFourteen], [FicChaSixteen],
[FicChaNineteen], [FicChaThirty], [FicChaThirtyOne],
[FicChaThirtyTwo], [TGTDTT]

[FicChaFourteen]    My thoughts on last night's Forum. Not quite sure how the good guys did ([FicChaTwelve], [FicChaFifteen] & [FicChaFourteen]) but I actually felt sorry for the others. Those three have been responsible for running [MCFLMosFB] these past 12 years or so? I never really paid attention to what they had to say, but last night, they all sounded like they had no idea what was or had been going on in [MCFLMosFB].

What were your impressions?

[FicChaTen]    [FBWC] Candidate Forum 12 was well attended. I counted 141. [FBWC]

Candidate Forum 12 attendance being the same, I am heartened by the interest and responsibility [MCFLMosFB] citizens s take with their governance.

However, whereas last week's forum was 90 minutes of [CCFLMosFBCan] answering questions of direct impact to [MCFLMosFB], last night's forum allowed citizens a mere 3 minutes to hear [CCFLMosFBCan]' answers to questions. It is unfortunate [FC020], [FC026] and [FC027] decided not to engage in answering 90 minutes worth of FB-specific questions, but rather felt more comfortable offering 3 minutes of their time and ideas to [MCFLMosFB] citizens.

[FicChaTwelve]

My thoughts are that a whole room of folks heard an intro, some confusion, and a conclusion...not much to base a voting decision on...but I (for one) didn't do well. I let [FicChaTwentySix] get away with 10 years of spending; I let [FicChaTwenty] get away with frivolous grant pursuits and tapping [MCFLMosFB] for 13 years. I don't know about you, but I was glad to see so many hands go up saying they had already made up their mind...I just wish I had the second data point—for whom?

[FicChaSixteen]

I saw those snakes squirm in their seats when you were talking [FicChaTwelve].

[FicChaTwelve]

I think I'd like to challenge [FicChaTwentySix] and [FicChaTwenty] to an open debate...they'd back down I bet. It would have to be either this weekend or next. Heck, I'd even include [FicChaTwentySeven] in it.

[FicChaThirteen]

I talked to Cahn Pollock about the "Press Release" that [FicChaTwentyTwo] posted. If [FicChaTwentyTwo] did actually did file a complaint with State Ethics and Election Board and the complaint is found to be groundless and/or frivolous, [FicChaTwentyTwo] is likely going to have to pay a $500 fine for doing so.

[FicChaTwelve]

I'm trying to understand what I did wrong and why my name was mentioned...but I guess that's beside the point. The Vice-Chair of [COFFEE] is certainly in a position to refute [FicChaTwentyTwo]'s claims...especially the part where "[CC] member [FicChaTwelve]" (versus [FicChaTwelve]) was on [COFFEE] and what we accomplished.

[FicChaFourteen]

[FicChaTwelve] . . . .don't beat yourself up . . . over 3 minutes . . . YOU DID JUST FINE . . . you made a very good valid point when you asked who has already made their minds up before you took your seat . . . I knew who I was voting for when I walked into that room and they certainly didn't change my mind. They won't do another one . . .

[FicChaThirtyOne]     HECK THEY DIDN'T EVEN SHOW UP WHEN THEY WERE INVITED to A FORUM DEBATE . . . .so get out there & talk one on one & tell the people your data . . . there was only 141 people there . . . you do real good with people one on one . . . I have seen you

[FicChaTen]     From my perspective, [MCFLMosFB] citizens learned a lot last night—or at least had their notions validated. The three [GOB] candidates confirmed they are all about "REVENUE GENERATION" (code for taxes), whereas [FicChaTwelve], [FicChaFourteen] and [FicChaFifteen] all spoke to controlling spending as being the primary mode to make [MCFLMosFB] fiscally sound, and generating revenue as opportunities permit (without raising tax rates—which drives away business and inhibits young families from moving into [MCFLMosFB]).

[FicChaSixteen]     [FicChaTwentySix], who spoke much more eloquently this year than last, led the "revenue generation" effort by discussing the potential for millions of dollars worth of taxes from the undeveloped [PelCo] property. [FicChaTwentySeven] read from his notes, saying the same thing [FicChaTwentySix] said off the cuff. [FicChaTwenty] joined in the fantasy of the near-term availability of millions of dollars of more tax money being available ('if only we'd work harder to find it').

[FicChaTen]     Unfortunately, none of the three of them, given their combined 35+ years of [CC] experience, said anything about why they hadn't made the changes or efforts to come up with these mysterious tax dollars during their previous time on [CC]. None of them answered the simple question "you had many years on [CC], why didn't you do it then?"

[FicChaEleven]     In the end, neither [FicChaTwenty], [FicChaTwentySix]          or [FicChaTwentySeven] said anything about their long-time involvement with the record [MCFLMosFB] debt, the [CRA] fiasco, the severely depleted [MCFLMosFB] reserve fund, the out-of-control [EMP] retirement and benefit debts, the problems of adding the [PelCo] property to [MCFLMosFB], and paying $1 million more for the property than it is worth, and the millions of dollars of tax payers' money they spent a lot to acquire "what they felt was best" for [MCFLMosFB].

[FicChaThirteen]     [FicChaTwenty] spoke angrily each time she had the microphone, dove deeper into the fantasy pool when she said the $5 million of [CRA] debt was not, in fact, a debt at all. She put her legal education and experience to good use making an obtuse and circuitous argument about why [USD] we all owe is not "debt." Huh?? After hearing her explanation, there was a large emotive groan throughout the audience. I believe the groan indicated [MCFLMosFB] citizens catching on to why and how [MCFLMosFB] has gotten into the fiscal situation it is in…with thinking like hers having been in charge for so many years, it's no wonder we're in such straits.

[FicChaTen]

[FicChaFifteen] made good points about new [CC]'s efforts to fix our spending problems, and his experience and education being useful to continue the trend. However, in my opinion, all three spent too much of their 3 minutes of total question-answering-time to countering the [GOB] candidates' mis-statements.

[FicChaEleven]

The three of you should have spent more time highlighting the good and constructive things current [CC] has accomplished, starting with the very successful and useful [COFFEE] whose results are being, and will be, used for running [MCFLMosFB] more cost effectively. Due to extremely limited time and their need to rebut misinformation, [FicChaTwelve] and [FicChaFourteen] never gave themselves the opportunity to highlight their efficiency, transparency and accountability efforts, including their efforts this year which resulted in the 7% operating [B] fiscal year 12-13 reduction, the 2% real tax rate decrease, the vast increase to reserve funds, requesting of proposals for use and sale of the property, solving the [CRA] debacle, etc . . . all while maintaining services!

[FicChaTen]  Given the shallowness of last night's forum due to the extremely limited time and few questions, I find it unfathomable that [FlaTo] decided to cover this forum vs. last week's forum. I believe better, more in-depth reporting of candidates' ideas and answers to citizens' questions would have come from the earlier forum. The fact 3 of the 6 candidates decided not to engage the voters in the more meaningful and in-depth forum last week should not have been a factor in [FlaTo]'s decision not to cover it. In fact, it should have been the MAIN STORY!

[FicChaSixteen]  Vote smart!

[FicChaTwelve]  I again grow weary of politics and imbeciles who waste and consume air and space.

(End [FicChaTwelve] [CC] campaign meeting)


(BeginTrans)

October 29, YR12

[FicChaTwelve]  To All,

[FicChaTwelve]  There is an Election Social at grassy strip at commercial plaza on Sunday, November

4th, [TSCMuniCom] 2PM. It's an opportunity to meet with [FicChaTwelve], [FicChaFourteen], and [FicChaFifteen] and engage in public interaction about the issues. It will be a tremendous opportunity to meet the candidates in person, have some food and "shave ice" (or water), and discuss in a visible, interactive forum the issues that [MCFLMosFB] faces presently and for the next few years of our economy.

[FicChaTwelve]     We'll stay until interest wanes! [FicChaThirtyOne] has graciously allowed us to gather at grassy strip at commercial plaza. The event is paid for and approved (in part) by the [FicChaTwelve] [CC] [ELCTN12]. Other vendors may contribute to the event. I hope all of you will join us on Sunday the 4th!

Very Best Regards,
[CCMFLMosFB] candidate [FicChaTwelve]

(EndTran)


October 31, YR12

(Begin the Shouting Match)

Best performed as a song and dance number. Musical score for full orchestra and road band written by Andrew Lloyd Webber.

| | |
|---|---|
| [FicChaTwelve] | The word needs to go out! We live in an ideal [MCFLMosFB] that is bound by ideals such as financial solvency, community, safety, and freedom of expression. There are candidates who are collectively advertising and mixing "facts" and "fiction": |
| [FicChaTwenty] | You and [FicChaFourteen] have less than 3.5 years of combined [CC] experience: |
| [FicChaTwelve] | FICTION: I have almost two years of experience attending and contributing to [CC] meetings...check the meeting minutes on line. [FicChaFourteen] is running for RE-election with over 3 years of [CC] member experience. |
| [FicChaTwenty] | You generated negative publicity and cut [B] fiscal year 12-13 to make a statement: |
| [FicChaTwelve] | FICTION: [B] fiscal year 12-13 was cut—yes—but services remain at 11/12 levels. There is no "cronyism" and we added a transparency link on the [MCFLMosFB] Web Page. [MCFLMosFB] is not DEVALUED...as a matter of fact, [MCFLMosFB]'s property values INCREASE this year by 1.5% ... the only [MCFLMosFB] in the county to do so! |
| [FicChaTwenty] | You built and planned for nothing ... |
| [FicChaTwelve] | FICTION: We revised [MCFLMosFB]'s comprehensive plan, revised [CRA] Plan and completed the Storm Water Drainage Project. |

[FicChaTwentySix]     You sought false economy by delaying wise investments:

[FicChaTwelve]        MOSTLY FICTION: We did not purchase a $750,000 ladder truck for [MCFLMosFB]. There is one in [MCFLMosIHB] and one in [MCFLMosMB]...two ladder trucks within 10 miles is PLENTY! [MCFLMosFB] does not have "essential software upgrades" ... they are functioning quite nicely right now.

[FicChaTwentySeven] You depleted reserves to dangerous levels:

[FicChaTwelve]        FICTION: We added $143,000 to the reserves this year after PAST [CC]s depleted them when they had to pay the bill for improperly using community Redevelopment Agency funds for General Fund use–a violation of [GVBMNTFL] Law163.

[FicChaTwentySix]     You falsely accused prior [CC]s of "misappropriating" [CRA] Funds:

[FicChaTwelve]        FICTION: Funds were not misappropriated, they were improperly transferred from the [CRA] Fund to the General Fund. We brought in consultants to FIX the [CRA] problem caused and perpetuated by past [CC]s.

[FicChaTwenty]        You and [FicChaTen] motivated [FD] to unionize:

[FicChaTwelve]     FICTION: [FD] tried to unionize before during past [GOB] [CC]s. It is their constitutional right. [MCFLMosFB] [EMP] were not INVESTIGATED but audits were performed to see what we were doing right and what we could improve upon.

[FicChaTwentySeven] It was a condition of selection that you not run for office:

[FicChaTwelve]     ABSOLUTE FICTION!! There was discussion in May during the process of selecting someone who had no intent to run for a [CC] seat, but [CC] was advised that it may not be legal to stipulate that. At the time, I had NO INTENTION OF RUNNING because a fiscally conservative candidate announced in March that he was running for [CC]. I supported him. Then, two days before the qualification deadline, he contacted me and said he would have to drop out for professional and personal reasons. He strongly urged me to change my mind and run in his place. Others followed suit with encouragement. I even called [CC] [FB], Mayor [FicChaSeventeen] to ask if I should change my mind and [FicChaSeventeen] advised me it would be okay.

So here I am...running on a platform of fiscal conservatism and full representation of you—the PUBLIC—with a full appreciation of our economic challenges ahead.

[FicChaTwelve]     PLEASE CALL ME or Write. I have
                   nothing to hide.

(End the Shouting Match)

Fade music.


(Begin Robo Caller Training)

November 05, 12

Hi, I'm [InsertNameHere] and a volunteer with
[FicChaTwelve] MCFLMosFB] campaign. Have you voted?

YES: Thank you for making a difference in our
national, state, county, and municipal elections.
[FicChaTwelve] hopes you favorably considered him
when you cast your [CC] votes and that you supported
both [MCFLMosFB] referendums. Tuesday will be an
historic day! Thank you for your time and making a
difference for our future!

END


NO: Tuesday's ballot is pretty large, but [FicChaTwelve]
would like you to know a little about his record
with just 5 months of experience on [CC], can you
spare thirty seconds for me to recap?

NO: Well, I completely understand and hope you will
favorably consider [FicChaTwelve] when you cast your
vote tomorrow. You can visit [FicChaTwelve]'s website
at [FicChaTwelve].

END

YES: Thanks and I'll make this short. In less than one year, [FicChaTwelve] and the current [CC] reduced [MCFLMosFB]'s [B] fiscal year 12-13 7.1%, brought in a 2% property tax reduction—the first real tax reduction in over 10 years, added $150,000 to [MCFLMosFB]'s reserves, brought back the [MCFLMosFB] quarterly newsletter publication, fixes the [CRA] issue with [GVBMNTFL], and did all this without cutting a single job or service. [FicChaTwelve] wants to continue this record of service in these tough economic times and hopes you will favorably consider him when you cast your vote on Tuesday!

Do you have any questions? Thank you for your time and have a wonderful Monday!

END

(End Robo Caller Training)

# [ELCTN12]

November 06, 12

[TGTDTT] has lived his entire life in preparation for the role he was to play in the 12 election. It was a role he did not seek and he was doing it for all of the right reasons and was helping someone he truly believed in. [TGTDTT]'s quest was righteous. God would certainly channel forth a well-earned victory for [CC] candidate [FicChaTwelve]

That was hopeful thinking.

Each [MCFLMosFB] voter had twenty-nine things to care about come Election Day 12 or there abouts when early voting and absentee ballots are considered. All [MCFLMosFB] voters demonstrated that virtually everybody cared that [FicChaOneSee] became [GovFLMosClkofC] but almost nobody wanted Peta Lindsay and Yari Osorio, the Party for Socialism and Liberation candidates, to become the next [USFG] President and [USFG] Vice President. About three out of four of the [MCFLMosFB] voters that made their inclinations known cared that [FicChaTwentySeven] became the Mayor. Just about 6 out of 10 wanted [FicChaTwenty] and [FicChaTwentySix] on [CC]. [MCFLMosFB] voters cared more about how a University Student Body President is appointed than they did about any of the things that [FicChaTwelve], [FicChaFourteen], or [FicChaFifteen] were talking about.

The fine [MCFLMosFB] voters decided collectively that Mitt Romney would be a better choice for President of the United States of America, but the majority of people disagreed with [TGTDTT] about who would best serve on [CC]. Parsing of the results indicates to [TGTDTT] that the likely reasons [TGTDTT]'s candidate were not elected are:

1. [MCFLMosFB] voters never heard of them
2. [MCFLMosFB] voters didn't know them
3. [MCFLMosFB] voters didn't trust them
4. [MCFLMosFB] voters didn't care

The above reasons are supported by the fact that 71% of the registered voters cast a vote for Referendum 1 (Board Consolidation), 74% cast a vote for Referendum 2 (4 to 1 majority for tax increases and special assessments), and 74% cast a vote for [CC] [FB], Mayor. None of the [CC] candidates received more than 38% as measured against the total number of registered voters.

When [TGTDTT] looked back at the portion of the campaign he was involved in, [TGTDTT] was always speaking to strangers because he doesn't know anyone. If there were others involved with [FicChaTwelve]'s campaign, or the campaigns of the [FicChaFourteen] and [FicChaFifteen] that had a more meaningful relationship with [MCFLMosFB] voters, [TGTDTT] never met them. None of [TGTDTT]'s candidates established key alliances with the leaders in the community.

If you have designs on a [CC] race, you have to make sure that:

1. Everybody has heard of you
2. Everybody knows you
3. Everybody trusts you
4. Everybody cares.

If you are not willing to commit to manageable set of tasks that confirms satisfaction of items 1 and 2 above, then whatever idea you have isn't something that everybody could ever be interested in. So you need an idea, you need to make sure you are absolutely right and then dedicate your life to sharing that idea with everybody you meet.

As far as [TGTDTT]'s advocacy, [TGTDTT] is spending some time not caring about what happens to [MCFLMosFB] and believing that people are pretty stupid.

But there is a second possibility as to why things turned out the way that they did. [FicChaTen] led the charge to appoint a known supporter on [CC]. [FicChaFourteen] had compromised his judgment by voting for the motion to put [FicChaTwelve] on [CC]. [FicChaTwelve] had turned his innocent mail group into a campaign tool. [TGTDTT] relied emotionally too much on the idea that because he was involved, he would win because he usually does. Bad Karma is just funny that way.

```
(BeginTrans [FBResMailGrp])

November 26, 12

Wednesday evening is the "change-over" evening
as [FicChaTwenty], [FicChaTwentySix] and
[FicChaTwentySeven] assume their positions as [CC]
members and the new [CC] [FB], Mayor. It is a light
agenda, but Item 18 on the agenda is very telling
as to what you can expect now that the election is
over. Here is a list of what I expect by 5 December:

[COFFEE] will be voted to disband (3 ayes and 2
nays) … even though it was responsible for finding
efficiencies and tax savings
```

[CC] attendance policy will be changed to only allow "extremely ill" [CC] members to call (or Skype) in to meetings…otherwise it's a missed meeting ([CC] members who miss more than four meetings in a calendar year can be voted off [CC]) (3 ayes and 2 nays) … even though this technology is used in successful meetings worldwide.

Current [CRA] board of 7 members will be disbanded (3 ayes and 2 nays) and the [CRA] will re-form as it has in the past, being the [CC] in their guise of [CRA].

Sometime next year, [CC] member [FicChaTen] will miss his 5th meeting and will be voted off [CC] (3 ayes 1 nay) and [CC] will vote in a replacement (3 ayes to 1 nay) giving them hand-picked, super-majority following to raise taxes.

I could be wrong-but I encourage you to look at the changes coming. Elections have consequences.

Sincerely,
[FicChaTwelve]

(EndTrans [FBResMailGrp])

# You Have Got to be Kidding

"Excuse me sir, can you tell him what time it is?"
"I'm terribly sorry, I can only tell you what time it was."

December 06, YR12

An article in today's local paper caught [TGTDTT]'s eye. "'Skullduggery' prompts council member to resign. Interim manager fired; [PD] Chief will fill in..." gave a somewhat hollow overview of the December 05, YR12 [CC] meeting that lasted some five hours and produced some rich material for gossip by the locals, debate by the constitutionalists, and fodder for a novel. [TGTDTT] believes this because he was there. [TGTDTT] listened to [FicChaTwenty] perpetrate a coup, [FicChaTwentySix] spew nonsense, and [FicChaTwentySeven] blather on in the hope that he would not be pegged as being in league with the other two. [TGTDTT] also watched a good man, [FicChaTen], fight the good fight on behalf of every [MCFLMosFB] citizen, [MCFLMosFB] [OwnProp] and [MCFLMosFB] [OwnBus]. The fifth member of the council, [FicChaThirty], was conspicuously absent due to an unspecified medical procedure.

The content of the article focused on the last issue of the evening, at midnight, where a decision was made to place the interim [CM] on administrative leave and have the [PD] Chief, [FicChaThirtyFour], take her place. In addition to leaving out all of the other agenda items that were discussed, the article failed to mention that even though the item was not on the agenda, it was clear that [FicChaTwenty], [FicChaTwentySix], [FicChaTwentySeven], and [FicChaThirtyFour] all had prior knowledge of what was going to happen and how they were going to deal with it. The problem is that it is a violation of Sunshine Laws for [MC] officials to collaborate on matters that affect the [MC] in private. So in addition to doing something that was unnecessary and spiteful, they probably broke the law.

Unfortunately, the likelihood they would ever be prosecuted is so small that if [TGTDTT] were to pursue, it would bring down so much unwanted trouble on him and his family that he couldn't justify the cost of seeking justice. The good news is that people love reading good stories and [TGTDTT] is a pretty good storyteller.

However, this tale is not one story with a beginning or end, but several intertwined stories of people and events that come together at a snap shot in time. There is a moral to this tale that the beauty of life can be found in the little stuff and that the big stuff seems to stay screwed up.

# My Fellow citizens

(Begin Farewell Speech [FicChaTen])

Dec 6, YR12

Fellow citizens:

I am resigning. In my opinion, last night we witnessed an epic display of [GOB] politics that [MCFLMosFB] has been infamous for for many years. Some in [MCFLMosFB] will take exception to this notion of the outside perception of [MCFLMosFB] politics, but I believe it to be true. Last night's display proves why many outside of [MCFLMosFB] (as well as many [MCFLMosFB] citizens) perceive [MCFLMosFB] politics in such a light.

My words will not do the meeting justice. Please review last night's meeting at http://www.youtube.com/ to witness the action for yourself and make your own decisions. It is clear to me the newly re-elected former [MCFLMosFB] leaders are on a well-planned, synchronized and rapid attack effort to curtail immediate-past [CC]'s efforts toward efficiency, transparency and accountability. If the video is not on the site, call [CMFLMosFB] clerk until it is.

What is most frustrating to me is my lack of ability to stop any of this regression. Last night demonstrated that common sense, procedural actions, and vigorous debate did, and will do, nothing to stop it. In fact, a review of coming agenda items suggests it will only accelerate. The shoe is definitely back on both "left" feet. [MCFLMosFB] voters voted it so, and so it will remain.

Elections have consequences, and [MCFLMosFB] is experiencing the same thing our nation is experiencing post-election. I sense many adverse things on our horizon. I have my own "predictions list" . . . let's see how many come true (including a new [CM] who has no business experience, is unproven as a leader, and is malleable by the [GOB]s).

While many herald the return to the old way of doing business (including, I believe, most if not all [MCFLMosFB] [EMP]), I fear for [MCFLMosFB]'s future…including the long-term jobs, benefits and retirements of the very [MCFLMosFB] [EMP] who support the regression. Short-term comfort via status quo may very well lead to long-term catastrophe via status quo. "Be careful what you wish for" comes to mind. I hope for [MCFLMosFB]'s sake I am wrong, and that the recently elected [CC] member and their supporters are correct.

Here's a little of what occurred regarding each agenda item.

1. Discuss/take action on "[CC] 12" issues:

   a. Elect [CC] [FB], Vice Mayor [FicChaTwentySix] won 3-1.
   b. Appoint a voting delegate and alternate delegate to the Space Coast League of Cities. [FicChaTwentySeven] — primary. [CMFLMosFB] accountant alternate.
   c. Appoint board liaisons. [FicChaTwentySeven]—Beautification, Library. [FicChaTwentySix]—Code

Enforcement, [MCFLMosFB] recreational area S. Island. [FicChaTwenty]—Comprehensive Planning, Retirement. [FicChaThirty]—Planning and Zoning. [FicChaTen]—Board of Adjustment, Recreation.

d. Appoint South Beaches representative. [FicChaTwenty].

e. Appoint [CRA] Board Chairman and [CRA] Board Vice Chairman. I did not think it appropriate for [CC] to make a decision on behalf of [CRA] board, especially since the board includes two at-large citizens. [CA] said it was appropriate, and [CC] [FB], Mayor and [CC] [FB], Vice Mayor were appointed to the respective positions… so much for the concept of separation between [CC] and [CRA] that the immediate-past [CC] worked so hard to establish to mitigate conflicts of interest.

2. Update on [MCFLMosFB] Special Events Coordinator activities. Lots of good things going on. As a member of the immediate-past [CC] who put this concept into place, I am happy with its progress toward promoting [MCFLMosFB] via [MCFLMosFB] Large Public Events.

3. [MCFLMosFB] Ordinance 1064: reducing side yard setback requirements for docks from 20 feet to 10 feet (First Reading). Sent back to staff to look at options as there were multiple issues with the ordinance's potential unintended consequences.

4. Discuss/take action on [CC] member [FicChaTwenty]'s proposed [CC] [FB], Policies and Procedures. Numerous changes are proposed, but major ones include:

a. Sec II. B. [CC] member will no longer be able to contact "outside entities" for guidance or legal interpretations after votes are made. After much discussion (again, see youtube for complete flavor), it was determined the wording would be reviewed by [CA] to ensure there were no Whistleblower or First Amendment issues before it is approved. Though other members didn't think so, I felt it limits [CC] members' abilities to question decisions, and makes doing so punishable in a punitive and vindictive way.

It also suggests to me that [CC] believes it is a power onto itself, controlling the flow of information as it deems best for the citizens, versus being accountable to the electorate. Additionally, to me, it also supports a "we will not tolerate dissent" mindset of [CC]...indicative more of a Duma than a duly elected body in [USA].

To the notion of "discrediting [MCFLMosFB]," the pertinent question: is it more "discrediting" for a member to not ask a question and allow [MCFLMosFB] to violate law, or to allow the [MCFLMosFB] member to ask the question, thereby potentially saving [MCFLMosFB] from discrediting itself via a violation? Imagine the savings in [CC] stature if a [CC] member would have asked outside questions of past [CRA] [FLMosFB] expenses over the many years they were occurring, rather than having citizens finally do so on their own, causing an adverse outside focus on [MCFLMosFB].

b. Sec III, C. [CC] members will no longer be able to attend meetings via electronic means while away on business trips. Watch the youtube video to see if you agree that all three new members believed this a good idea, and though they initially claimed it was not directed at my status, they all eventually spoke to the fact I should have known I was going to be away a lot during my campaign and therefore I should not have run.

They said I should show a "sense of duty" to [MCFLMosFB] by being physically present at meetings. I countered that I demonstrate my sense of duty by making the extra effort to be present at meetings while away on business, working my hectic schedule on the road to accommodate time changes and meeting lengths in order to serve [MCFLMosFB].

Additionally (and most importantly), I pointed out that by negating the ability to use electronic media to attend meetings while on business trips, [CC] was denying the opportunity of any business professional to EVER serve on [CC]. Given that such people tend to internalize efficiency and organization, they would be mitigating the positive impact such people could have on [MCFLMosFB].

After multiple citizens stood to speak against the effort (with counter speakers, as well), the three members decided to "grandfather" me into the rule. I objected on grounds it wasn't about me or my situation, but rather about the ability of future business people to serve [MCFLMosFB]. They decided the policy will stand with the "grandfathering" statement added. I do not view this as a "victory" in any sense . . . this is a distinct loss for [MCFLMosFB] over the long term.

5. Discuss/take action on [CC] member [FicChaTwenty]'s request to disband [COFFEE] and cancel study to determine whether the dog park needs to be staffed at its current level. Passed 3-2.

6. Discuss/take action on [CC] member [FicChaTwenty]'s request to disband Blue Ribbon Panel (FYI…this was already accomplished by prior [CC] on 04 Apr 12). No action after I pointed out the previous vote had already occurred.

7. Discuss interviews for permanent [MCFLMosFB] [CM]. It was agreed the current list of candidates was problematic. [CA] allowed that the 180-day requirement to name a permanent [MCFLMosFB] [CM] was not, after all this time, applicable in our case since the past permanent [MCFLMosFB] [CM] had not been fired but had decided to retire. The long-term impact of this decision is so great, it was agreed we should take the time to use a professional service to conduct a nation-wide search. In retrospect, I believe this search is a delaying tactic for the individual the controlling members already have in mind… someone they can control.

While the agenda item was supposed to limit the discussion to the interview process, it rapidly devolved into what (in my opinion) was a well-planned ambush of [CMFLMosFB] newsletter[FicChaOneA] — with no pushback from [CC][FB]Mayor to reign in the not-on-the-agenda effort. In what seemingly was a coordinated effort between the newly elected former leaders and [PD] head, (the discussion flowed in way too coordinated a fashion, in my opinion), [FicChaTwenty] moved to immediately put [FicChaOneA] on leave pending the end of her contract and appoint [PD] head, [FicChaThirtyFour] acting [CM].

[FicChaTwenty] publicly chastised [FicChaOneA] for non-specific "personnel issues" that had never been brought to [CC] or that [FicChaTwenty] had never before expressed. When I asked [FicChaTwenty] if she had discussed her concerns with [FicChaOneA] in private before the meeting, [FicChaTwenty] said she had not.

[FicChaOneA] professionally and eloquently addressed [FicChaTwenty]'s out-of-the-blue accusations and removal effort. You may find the video of this enlightening (and entertaining) and a good representation of why many folks believe what they do about [MCFLMosFB] politics.

I pointed out multiple violations by [FicChaTwenty] of the very [CC] [FB], Policies and Procedures [FicChaTwenty] had rewritten, and that we had just completed reviewing in item 4 above, including a [CC] member speaking directly with a [MCFLMosFB] [EMP] on [MCFLMosFB] matters ([FicChaTwenty] admitted she had pre-discussed this effort with [PD] head, [MCFLMosFB]). I do not hold [PD] head, [MCFLMosFB] responsible for [FicChaTwenty]'s successful effort, as [FicChaThirtyFour] has his job to worry about.

During the discussion, [FicChaTwenty] said something about [FicChaEighteen]'s [CC] replacement actions. I asked about political payback being the basis of her comment, which she denied.

[FicChaTwenty] dropped her bombshell at 11:50 pm, after an already very long meeting with most citizens having (smartly) left for their beds. The meeting ended at approximately 12:30 am.

As an example of the nature of [MCFLMosFB] politics, please pay attention in the video to [FicChaTwenty] verbally chastising a long-time [MCFLMosFB] citizen when he made a remark about [MCFLMosFB] debt. [FicChaTwenty] made a flurry of accusations against the notion of [MCFLMosFB] debt, and chastised the [MCFLMosFB] citizens and others for continually bringing it up. [FicChaTwentySeven] allowed this activity to continue until I spoke to correct her position by quoting from [MCFLMosFB] Financial Audit FY11-12. As I started to read from [MCFLMosFB] Financial Audit FY11-12 that I keep in my notebook, Mayor [FicChaTwentySeven] summarily shut the conversation down.

It became very apparent to me after experiencing last night's meeting that current [CC] will not allow the continuation of efficiency, transparency or accountability in [MCFLMosFB]. We are rapidly regressing to prior status quo and, in my mind, should frighten every [MCFLMosFB] citizens and [MCFLMosFB] [EMP].

In my opinion, we are a community of [GOB] politics, high taxes, bloated payroll, and over-promised [EMP] retirement and benefits. I suspect we are also a community of personal political payback, but only time will tell on that score.

I am sorry to all of my supporters, but I cannot be part of a body that is rolling back the advances and hard work that [MCFLMosFB] citizens, [MCFLMosFB] [EMP] and [CC] have done—and all that has been accomplished over this past year. My voice has no impact, my thoughts no regard. I am resigning effective today.

I am also resigning in protest of the way the interim [CM]'s termination was handled, as well as my perception of [CC] [FB] Mayor's failure to properly run meetings from the dais. Life is too short to bang my head against the wall of inefficiency and status quo while missing the good things in life like time with family and friends. If the former wasn't so, missing the latter would be easier to do.

I have too many other professional and family responsibilities to spend so much time and effort in what will always be a failed attempt to govern efficiently via accountability and transparency.

It has been my privilege and honor to serve every [MCFLMosFB] citizens in the best way I know how. If I have made you uncomfortable, or distressed you in some way, by things I have said or done in the pursuit of efficiency, transparency and accountability, please know I did not do so out of personal animus... it was merely a result of policy differences. Good, well-intentioned people can aggressively disagree on policy...and we have! If I have been supported by you, please accept my heartfelt thanks and be mindful that your fiscally conservative mindset does not currently rule the day in this [MCFLMosFB]...but that doesn't mean it won't eventually.

God bless this wonderful [MCFLMosFB] and all [MCFLMosFB] citizens. I wish EACH and EVERY one of you well.

[CC] member [FicChaTen]

PS. Since I will no longer be able to do so, I suggest all [CC] members donate their monthly paychecks to the city Police Athletic League. This organization does a world of good for our city's youth.

(End Farewell Speech [FicChaTen])

# Filling the Seat

The [MC]'s charter allows 30 days to fill a council seat that is vacated due to death or resignation. [FicChaTen]'s resignation comes just six months after the council had to fill the seat vacated due to the death of [FicChaEighteen] so there was some memory of what needed to be done and the criticism of how it had been done in the past. This new council wasn't going to make the same mistake of immediately filling the seat and they wanted to give the appearance that the matter had been dealt with publicly and properly.

A decision was made to get the band back together with bringing [FicChaTwoA] back to [CC]. [FicChaThirty] was the last remaining voice of reform, and she was a second string player on her best days. So most of the people went home and back to their lives as the decidedly uninformed. [TGTDTT], for one, looked at whether the crusade for a [GVBMNT] of his dreams is a fight [TGTDTT] was meant to lead.

[FicChaTen]'s resignation came with the realization that [TGTDTT]'s efforts were to help people accomplish what they believe is right as long as their right was the same as his right. All the people that [TGTDTT] was willing to vouch for and actively support were either voted out, lost, or quit. [TGTDTT] believes it was disheartening that the merits of an idea were dependent on the source of the idea so much so that group think runs [MCFLMosFB]. [TGTDTT] figures that if [FicChaTen] was right about why stuff needed to change, then the worst thing that happens is the dissolution of the [MCFLMosFB] and a return to being governed by [GovFLMos] which is one less layer of [GVBMNT] in [TGTDTT]'s life. If [FicChaTen] is wrong, then [FicChaTen] can join the club of the Great Wrongnosticators. They are having jackets made.

# [FicChaTen]'s Predictions

As his resignation letter stated, the manner in which the interim [CM] was relieved of duty was merely the last straw in [FicChaTen]'s decision process. [FlaTo] has reported it was THE reason, and that is false. Though the timing makes the perception understandable.

(Begin Dialogue)

Monday, December 17, 12 1:39 PM
Subject: Predictions
[FicChaTen][FicChaTwelve][MicBil][TGTDTT]

[FicChaTen]              Tell me what you think. [FicChaTwelve], I am especially sensitive to using you as an example in my final point . . . tell me if you want me to delete it.

[FicChaTwelve]         I am okay with it. Everything that could be published about me has been published about me. So I can't be embarrassed. [FicChaThirteen] is a different story. We are already closing on a house in a differentcity.

[FicChaTen]              Thanks. I have heard [FicChaSeventeen] is moving out of [MCFLMosFB] with his girlfriend.

[TGTDTT]  Okay. This might sting a little bit, but you need to "hear" it.

First, you should feel somewhat better by having taken the time to articulate your thoughts and give some voice to where you see things going.

I believe this is healthy, even if you were the only one to ever see it.

Expanding the audience beyond the author is where my confidence begins to diminish. I am not the least bit confident about general publication. My experience has been that [GenPub] either completely forgets the guy that cries "foul" and quits or has a memory that evolves into a satire or parody of the actual person. The probability that you will be remembered as a guy we should believe in is virtually nil.

[MicBil]  Since we are piling on... My concern is one of credibility and perception for potential future service possibilities.

[TGTDTT]  Imagine sitting in a local restaurant a couple years from now and you overhear someone at a table nearby saying to their dinner companion "See that guy over there. He used to be a [CC] member. When things weren't going his way, he resigned and published this long doom's day letter about how [MCFLMosFB] was going to crumble under its own weight and telling the voters how stupid they are. The guy's a loon.

[MicBil]

Those are concerns.

[TGTDTT]

That is only one possible scenario and it has nothing to do with your actual intent or the merits of what you wrote. It has to do with how people generally process [REALITY].

[MicBil]

I agree with the predictions. They will most likely happen, but don't believe they will deter and could actually serve to harm future ability to effectively argue the common sense position.

[TGTDTT]

If it were me and I resigned from [CC] under the same circumstances and for the same reasons you have stated, I would not release this letter and I would discontinue any statements for public consumption under the umbrella of "civic duty." I would channel my efforts in a different direction. I tell you this because you gave up the moral high ground when you resigned. It is time for you step off the stage and let the world run its course.

[FicChaTwelve]

I think the ground you gave up was the ground you were going to lose anyway… not the moral high ground. Let's move to a happy place.

[FicChaTen]

Thanks, as always. I still think getting this info out may tend to deter some of

|  | these things from happening . . . but probably better from a different author, i.e. Not from a Quitter. |
| [MicBil] | Love ya like a brother (which has odd implications coming from WV) and while I believe you are likely right, publication would not likely have an impact and could serve to diminish your voice in the future. |
| [FicChaEleven] | The question you have to answer for yourself is whether the publication of the letter will put your mind at ease regardless of how it is received by the public. |
| [TGTDTT] | That doesn't mean you should not help me write a book or write books of your own. It just means that you have given up your position of leadership in [MCFLMosFB]. You can vote and from time to time people might solicit your counsel, but you quit. If you still had something to say that might help [MCFLMosFB], you should have said it before your term was over. |

(Begin Farewell Speech [FicChaTen])

My main reason for resigning was that I no longer have the ability to make positive impacts, as the concepts of small, unobtrusive, efficient, transparent, and accountable [GVBMNT] are no longer priorities. Recent actions demonstrate no amount of effort on my part will make them so again."

In other words, I foresee the following stuff occurring, and given shifting alliances and the well-coordinated and rapid-fire nature of policy changes evident in the first two meetings of new [CC], I realized I had absolutely zero ability to keep these things from happening. Occur they will, and in my opinion, to the detriment (and potential demise) of our fair [MCFLMosFB].

I did not want to be a part of (if only a dissenting voice) the body that will, in my opinion, re-start the inefficient [GVBMNT] processes that may very well eventually bring down [MCFLMosFB]. I believe I can do more as a [MCFLMosFB] citizen than as a lone dissenting-[CC] member… but it's going to take all [MCFLMosFB] citizens who believe in small, limited, efficient, transparent, and accountable [GVBMNT] stepping up and being heard.

If [ELCTN12] is any indicator, I fear this may not happen, as those who wish for that sort of [GVBMNT] either don't exist in great enough numbers in [MCFLMosFB] (and in their nation) or failed to vote. By and large, it seems [MCFLMosFB] voters want bigger, more "gimme" [GVBMNT] at all levels. If that's the case, so be it. To paraphrase our nation's Founders, 'the people get the [GVBMNT] they deserve.'

Here's what I think will occur over the next year as a result of the newly elected [CC], that will – eventually – lead to [MCFLMosFB]'s demise (I hope beyond hope I am wrong):

1. Permanent [CM] – a relatively young and inexperienced candidate with zero [CM] or business experience, whose closest qualification includes being a development director for a town who's development has been anything but a success and who's businesses are leaving in droves, will somehow make the short list and

be chosen over more highly qualified, broader based candidates who would be less apt to be controlled by [GOB]s. This person's relative young age, inexperience and established relationship with [GOB]s will allow [GOB]s to manipulate [CM] for many more years...or until they cease to exist as [CM].

Additionally, the fact that [PD] is running just fine with the [PD] chief being acting [CM] will be lost on [CC]. [CC] will not choose to continue to operate [MCFLMosFB] with one less highly paid [EMP] position via keeping the [PD] chief as permanent [CM] and allowing the commander currently running [PD] to become [PD] chief.

2. My replacement on [CC] -- regardless of the process designed to do so, will be a died-in-the-wool [GOB] who has spent many years on past [CC]s, thereby buttressing the return to past practices. This will stand in stark contrast to past [CC]'s naming of a reform-minded [MCFLMosFB] citizens who had just led the highly successful [COFFEE] to replace a deceased council member. Past [CC]'s act was one of reform, whereas this [CC]'s act will be one of cementing the [GOB] network back into [MCFLMosFB] politics.

3. [MCFLMosFB] Personnel Policies – rather than continuing immediate-past [CC]'s effort to review and modify the long-time policy to align pay and benefits with local industry standards (e.g. no sick time payout, limiting late employment buttressing of pay for retirement purposes, etc), council will employ an outside agency to provide fodder for giving pay raises and increasing benefits. DROP will be maintained vice opening up positions to younger faces with fresh ideas at cheaper labor costs. [FD] and [PD] will remain top-heavy with supervisors.

4. Transparency efforts will recede – though I don't believe council will be so rash as to immediately rescind all of the transparency efforts instituted by the immediate - past[CC], transparency efforts will fail over time from lack of maintenance (updating of the transparency page) and failing to exploit technology (real-time streaming and you-tube recordings of [CC] meetings).

5. [FD]'s use of pump technology to protect their Professional Fire Firefighters' lives and save salaries on 3 positions over the next few years (via attrition) will not occur. [FD] chief will determine, after much research that proved the life and [USD] saving value in the technology, that the technology is, after all, not mature enough (even though he expressly stated it was--numerous times--during efficiency discussions in the last council). This will please his staff and the union.

6. [CRA] board – the at-large [MCFLMosFB] citizens appointed to [CRA] board by the immediate-past [CC] to mitigate exclusive control of [CRA] board by the [CC], and board/council conflicts of interest, will be relieved of duty. The [CRA] board will return to its prior makeup of only [CC]... which contradicts [GVBMNTFL] guidance that a [CRA] should be as disassociated with its governing body as possible. [CRA] board will once again be able to indebt taxpayers by virtue of their Board positions vice their legal inability to do so as [CC]. Only possible saving grace is the current Governor's effort to review [CRA]s (and other special districts) state-wide for potential dissolution.

7. [MCFLMosFB] Members – the same long-time group of folks will return to serve on boards they have long served on. New faces and ideas will be less welcomed.

8. [MCFLMosFB] revenues from grants, [MCFLMosFB] expenses associated with the research, preparation, follow through, and management. Newly elected (and former) [CC] member [FicChaTwenty]'s past business partner [FicChaTwentyOne], which had a long-standing contract with the [MCFLMosFB] at almost $60k/year, will be awarded a contract for standing grant writing services (even in this time of grant [USD] dearth). Past [CC]'s and interim [CM]'s request for proposal effort to obtain more efficient, on-demand writing services will be disbanded.

9. Business executive experience on council will be non-existent due to attendance policy changes, and lack of interest by the [GOB]s to deal with making [GVBMNT]as efficient as possible

10. The $750,000 ladder truck will be purchased – even though it was deemed an unnecessary expense by immediate-past [CC] which decided to simply repair the broken current truck for approx $26k, and even though the county decided to pay for a ladder truck on its own and station it beachside after past council had made the repair vs. purchase decision (which the county did soon after the repair decision was made by the past [CC]).

11. [B] FY13-14] will increase in excess of the immediate-past [CC]'s 7% decrease... I predict approximately 15%.

12. [MCFLMosFB] [Emp] cost will exceed the current 80% of [MC] expenditures and will rise at least 2% per year until they account for so much of the [B] that assessments and fees are forced upon [MCFLMosFB] taxpayers to accommodate both [EMP] costs and normal operating expenses.

13. Ad Valorem Tax Millage rate for [MCFLMosFB] will once again be the highest in the county, because

even though they have very low infrastructure requirements (as compared to other cities with lower millage rates), [MCFLMosFB] [EMP] cost and [MCFLMosFB] operation cost will continue to rise. The introduction of assessments and fees will slow millage rate rises but not stem them. Regardless, more [USD] will be taken from [MCFLMosFB] taxpayers at increasing rates over the coming years to pay for increasing personnel costs (see the many news reports of cities throughout the nation who have experienced this trend if you want to see where this ends up).

14. Even with increased millage rates and the introduction of assessments and fees, the [MCFLMosFB] reserves will continue to dwindle. [MCFLMosFB] reserves will not see another annual increase like the $143k addition by the immediate-past [CC] for years to come. Even in future fiscally strong years, if the past is any indication, the tendency will be to spend the excess [USD] versus saving it for leaner (or crisis) times.

15. Various personal paybacks will occur against [MCFLMosFB] citizens who dared challenge the [GOB] network over the past 2.5 years. These may not occur right away because that would make the actions too easy to attribute. They will occur over a period of months and years to mitigate the possibility that others ever again challenge the [GOB]s' sovereignty over FB. Evidence of this tactic being SOP for the [GOB]s throughout the years exists…just ask [FicChaOneBee] (who tried to bring efficiency to [MCFLMosFB] fifteen years ago) or [FicChaTwelve] (who has recently attempted to do so).

[FicChaTwelve]'s experience stands out as the most recent and egregious… though one can speculate on a direct quid-pro-quo, the timing suggests a strong correlation to me. After [FicChaTwelve] conducted the research pointing to the misspending of [CRA] [MCFLMosFBF] and his subsequent interviews with media about it, his work place received visits by an [MCFLMosFB] [EMP] to denounce his efforts. In addition, his workplace supervisors received (in an envelope sans return address) a copy of the citation and dash-cam video of a traffic stop conducted on [FicChaTwelve] by [PD] the year prior. Coincidence?

I believe personal payback has been, is and will be standard operating procedure for those in power in [MCFLMosFB]. "Check your six" if you've been part of the effort to transform [MCFLMosFB] into an efficient and transparent entity over the past couple of years... and, by the way, thanks for your effort and support. It was a valiant, if eventually unsuccessful try!

(End Farewell Speech [FicChaTen])

# Interlocal Agreement

June 13, YR13

"I have this great idea!" exclaimed permanent [MCFLMosFB] [CM] [FicChaTwoBee] shortly after a mid day climax in a discrete location between two consenting adults. "I will get [GovFLMos] county commissioners to sign a letter that says that they will not sue [MCFLMosFB] for [USD] that we don't owe them but are planning to pay them back if we get around to it."

The new [GovFLMos] Clerk of Courts used to be the [GovFLMos] Clerk of Courts and had a reputation for scrutinizing how the county's [USD] is being spent. His tool of choice is the lawsuit and he is pretty good at getting them filed in a hurry. He also has a reputation for using that tool effectively. [FicChaOneSee] returned to [GovFLMos] Clerk of Courts was compelled by the perceived irregularities associated with the incumbent [GovFLMos] Clerk of Courts. The incumbent lost the election and is now under indictment on charges of bid tampering and bribery.

As of late, [GovFLMos] Clerk of Courts has turned his attention to the [USD] paid by [GovFLMos] to [CRA] that was then paid to [MCFLMosFB] instead of being returned to [GovFLMos]. [GovFLMos] Clerk of Courts wants [GovFLMos]'s [USD] back and is making some pretty serious noise in that direction.

Permanent [CM] [FicChaTwoBee] needs three of the five commissioners to approve the agreement so that there is one more line of defense between her and [GovFLMos] Clerk of Courts. One of the votes will come from the father of a high school buddy. The second vote will come from the commissioner who would make special trips to see her at her last job in the northern end of the county. The third vote will come from the principal mechanism that facilitated the conditions that inspired the idea.

It is a week or so before the meeting to vote on the agreement and [TGTDTT] sees [FicChaSixteen] crossing state road A1A to get some cigarettes at the corner drug store. [TGTDTT] pulls into the parking lot to say hello.

It is a little after one in the afternoon and [FicChaSixteen] has all the outward symptoms of someone who has already raided the liquor cabinet. As soon as [FicChaSixteen] started talking, [TGTDTT]'s suspicions were confirmed.

[FicChaSixteen]: I have been told to lay low until after the [GovFLMos] county commissioners Meeting.

[TGTDTT]: Who told you to lay low?

[FicChaSixteen]: I'd rather not say.

[TGTDTT]: You are so full of shit [FicChaSixteen].

[TGTDTT] had good reason to believe that [FicChaSixteen] was following the developments very closely, but if he was "helping" in the same way that he "helped" write the [COFFEE] report or actually did make available the materials he promised to produce every time he spoke at a [CC] meeting, [TGTDTT] believed that [GovFLMos] Clerk of Courts [FicChaOneSee] might know [FicChaSixteen]'s name but doesn't ask for [FicChaSixteen]'s "help" or advice.

Football 12-13 season has begun and [ELCTN14] is thirteen months away. The seats on [CC] currently held by [FicChaThirty] and [FicChaTwoA] will be just part of the festivities that might try to bill itself as the main attraction. I wonder if any of the following terms will be mentioned.

[MCFLMosFB] debt
[MCFLMosFB] reserves
[CRA] debt
[CRA] reserves

Or will we hear all of those other words which mean that you are either behaving like someone else wants you to or you are not.

While we may not hear them from the [MCFLMosFB] [CC] or anyone else who is an [MCFLMosFB] [EMP], the words just were used—and not in a flattering way with regard to the [MCFLMosFB]. They were words from a report of the [GVBMNTCNTY] Clerk of the Court, whose investigators had just sent the former [GVBMNTCNTY] Clerk of the Court to jail for fund mismanagement issues (so [TGTDTT] believes these pros know what the hell they're doing and the [MCFLMosFB] [CC] and [CM] should be twitching with anxiety right about now!). In summary, the investigators' report said, "hey, [MCFLMosFB], you got some 'splainin' to do about spending that [CRA] money over the years! Oh, and by the way, we don't care what sort of deal you and your [GOB] cronies at the [GVBMNTCNTY] decide to cut to give you a 'Get Out of Jail Free' card, we will see you in court so we can protect all of the [GVBMNTCNTY] citizens' money."

# Solving for [X]

The [X] that we are talking about is the aggregate control of people by [GVBMNT]. On the one extreme, [X], stands for the complete abolition of those imperialist capitalist dogs and [GVBMNT] controls the spending of all [USD] and people are allocated sustenance in accordance with individual advocacy of [GVBMNT]." On the other extreme, [X] is a [GVBMNT] that cowers in fear at the mere thought of offending people and that people know as much about [B] as [GVBMNT]. Currently, [X] is somewhere in between. All people believe one extreme is better than the other. Over the course of their life, that belief may get reinforced or shifted somewhat. There might even be times when a person doesn't know what to believe in. But stuff never seems to stop.

| | |
|---|---|
| Producer: | Cue Music |
| Sonny: | The beat goes on. The beat goes on. Five mouths in the front making some noise. |
| Cher: | The beat goes on. The beat goes on. Screaming mouths just wanting to be heard. |
| Sonny and Cher: | The beat goes on. The beat goes on... |
| Producer: | Fade music. |

The author would like to give a special shout out to the late singer, songwriter, and former Mayor of Palm Springs, CA, Sonny Bono for being the inspiration for those closing words.

And one last thing. Never forget that [B] is an imaginary thing and anyone can make a [B] as beautiful as they want to make it. The trick is to use [B] to create a [REALITY] that doesn't suck.

# Epilogue

To wrap up the story in a way that will help you believe in Truth, Justice, and the American Way, ELECTION 2014 was something like we have never seen before. At the local level, every candidate spoke to the exact manner in which their actions would influence the financial health of the [MC] and that every aspect of [GVBMNT] would be openly visible to shareholders (taxpayers). Those candidates who articulated the clearest understanding of the technical issues were elected by an upswell of voter turnout and citizen participation in being an integral part in the understanding and solving of technical problems. In the process of optimizing the systems, past indescretions were identified and the documentation was submitted to the relevant governmental offices at the county, state, and federal level.

One result of those efforts were that the fortunes and freedoms of some individuals were reduced to levels that could be ethically justified. Another result was that all of the shareholders of the [MC] began to understand that it would be cheaper, much cheaper, to dissolve the [MC] and be absorbed by the county. There were some that believed that it would not be better if the [MC] went out of business, but every single person who lives or conducts business within the [MC] agreed that their ongoing costs would be less if the books on the [MC] were closed for good.

Economic conditions continued to worsen overall and the reality that there was not enough money to fund things people did not absolutely need became clear and inescapable. The people of Fujiwhara beach began to cultivate backyard gardens and fish the river more than had been done in the recent past. Each individual was taking inventory of their own lives and slowly realizing that the problems they were having were the result of artifically relinquishing their responsbilities to elected officials who create departments that take care of the people. These people also began to realize that everything they want in their lives can be had at less cost and better quality if they just do it themselves.

ELECTION 2016 resulted in a continuation of the informed dialogue that produced a voter referendum to liquidate all [MC] assets and dissolve the [MC], to include all subsidiaries such as [CRA]'s and economic development zones and all financial obligations such as loans and pensions.

Through active citizen involvement, all real estate held by the city, including City Hall, was sold to the highest bidder. The proceeds of those sales were applied to all outstanding debt. Government operations were moved to a storefront in a strip mall and council meetings were moved to parking lot. All government operations, except the City Clerk and City Manager were contracted out until the county would agree to assume governance and the state would approve the transition, to include paying off the remaining debt.

On September 30, 2017 the [CC] met for the last time to sign the final transfer of governance to the county and to formally dissolve the [MC]. On October 1, 2017 [FlaTo] reported the story on page 3 of the Space Coast section.

It took a while for the differences between [MC] and county governance to be noticeable to anyone but those who who lived and breathed [MC], [CC] and [CRA]. But the changes were not what the detractors predicted. Taxes were reduced by a reasonable percentage. Police, fire, and ambulance services became sherrif, fire, and ambulance services (when a person dials 911, do they have any knowledge or control of who is actually going to show up?). Public works functions went on without any major upheavals.

What did change is that there is one less small group of housewives and their husbands have a club that they run using other people's money. At least for the time being...

# Author's Note

I do hope you enjoyed this tale. If you are like those who had the opportunity to comment on earlier drafts, then your experience was not considered a total waste of time but you did read items that did not speak directly to your interests at that time. If you are reading this note at the end of the book, I suspect you are thinking about "What's next?"

Do people behave the way they behave because they don't know any better? Or is their way of behaving a better way? I have seen people modify their behavior to be successful in a situation and then revert to some other behavior when the situation was over. Getting their game face on so to speak. But what is at their core?

There are stories of professional American football players who admitted to trying to hurt other players with the implied understanding that the act was justified for the good of their team and the goal of winning. The prevailing strategy to win any war is to destroy the enemy's will to fight.

Winning is good and doing whatever it takes to win is the trait of a champion. I believe in winning with all of my heart and soul and do whatever it takes to accomplish tasks and achieve goals every single day of my life. As I have matured, I see only one game that is worth sacrificing everything I have here on earth to win. The paradox is that in order to win at the thing I am willing to sacrifice everything for, I must exhaust every ounce of will I can muster to make everything I have here on earth better. Family, friends, acquaintences, houses, machines, businesses, teams, boats, food, parties, my marriage, my bank account, and myself to name just a few things on the list. I must be willing to sacrifice it all in an effort to make all of those things better.

There are many people who believe the same way as I do but we differ in what we believe is better. I have come to believe that if I have to destroy your will to live in order to reach my goal, then the result will probably yield some short term satisfaction but will not really be better.

Many authors before me have written many things with the purpose of winning whatever game they were playing at the time. In the case of this book and this author, I have just answered all the questions that could ever be asked of me as to why I wrote this book and what I am seeking to accomplish by publishing it. If by chance you have a thought that was clear and made you smile, then you understand the answer I have given. Whether you can and should explain the answer I have given to anyone else is something you might want to think long and hard about. If you come across someone who claims to be able to explain my answer, don't give them your money to explain it to you. Instead, give me your money and I will tell you another story.

W.C. Andrew Groome
Author
October 12, 2013

# Glossary of Terms

| Term | Definition |
| --- | --- |
| [] | Open and close bracket identifying a key term. |
| [ActorPorn] | A person who participates in the performances of a pornographic production. |
| [APCSS] | Authentic Philadelphia Cheese Steak Sandwich |
| [B] | Budget, budgetary |
| [BST] | Beachside trailer or RV Park |
| [BusRestLocal] | Local Restaurant |
| [CA] | City Attorney |
| [CapEq] | Capital Equipment |
| [CC] | City Council |
| [CCAS] | Cape Can Air Station |
| [CC] meeting | [CC] [FB] meeting |
| [CitComm] | Citizen's Comments |
| [CitSys] | [PD] E-Citation System in use by the Police Department of the Municipal Corporation |
| [CM] | City Manager |
| [COFFEE] | Citizen's Fact Finding Exercise |

| | |
|---|---|
| [CFFEERpt] | [COFFEE] Report (The only one that was ever published for [MCFLMosFB] |
| [ColUSAF] | Colonel, United States Air Force |
| [CRA] | Community Redevelopment Agency |
| [EGO] | The core obstacle to any truly good decision or of seeing the truth |
| [ELCTN11] | Election 11 |
| [ELCTN12] | Election 12 |
| [ELCTN14] | Election 14 |
| [EMP] | Employee |
| [FB] | Fujiwhara Beach |
| [FBLC] | [FB] Lions Club |
| [FBResMailGrp] | [FB] Resident Mail Group |
| [FBWC] | [FB] Woman's Club |
| [FD] | Fire Department |
| [FDMCFLMosIndia] | [FD] [MCFLMosIndia] |
| [FicCha] | Fictional Character |
| [FlaTo] | Daily Newspaper |
| [FOP] | Fraternal Order of Police |
| [FY11-12] | Fiscal Year 11-12 |
| [FY12-13] | Fiscal Year 12-13 |
| [[FY13-14] | Fiscal Year 13-14 |
| [GenPub] | General Public |
| [GOB] | Good Ole' Boy |
| [GSoF] | Great State of Florida |
| [GVBMNT] | All Government |
| [GVBMNTCNTY] | County Government |
| [GVBMNTFL] | The Government of the Great State of FL |

| | |
|---|---|
| [GovFLMos] | The Government of Mosquito County FL |
| [GVBMNTSTATE] | State Government |
| [HurcanAndrw] | Hurricane Andrew |
| [HurcanFran] | Hurricane Fran |
| [HurcanJean] | Hurricane Jean |
| [JLACFL] | Joint Legislative Auditing Committee State of FL |
| [JoeBob] | Fictional character |
| [KoolAid] | KoolAid. In reference to the Jonestown Murders in Guyana. It is a metaphor for loosing all perspective for the sake of the group. |
| [LCF] | A political action group |
| [LOVE] | The word love when used as a noun. |
| [LG] | Local Government |
| [Lt2JAGUSA] | First lieutenant in JAG Corps [USA] |
| [MajUSA] | Major [USA] |
| [MC] | Municipal Corporation |
| [MCExp] | [MC] Expense(s) |
| [MCFLColNA] | A specific [MC] |
| [MCFLLakOca] | [MC] Lake Oca |
| [MCFLMarLnd] | Mid-central Marsh Land |
| [MCFLMosFB] | Municipal [FB] |
| [MCFLMosIHB] | Municipal IHB |
| [MCFLMosWM] | A specific [MC] |
| [MCFLOraOr] | A specific [MC] |
| [MCFUND] | One or more specific buckets of money that an MC uses to store and distribute money. |

| | |
|---|---|
| [MCPWFP] | [MC] [PW] Field Personnel |
| [MCRLE] | [MC] Real Estate, current value held |
| [MCRev] | [MC] Revenue |
| [MFCU] | Mirror Fogging Carbon Unit |
| [MicBil] | [FicCha] - Radio Talk Show Host Local AM |
| [MosConCoa] | Mosquito Conservative Coalition |
| [OBandSD] | Old Beach and Surfer Dude |
| [OptProj] | Projects funded by [B] that are not absolutely necessary to ensure public safety and reasonable health standards. |
| [OwnBus] | Any Business Owner |
| [OwnProp] | Any Property Owner |
| [PD] | Police Department |
| [PelCo] | Pelican Coast |
| [PenBen] | Pension Benefits |
| [PFB] | Pat Air Force Base |
| [PubServ] | Public servants |
| [PW] | Public Works Department |
| reader | The individual(s) reading this book |
| [REALITY] | Your guess is as good as mine. |
| [RecMCFLMosFB] | Recreation department [MCFLMosFB] |
| [StarPorn] | A person who has achieved celebrity status in the Pornography Industry. |
| [TGTDTT] | The Guy that Does the Thing |
| [TSCMuniCom] | Municipal Complex |
| [UoF] | University of Florida |
| [USA] | United States Army |

| | |
|---|---|
| [USAF] | United States Air Force |
| [USD] | United States Dollar |
| [USFG] | The United States Federal Government |
| [USMC] | United States Marine Corp |
| [USN] | United States Navy |
| [WhiRob] | Fictional character |